## THE "FEELING" OF VICTORY . . .

He "knew" he was getting close to his quarry, and he couldn't help pausing a moment to savor the feel of heightened senses, the excitement of anticipation. Then Cord aimed the want at the door and pressed, vaporizing the lock mechanism instantly. He jerked the sliding panel open, sinking into a crouch and bringing the wand to bear on—an empty room! But if his quarry was not safely there, then . . .

Cord dove to the floor as the first of many projectiles cratered the door jamb, showering him with splinters and blood . . .

# THE ALIEN TRACE

# SIGNET Science Fiction You'll Enjoy

# ✦ THE ✦
# ALIEN TRACE

## H. M. Major

A SIGNET BOOK

NEW AMERICAN LIBRARY

NAL BOOKS ARE AVAILABLE AT QUANTITY DISCOUNTS
WHEN USED TO PROMOTE PRODUCTS OR SERVICES.
FOR INFORMATION PLEASE WRITE TO PREMIUM MARKETING DIVISION,
NEW AMERICAN LIBRARY, 1633 BROADWAY,
NEW YORK, NEW YORK 10019.

Copyright © 1984 by H. M. Major

Cover art by Kevin Johnson

SIGNET TRADEMARK REG. U.S. PAT. OFF. AND FOREIGN COUNTRIES
REGISTERED TRADEMARK—MARCA REGISTRADA
HECHO EN CHICAGO, U.S.A.

SIGNET, SIGNET CLASSIC, MENTOR, PLUME, MERIDIAN AND NAL
BOOKS are published by New American Library, 1633 Broadway,
New York, New York 10019

First Printing, July, 1984

1   2   3   4   5   6   7   8   9

PRINTED IN THE UNITED STATES OF AMERICA

*For H. B. Buckley*
*They also serve who sit and type*

# Prologue: Now

The city was alien, as all cities were to him in his exile. This one, on the planet Brunan, was mostly human-populated, but there were a sufficient sprinkling of other races so that Cord attracted no notice. His erect, pointed ears twitched occasionally as he caught a few words of importance. Under the tunic and robe he wore, his tail twitched too.

He strode under the pink arches of a luxury hostel and found himself amid a group of trisexuals from one of the lesser-known worlds. As they pored over a compumap, their feelings were a jumble in Cord's mind: irritation from the male, anxiety from the female, a wish to mediate from the neuter being.

A human would not have paused or even realized that they needed help. He need not stop—no one would think it strange if he passed them by, and he had his own affairs to tend. Yet it would not take long, and there was no need to hurry now, not until he located his quarry.

In Multi-Lang, polished by long lonely days among aliens, Cord said, "Gentles, may I aid?"

"No, we thank you," the male replied, as the female said, "Yes, gracious one, please," and the neuter finished,

"If you could direct us to the Jewelers' Section? It is famous but I do not perceive it on this otherwise excellent map."

"That is because it is not really within the city at all, but in a suburb not shown. Dial for the northern suburbs and you will find it."

They thanked him, more or less in unison, in their various ways. He took in their psychic reactions as well. The male was sullen with embarrassment that it had been necessary to accept another's assistance. The female was grateful, happy to be extricated from an uncomfortable situation, and full of

7

pleasant anticipation. The emotion was so clear that Cord felt sure she was thinking of the dragon stones and flame beryls to be bought. Any visitor to this world would think of those gems. The neuter was glad to be removed from difficulty. Its thoughts settled into contentment.

Cord dismissed the trio from his mind even as he turned to leave, but in its way the encounter was satisfying; for once he had not been seeking information or been wary of a trap. For a moment he felt an overwhelming homesickness for the innocence and peace of his home planet, Mehira. His guard was down—if there had been another Mehiran in the city, that outburst would have brought a response, but there was nothing.

Not surprising, Cord thought. His race stayed planetbound, not courting friendship with aliens. Since they had never developed spaceflight, they were dependent upon space-faring breeds, but they fiercely limited that contact, managing to keep all aliens ignorant of Mehiran secret abilities. So far as Cord knew, he was the first—perhaps the only—Mehiran to travel offworld. No one on this planet would know it, of course. Who could remember all the races that fared up and down the galaxies? He was humanoid, like fifty other species. He could speak Multi-Lang. And he was very good at avoiding detection.

He passed another neon-colored building crowded with tourists and scanned them quickly. No trace of his quarry there. The tourists' thoughts were of red-gold and glowing green jewels, the kind sold by master craftsmen in the teeming markets. A few years ago, Cord reflected, he would have bought a pair of rings to take home to his parents or to his love-partner. His parents had loved beauty for its own sake as the natives of this world did. He himself had once felt the same; most Mehirans enjoyed loveliness. Now it was only a distraction—as well as dangerous.

Other tourists thought of sampling the unusual delicacies sold from small pushcarts. Still others dreamed about buying new faces and bodies, having themselves sculpted like clay and molded into handsome, muscular men or lusciously curved women. Each one had an important thought uppermost in his or her or its mind—but there was only one thing of importance to Cord, and he was near it. So near. It meant more to him than flame gems or the medical marvel of body-sculpting.

Yet these were the planet's ultimate artistic achievements. The latter was Brunan's most famous art form, and its most expensive: molding flesh, not metal, cutting tissues rather than stones.

The Brunani were the most skilled plastic surgeons and biochemists in this galaxy. Hundreds of thousands of the wealthy came each year to buy new faces, new figures, new metabolisms. The concubine of the Space Guild's Grand Master has a tendency to gain weight? Two days' treatment and she could be slim forever—or until she was tired of her new body and could afford another one. If the heir to a solar system's industrial empire was unhappy with his skin color (olive, perhaps, rather than a high-caste leaf-green), it could be changed in a moment. Others came also: those who did not want to improve upon nature but rather conceal it. Any identifying feature could be altered by a Brunani artist—for a price. Well, almost any. Cord's lips quirked a little. The one feature which could not be changed was the one only he and his fellow Mehirans could detect. And they had kept it a secret from the rest of the universe. . . .

Still no trace. This teeming section was packed with visitors eating, drinking, buying souvenirs. The trisexuals were sensible to travel to the Jewelers' Section, where prices were said to be lower. Calling to memory the map he'd studied earlier, Cord left the neon-bright amusement area. He did not turn away from the spaceport, however. Though he had nothing to go on at present but intuition, he was sure his quarry would not venture too far from the ships.

Late-afternoon sun felt good on his torso. The scarlet tunic he wore left bare large sections of his muscular chest and shoulders. If not for the softly tanned belt pouch he wore, and the ray wand concealed in one high boot, he would have been hard pressed to hide his weapons in such skimpy clothing. He *was* attracting a certain amount of feminine attention, he noted with satisfaction. He was in better physical condition than most of the tourists and locals, and sufficiently exotic yet acceptably humanoid to prove irresistibly appealing. (And the robe did hide his tail!) Unfortunately, now was not the time for pleasurable dalliances, but the thought was attractive.

The next arcade was a flesh show, with "No Minors Permitted" posted at the entrance. Well, if he couldn't touch, he could at least look. He walked in. Here the eye-catching wares were displayed inside, out of view of the street. A tourist trap, of course, with the usual assortment of multispecies prostitutes, some whose sole attraction was their alienness.

In one window a woman with a mane of black hair, her nipples pierced with several small gold rings, danced lasciviously if ungracefully. She wore nothing more than long beaded fringes of fire gems around her hips. Her gyrations allowed frequent glimpses of her pubic hair and even of her labia. A continuous electronic advertisement above her cubicle proclaimed her to be a "Wild Woman from a Primitive World." She snarled and bared her teeth, virtually all she had left to expose.

For those who preferred them young, there were two Tii; billed as twin sisters, but Cord had his doubts. The Tii had none of the secondary sex characteristics humans associate with adult sexuality. These two looked like prepubescent girls, with slim hips, tiny buds of breasts, and hairless skin. Their faces were cherubic and flawless, their eyes large and innocent. One pouted and sucked her thumb. Definitely not to his taste.

Of the two dozen or more bodies on display, the only one which interested Cord was a lithe young woman who was obviously a professional contortionist. She had long striped yellow-and-red hair and wore nothing but dark stockings held up by red garters with yellow rosettes. In her small cubicle she slowly bent her body in a variety of poses, all of them highly erotic. A crowd had gathered to watch her, an unusual tribute to her abilities. Teasingly, her back to the audience, she leaned over, legs spread wide, hair brushing the floor. A pink, moist tongue traced a wet line up the inside of one sleek thigh. Cord's tail twitched in reaction. Two or three male spectators turned toward the admission booth; one sprinted through. A moment later, a pink light appeared in the cubicle, tinting her skin peach. She smiled, straightened up, and leisurely walked through the back door into the private rooms beyond. The cluster of watchers broke up slowly.

Cord smiled and shrugged. She would have appealed to him at any other time, but he was not interested at the moment. A woman had to be unusual indeed to pose a distraction while he was hunting.

Cord had followed his quarry from Mehira to E'aij, lost the trace, picked up the trail again, had taken a freighter bound for Dragon IV, caught up with the other on Keli—and found himself tricked again. This time he was only hours behind. He had spoken to those who had seen the other leave the spaceport. Striking, all agreed, with eyes like malachite and hair like flame beryls. Such features were a liability when trying to melt into a crowd; it would explain the detour to Brunan.

So he would find his quarry in some Brunani body shop—sedated and oblivious while an artist's instruments altered face and form—and then he would kill. The Brunani would not object, not when Cord could pay for an "inconvenience." What aliens did to each other was no business of theirs, as long as no Brunani property was damaged, or as long as the damage was made good with money.

Cork stalked the streets methodically, giving only cursory attention to his physical surroundings. He was nearing the section of the clinics and biochemists, cynically called "body shops."

Someone—a fat, human male, a tourist—bumped into him, Cord smelled the unmistakable odor of alcohol and sensed unfocused hostility: someone not happy with himself, wanting a scapegoat.

"Why doncha watch where ya goin'?" the man snarled out.

Cord did not like brawls. They attracted attention. He was in no mood, however, to tolerate fools.

"You are drunk and stupid," he stated flatly.

"Who you calling—?"

"If you force a fight, either I will kill you or you will spend the rest of your vacation being repaired."

Something in Cord's staccato voice and in his harsh face penetrated the man's alcohol-induced anger. He backed away a step or two, muttering, "No offense . . ."

Cord passed on. As he walked, the strange multicolored buildings, all angles and planes, were filled with a jumble of emotions: fear, pain, pleasure. Cord succeeded in muting even the most anguished calls so that the sounds/feelings were a dull roar in his conscious mind. As night fell on this part of Brunan, the cacophony was joined by the colors of garish streetlamps, so that his senses reeled under the constant onslaught. He steeled himself, recalling the ancient hymns, and recovered control.

He threaded his way around the knots of tourists, prospective patients, doctors, artisans; through the winding streets, seeking the one cold emotion that did not match; like the last piece of a jigsaw which would not fit into place no matter how you turned it. His quarry was like that puzzle, with a "scent" like no other.

Very slowly, an icy tendril of feeling crept into his nearly numb mind, distinct from all the other psychic impulses. Its touch was a crisp thrust, shocking him alert.

It was the one. And it was near. The closer he came, the stronger the scent.

Cord broke into a run, dodging easily around the few people who were still out in this quarter. Except for those coming steathily to the face artists who kept office hours at night, the streets here were deserted. All the amusement arcades and pleasure palaces were behind him, with the markets and businesses that supplied the port. This was a quiet professional section.

Cord slowed. He was very near now. He opened his mind, heedless of the increased clamor of other brains. This section was not as bad as the thronged areas nearer the port; it was isolated, empty except for many who were in a drugged sleep. Intently he followed the thread of emotion, as one in a dark maze might follow a bright string. Past large, brightly illuminated clinics, past smaller body shops and face artists, to a large but plain building almost at the street's end.

He knew his target was inside.

Cord paused at the entrance to damp down the exultant feeling coursing through him. Until he had caught and killed his elusive quarry, until a corpse lay at his feet, there would be no real triumph.

He pushed through the sun-yellow portals of the Xavier Clinic. He calculated that he had allowed enough time for his quarry to have gone through whatever paperwork and payment arrangements might be necessary. Now the prospective patient would be in a room and anesthetized. These places were strictly assembly-line and, to his advantage, very private. The clinic had this one main entrance and at least four interior exits; a patient came in one way and went out another. Leaving here, once he was done, would be easy.

The receptionist, a blue-smocked man wearing a name

badge, rose to greet him. "Do you have an appointment, sir?" he inquired, reaching for a medical questionnaire.

"No," said Cord, drawing his ray wand from his boot in one fluid motion. It resembled a wizard's magic wand, hence the name. It was not quite as long as Cord's forearm; it was slender, crystalline, the pale purple of the base shading to mauve and pink. He pointed it at Med-Tech Nin's stomach.

"Someone arrived here recently. I am here to see that one."

The med-tech's face sheened over with sweat, though the room was cool.

"Sir, information about our clients is confidential. The Xavier Clinic prides itself on ethical behavior and on protecting the pri—"

"Objection noted. However, my argument seems decisive." Cord nodded gently toward the wand, which was firmly pointed at Nin's middle.

"Whatever quarrel you may have with this person should not be pursued here. This is a medical facility."

Cord gave the man full credit for courage. "Med-Tech Nin, if you do not do as I ask, I will regretfully perform an impromptu operation on your internal organs. A hospital is the place for that, is it not?"

The med-tech acknowledged Cord's request. "Which—which one of our patients did you wish to see?"

Cord smiled. "How many have come in today who appeared to need no surgery?"

The med-tech forgot his situation and laughed. "Half a dozen since lunch, sir." At the reminder of the ray wand, his grin vanished abruptly.

"The one I'm looking for carries Voskian papers."

"Oh, yes. Of course. You want room A-6."

"You will lead me there," Cord ordered.

"Ah, certainly. If I may turn on the autoreceptionist?"

Cord gestured permission. Now that the man had gone through the motions of resistance, he would be cooperative; Cord could tell.

Moving very carefully, the med-tech switched on the system. Now, if someone came in, he or she would be asked by a pleasant but disembodied voice to please be seated and wait.

Cord let the med-tech lead him out of the reception area, past a heavy door. The understated luxury of the outer office turned to stark simplicity. Doors opened off the dim hall on both sides. Cord noted four discreet exit signs as they went down the deserted corridor. There seemed to be no one in the building but the two of them and the sedated patients behind closed doors. Good; so far everything was going as planned. From now on, the med-tech would be a liability.

As they passed a door marked "Supplies," Cord's free hand stole into his belt pouch and withdrew a small capsule with a tiny, almost invisible needle at one end. With one quick movement, Cord slapped it against his prisoner's neck and squeezed the bulb.

The man jerked once and swayed. Cord caught him before he collapsed and carried him to the supply room, using the mid-tech's now flaccid hand to open the door's palm lock. Cord dragged him inside and lay the unconscious med-tech behind a row of shelves. The drug would keep him quiet for hours, and he would eventually wake up on his own, unless some prospective customer, bored by the autoreceptionist, called for a guard.

He slipped out of the storeroom, carefully closing the door behind him, and went looking for room A-6. He found it almost at the end of the passage.

Its door was closed, like all the rest. A lighted panel in the door proclaimed "In Use," a superfluity, since the door, when shut, was automatically locked against intrusion, accidental or otherwise. Cord knew from previous research what lay behind.

Each surgical suite in a reputable clinic had to be self-contained, with robo-med units in constant attendance, a bathroom, meal dispenser, computerm, and molded bed, where the patient could recuperate before showing the world a new face or figure.

His quarry would be lying on the surgical table surrounded by the metal shell of the robo-med, unable to resist, unaware of his approach. Satisfaction rose in him. He paused a moment before the door, savoring the feel of heightened senses, the excitement of anticipation. Then he aimed the wand at the lock and pressed, vaporizing the lock mechanism. Cord jerked the sliding panel open, at the same time sinking into a crouch and bringing the wand to bear on the robo-med—

—which hung over the table, unengaged. The table was

empty. If his quarry was not safely inside the robo-med, then—

Cord dove for the floor as the first of many projectiles cratered the doorjamb, showering him with splinters and blood. . . .

# Chapter 1

Cord was still a youth when the Terrans came to Mehira.

It seemed like a dream, a made-up story from some fanciful book, especially when the aliens were kept in isolation, as though they had some dread disease. Rumors spread instantly—not surprisingly, given Mehiran mental abilities. Some said the Terrans were misshapen monsters. Others said the Terrans were far too uncivilized and grotesque to mingle with real people.

Within a week, though, a televised meeting, heavy with Mehiran tradition, was shown throughout the planet. The Terrans, or "humans," as they called their breed, were not unlike the Mehirans, at least superficially. They had a head in the right place, two arms, two legs, and an interesting variety of skin, hair, and eye colors—although in a different spectrum. These humans wore identical silvery uniforms and wide smiles: they were friendly, eager, and not unattractive in their way. But they did lack tails, so their sex lives were clearly deficient.

That one news program was the only time Mehirans were allowed to view the aliens, who remained confined in the hastily built enclosure erected on the spot where they first made planetfall. Only a chosen few—the ruling Council and some scientists—made contact with the Terrans. And in the days that followed the aliens' arrival, Cord wondered if he and his parents would ever see the humans in the flesh.

Then one of his father's lovers came to visit unexpectedly, not long after the aliens' arrival. She was a small, delicate woman, with topaz skin and blue eyes. She favored the short multicolored shifts that were now in vogue and preferred to weave stones through her hair. She was also a woman with some political connections; one of her other love-friends was a Council member.

"I can't stay long," Finola said, when they offered her

refreshments. Her excitement was palpable, and she was clearly delighted about something. After a pause for dramatic effect, Finola announced:

"I've met the aliens."

Cord's father, Fyrrell, sat down beside her on the soft couch and placed a muscular arm about her shoulders; his anticipation level rose. His wife, Neteel, leaned forward in her seat, her finely shaped ears swiveling toward Finola to catch every word. Cord hung back, and took a pillow seat off to one side; he sat silently, trying to control himself, until her next words:

"And I can arrange it so you meet them too."

Cord's sudden emotional leap of pleasure bounced off the mingled glad surprise of his parents, making the room nearly reverberate under the onslaught of feelings. Finola flushed with satisfaction at the reaction to her news.

"The aliens have come to trade with us. Even though they are technologically more advanced than we, Mehira still has things the Terrans will accept in exchange for information and material goods. I can get you the sole license to trade crime-detection information with the aliens."

Another emotional spike of surprise filled the room. Cord's family, and the few others in the area who were Catchers, were tolerated for their usefulness, but they were not admired. They were not even welcomed, unless they were needed. As a child, Cord was acutely aware of this isolation and ostracism, but he was also aware that nothing would be done about it. He would be a Catcher, as his parents were, and like them, he would be shunned by most Mehirans.

His gentle mother, Neteel, an engineer, seldom saw her relatives because she could not bear their feelings of pity for her marriage to a tainted inferior and for her poverty. If it had not been for the moral support—and the more tangible aid given Cord's parents by their lovers—Cord did not know how they would have lived. Yet his parents were successful in their work. Although Mehirans were nonviolent and law-abiding, there were always some deviants and criminals. The Catchers existed to track them down. And Cord's parents were most efficient about it.

"Meet the aliens," Fyrrell mused. "Why us? What do we, lowly Catchers that we are, have to offer these powerful starfarers? There's something you aren't telling us," he admonished.

"We'll take it," Neteel interrupted, her topknot swinging in emphasis. "Finola wouldn't have offered it if she didn't think it was to our advantage." She and Finola smiled at each other in perfect agreement.

When Fyrrell continued to glower at them both, his disapproval evident, Finola sighed.

"All right, I'll explain. First, you'll receive instructional materials from the Council and be placed under formal oath."

"We've kept many secrets in our work," Fyrrell pointed out. "You know that, Finola."

Finola nodded. "But this is a secret that must be kept not only from other Mehirans but from the aliens themselves."

Neteel raised an eyebrow at this remark. Cord sat up straighter, tail twitching.

"The aliens," she continued, "are under permanent quarantine by order of the Council. They keep to their compound because we won't let them out, and the aliens are still unsure of our power to keep them in. Besides, they say their primary reason for traveling between the stars is to gain knowledge. They've come to trade!"

"And the Council . . . ?" prompted Neteel.

"The Council is allowing trade with authorized persons only, as few of them as possible. Neteel, Fyr, it's going to be very lucrative for those chosen few!"

"But why aren't the Terrans allowed to travel freely—and why us?" Cord finally spoke up, and all heads turned toward him.

"I was coming to that point," said Finola. "When the aliens first communicated with us, it was quite a shock. Not the appearance of another sentient race—but the terrible diffferences between us and the Terrans."

"There *were* rumors," said Fyrrell.

"It's not their physical appearance. Our scientists have discovered that they can't 'feel' us. They have the other basic senses, but they are not empaths. They're hardly better than beasts in some ways," she added frankly, "but they are technologically superior, and therefore stronger."

"I'm stronger than most of my neighbors," said Fyrrell logically, "but they have nothing to fear from me."

Finola squeezed a muscular thigh in appreciation. "I know

it, and among our people that would be a reasonable argument. But there's more I haven't told you.''

They all felt her reluctance and embarrassment quite clearly.

''We're peaceful because it's too painful to live around those who are in pain, or dying, or even terribly unhappy. The more a mind can feel anguish, the worse it is for everyone. Over thousands of years, we have been forced to evolve a society governed by strict laws as well as etiquette. We 'listen' for others' feelings, so as to avoid causing them anguish or embarrassment. And we let them feel our emotions for the same reason. The only time it's permissible to mask emotion or to refuse to receive it is when the sender is in terrible distress. Even then, it's not possible to block it out completely. Our being able to feel the suffering of others makes us unwilling to cause unhappiness. We have had peace on Mehira for generations. We've had to. But have you ever thought how things would have turned out if we hadn't been empaths?''

She gently disengaged Fyrrell's arm and stood up. She paced in front of the pillowed couch, her tail jerking spasmodically in agitation.

''If we had never been empaths . . .'' Neteel began. Her emotional signal wavered doubtfully. ''Then we might not have evolved away from aggressive behavior.''

They read Finola's answer in her feelings. ''Let's not use euphemisms,'' she said at last. ''For 'aggressive behavior,' we should say 'violence.' The aliens are violent. And they are strong. They know we are weaker technologically—but that's all they know. Right now they are not in a position for conquest; there are too few of them and they are too far from their home worlds. Perhaps it's not even politically or materially expedient for them to expand their empire right now; we don't know. But if they learned the true extent of our abilities, not only would they become our masters, but we could become their slaves, their pawns in other interstellar wars.''

Her words were as stunning as any blow made by a fist. Cord's parents were deep in thought over the ramifications; they did not notice his reaction of near-lust, a craving for excitement such as often came unbidden during a hunt, which he damped down quickly. Finola did not appear to notice either, though she had paused in her tirade to eye his father speculatively.

"The important thing," Finola concluded, "is that the humans are incredibly wealthy and eager to trade. You, my beloved friends, are among the best Catchers on Mehira, and you're close to the port. It's time for you to profit from your talents."

Fyrrell rose gracefully and embraced her, his fingers gently stroking her golden skin; they stood quietly, entwined. Neteel rose and embraced them both.

"With extra income we could move to larger quarters," Neteel said slowly. "If we had a larger workshop, we could complete the . . . project we've been working on."

She and Fyrrell exchanged nervous but excited glances.

"What is this project, anyway?" Finola asked. "Fyrrell has spoken of it, but he's always made a mystery of it."

"I haven't meant to," Fyrrell replied. He raised her hand, palm upward, and nuzzled it with his lips. They all could feel a tremor pass through her body. "It's too soon to talk about it, that's all. It's based on a wholly new approach to the problem of detecting criminal tendencies—"

"And we're still afraid we've made some enormous miscalculation, that it will be worthless," Neteel finished. She stroked Finola's arm and then rested her hand on her husband's forearm.

The mood in the room was shifting. Their words were now tinged with desire and need for a generous friend. For a moment Cord thought of the warm, soft body of Bird, quick and light as her name. He also thought that the three of them had forgotten he was there, and now their foreplay was bathing him with fiery caresses. He groaned, and an obvious bulge appeared in the front of his tunic.

They turned to him in amusement. "Why don't you pay Bird a visit?" his mother suggested. "You can tell her the news—if it's all right to speak of it," she added to Finola.

"Only if he speaks of trade—and love." Finola smiled, a sly, secretive smile that was one of her most attractive characteristics.

"Bird is the daughter of the Third District Speaker."

"That's all right. Fyrrell told me as much. My love-friend on the Council is a bit more powerful than the Speaker."

Fyrrell and Neteel laughed a little. Even Cord knew that Finola's friend was the Council's head. Thanking her, Cord took his leave. Not only was he anxious to see Bird, but he could tell from the heightened emotional coloration in the room that his parents and Finola were interested in being alone to pursue their own amorous bent.

As he left the dwelling, their rising tide of lust caught him in a backlash, making his blood pound and his loins ache. His tail whipped in anticipation.

Before he boarded the intercity transport, he took care to close down his mind to those he would be encountering. Probably none would recognize him for what he was, but if they did, he preferred not to feel their contempt. He recited a brief but calming ancient hymn.

The jointed, wheeled bus came quickly, and he joined the throng boarding. It was crowded but cheap.

He spent the journey to Bird's suburb watching the other passengers. There were many lovely young women, he noticed. All had long, slim legs and soft, tinted skin. They favored short, colorful shifts that came close to revealing all their assets. And many returned his appraising stare frankly. He'd already learned that his smooth, muscular chest and bulging arms excited many women. He had kept in top physical condition; he had to, to be ready to hunt at any time. Women found him quite attractive—until they learned of his profession.

He closed down his mind even further. Eventually the few women who had returned his stare turned their attention elsewhere. If he maintained such control, as well as his posture and mannerisms, then he would remain invisible to notice. Being completely inconspicuous was part of his work, and, like his parents, he was very good at what he did. Besides, Bird was waiting at the end of the trip. And while she was no more fond of his work than most Mehirans, she was more understanding and certainly more loving.

She and her father lived outside the main part of town, in an area consisting of single-family houses, not like his family's teeming building. Many of the single houses were built around garden courtyards, with beautiful sculptures, fish ponds, elaborate garden furniture. The Third District Speaker's home was less rich than some, as he made no effort to compete with those in the medical or entertainment arts. He was said to have simple tastes. All the same, Cord envied the ease of Bird's existence.

She was still in school, studying speech and history, intending to take up politics. At present she acted as her father's aide. It was only the luxury Cord admired, however. He would not want to be a Speaker; the job entailed not only presenting his constituency's desires to the Council but also determining them by being available to the people of his district. That meant a great deal of emotional sharing. Cord was afraid to share his feelings completely. Not even his parents really knew of the forbidden delight that gripped him during a hunt.

"Cord, I'm so glad you came this evening," Bird said, greeting him warmly. She had opened the door even before he knocked; his desire had certainly alerted her in advance. He could feel the surge of her gladness underlaid with a yearning as great as his own.

She put her arms around his neck and whispered into his left ear, tickling it. "My father's out tonight." There was a throb of relief behind the words.

Cord was surprised. He'd felt no other emotional signal in the house, but he'd assumed the Speaker was at home; he often veiled his feelings. Cord shared Bird's relief. He was uncomfortable with her father. The Speaker was courteous, of course. He had never shown by the least sign that he disapproved of Cord. But Cord did not think he viewed his daughter's attachment to a criminal catcher with pleasure.

Bird took him up a polished wooden staircase to her room on the second floor. The walls were tinted in pastels, the floors covered with thick carpets. Her bedroom was strewn with beautifully hand-painted cushions. She pushed him down onto a cushion and poured something from a small jug into crystal cups.

"I know you'll like this," she said, offering him one. It was a spiced fruit drink laced with the aphrodisiac sap of a cold-climate tree. Cord stirred it idly; the beverage was the color of Bird's skin: a rich gold. He liked the way she wore her scalplock braided down her back. The velvet on her ears and spine, which ran nearly halfway down her back, was the same color as her hair, a deeper gold.

It was easy to forget the difficulties between them at times like this. He could even convince himself that it would all work out. After all, his mother and father had married in spite of similar obstacles. And at the very least, Bird would continue to be his love-friend, surely. And now that things were looking better for his family. . . .

He wanted to tell her, but she had other things on her mind. When he felt her sensations, all thought of talk left him.

"It's warm in here tonight. And getting warmer." She smiled and unclipped the jeweled fastening at the breast of her downy wrap-gown. Her nipples were like topazes. Rising from her own cushion, she pulled him to her. Caught up in the flow of her passion, Cord cupped her thrusting breasts and kissed each one in turn, too preoccupied to think about undressing. That was no bar to Bird, who stripped him enthusiastically of his tunic and pants.

The tip of her tail stroked his loins, causing his tail to twitch uncontrollably. He didn't know why she bothered with an expensive aphrodisiac; with her it was quite unnecessary.

She kissed him, thrusting her fruit-stained tongue into his willing mouth, while her hands never stopped moving over his body. He stroked her roughly, while his tail curved up between them and caressed the soft, tender area between her legs. Slowly the furry tip intruded farther, as Bird relaxed her interior muscles. The farther the tip explored, the more she writhed in pleasure.

She pushed him away, the tail withdrawing, and then she knelt before him. Using mouth, hands, and tail, she teased the pouch hanging there. Slowly, his organ snaked out from the protective pouch and uncurled.

Cord drew her down on top of him, entering her carefully as she straddled him. Bird arched her spine and threw back her head, scalplock swinging. Her pleasure coursed through him, engorging his organ even more. He grabbed her, twined his legs around her, and flipped her on her back. The aphrodisiac flowed to every sensitive part of their bodies. Using the strength she so much admired, Cord took her legs and spread them apart in the air while he began thrusting in earnest.

His tail curled up under him and probed her anus while hers did the same to him. He felt the ache in her loins, the contractions of delicate muscles. She felt the moist, hot friction and his delight in piercing her soft flesh. His tail began thrusting in matching rhythm while her tail pressed incessantly upon a most important gland, the pressure driving him to frenzy.

The reverberation of emotion peaked as they reached fulfillment together. They lay there gasping, while their spiking ecstasy subsided.

"I wish you would come to a passion party sometime," Bird murmured later, when they lay close, unmoving.

"You know how it is," he answered. As a sex partner, he was not desirable to many because of his occupation.

"I went to one last week where one of the guests filled eight girls, one right after the other. He had fortified himself with several cups of that"—nodded at the jug—"before he arrived—or should I say 'came'?—and drank more afterward. Someone told me today that he's still out of commission. Serves him right for showing off. He wasn't the only one. The award for the most acrobatic performance must go to the young lady who contrived to have herself plugged front and back, while stimulating a third with her tail and a fourth to greater heights with the only available orifice. Though, I suppose if she hadn't needed her nose to breathe . . ."

Cord shook with laughter. "Oh, stop it, Bird! Tell me how she did it."

With unexpected swiftness, Bird sprang to her knees and leaned over Cord. His sexual apparatus had retreated into his pouch, but Bird's tongue found the opening and obligingly followed it in. After an interval during which Bird demonstrated some rather advanced techniques, she stopped and said suddenly:

"You're certainly happy tonight."

"I'm always happy around you," he replied. It wasn't wholly true, and both of them knew it. But he tried to tell her of his family's good fortune and felt her withdraw slightly, as she always did when he mentioned the source of his family's income.

"I'm pleased for you," she said carefully. "I know you aren't—well provided for. But it's not an appointment to be proud of, is it? If your work were the arbitration of disputes, or entertainment, it would be wonderful. But it's almost as bad as being a criminal yourself. You use force, you hurt people—and you enjoy it."

Cord sat bolt upright. "I *don't* enjoy hurting people!" She was accusing him of being a deviant!

"I'm sorry," she said, a backlash of remorse washing over him. "I didn't mean that, exactly. You like hunting them, though. It excites you. I've felt it, Cord. You can't hide it completely.''

He felt a stab of alarm: he could think of no response. He had been able to deny truthfully any pleasure in others' pain, but he could not deny the second accusation, because it *was* true. The chase thrilled him. And it did border on forbidden behavior.

"Don't worry," she reassured him. "I won't tell anyone. But I can't help remember the time you caught that . . . that child mutilator.''

Cord plainly felt her psychic shiver. It was the proper response to a violent crime. Anyone who was not sickened by the idea of hurting others would have to be a hardened criminal himself. To any normal person, the victim's anguish and fear would be as painful as if they were his own.

And emotional backlash could be bad, very bad. Cord dismissed the case of the mutilator of children: she had been vicious, but her capture had presented no great challenge. Of many pursuits, the one Cord remembered was that of a murderer whom Fyrrell, with Cord's assistance, had cornered in a walled garden in the wealthy section—not far from Bird's home, in fact.

Their quarry expected to duck through and out another entrance in the dark, only to find that his means of escape had been locked. Cord recalled clearly how the criminal had felt, searching for a way out and realizing there was none. Then came the interior cringing he had not bothered to conceal. By then he was probably not able to govern his mind. Ordinarily, one could choose to make one's feelings opaque if it was necessary to hide them for others' comfort—that was why it took professionals to locate the committers of crime.

The episode was still vivid in Cord's memory. It was one of the first captures in which he had played an active part. But what he remembered was the malefactor's terror, apprehension, and desire to hurt them, which were strong enough to make Cord physically ill until Fyrrell shot the trapped man with an anesthetic. Then they'd turned him over to the Council. The murderer was of influential family, which was not sufficient to save him, but in such a case the Council would carry out the execution. While still unconscious, he would be given a lethal drug, and the Council would see to it that his death was ascribed to a seizure. Possibly some would guess the truth, but appearances would be maintained, to spare the family. For the less prominent, it was not necessary to go to such lengths. Then Fyrrell would have administered the poison on the spot, and they'd have presented the corpse to the Council and been paid their fee.

"Do you want to stay here tonight?" Bird inquired softly. Her eyes were full of sympathy: she could tell he had been thinking of something unpleasant. There was also hopeful anticipation of a night of lovemaking.

Drawn back from his memories, Cord said, "No, I'd better leave now. I've got to be there if my parents have a project on for tomorrow." He wished he could recapture the happiness he'd felt earlier in the evening.

"Oh, that's too bad. I'd thought we might sleep for a while, and then . . ." Her tail snaked over to curl around his. "That's all right, Cord, I know you have to make a living. There's always another opportunity, anyway." She ran her fingers down Cord's spine, caressing the velvety strip there, down to the base of his tail. "I didn't tell you *my* news, did I?"

What news?" His hands toyed with her golden breasts and began to roam downward. Not a smart move if he really did plan to leave soon. . . .

"Maybe you'll see me at the spaceport too."

Her words startled him. "You? How? We're going to trade, but you—"

"The spaceport is in the Third District. Who's Speaker of the Third District? My father suggested that he should receive clearance to visit the humans so he could assess their impact on the region and reassure his constituents if necessary. A District Speaker has the right to have an aide—even when inspecting dangerous or restricted areas—so I can have a pass, too."

Cord hugged her. He did not need to say anything. She would be able to feel how happy he was for her, for both of them. Regretfully, after a few more caresses and tongue thrusts, they washed and dressed.

It was a pity, the way working for a living cut into one's sex life.

It was late when he entered his parents' unit of the multi-residence. Most of the tenants were asleep, their emotional signals muted. But strong psychic impulses came from Neetel, Fyrrell, and Finola.

Cord grinned. Obviously he had returned too soon. He checked his shielding; why distract them from their pleasures by letting them know he was home? Their mental output showed no sign that they had heard or felt him come in, so he moved silently to his own room.

It was surprising that they hadn't aroused the entire building with their, ah, activities. And Cord could hear, as well as sense with his mind. Their unit was minimal housing; the walls were not as soundproof as they might be. A soft moan . . . an arpeggio of desire . . . a murmur of laughter . . .

Cord wondered how his father was able to keep two playful women entertained. It was, perhaps, an ability gained with practice and wide experience. Cord looked forward to the learning process. . . .

There was an explosion of passion, sustained for what seemed like eternity. Caught in the backwash from three orgasms, Cord lay gasping on his bed, hands pressed between his legs, loins aching, until all that remained was a feeling of satiation and drowsy contentment.

Cord gave in to it and fell asleep, dreaming of sexual prowess and a lengthy education.

# Chapter 2

The data Finola had promised arrived next morning by messenger. Fyrrell, Neteel, and Cord were all sworn not to show or reveal the material to any person not authorized to deal with the aliens. Then they were issued passes admitting them to the spaceport, and the formalities were complete.

"Let's get to work," Neteel said, securing the entrance to their unit. "The sooner we can communicate with them, the sooner we can sell them some technology."

The furnishings of their quarters were sparse, but they all had quick-study headsets. Fortunately, there was no case in progress at the moment; that left them free to absorb the alien language and the background materials. The quick-study headsets permitted information to be stored in the brain faster than it could be taken in by eye or ear. It would not make them fluent linguists, but would provide the vocabulary and grammar to understand the language. Speaking it would require some practice. Still, it would be enough for their needs.

By early evening, when they laid aside their headsets, they were all ready for a well-deserved rest.

"Here's a 'drama,' " Fyrrell announced, rummaging in the box of Terran material they'd been supplied. He passed the cylinder to Neteel.

"This will be a treat," she remarked, inserting the cylinder in the viewer. They seldom had the time to watch entertainments, even if their budget had permitted. Their viewer was used mostly for business.

"Are you sure this is fiction? 'The Theft of the Imperial Treasure' sounds more like a documentary. . . ."

Fyrrell shrugged and opened his mouth to reply—it stayed open as the first scene unfolded and skin-clad savages appeared, swinging swords.

No one said a word until the adventure had played itself out.

The aliens obviously were different, to judge by the casual violence of the main character's encounters. He was threatened with death half a dozen times, was beaten, inflicted assorted injuries upon the gang of thieves, and finally was rewarded by the alien equivalent of the Council.

"They really can't feel each other, can they?" Neteel marveled. "I thought Finola was exaggerating."

"You know," Fyrrell observed dispassionately, "I don't think I've seen that much violence in my life."

"I thought it was disgusting—deviant, in fact," Neteel said. "But it's clear that those people need our skills."

Cord said nothing. He was shocked, of course: the Third District didn't see that much crime even spread over many years. And he was glad that the alien drama did not have an emotion channel, as a Mehiran recorded play would. The assault of violent emotions and the anguish of many deaths would have prostrated a Mehiran. His parents, hardened to aggression, looked pale, and Cord was sure he did, too. At the same time, he could sense that they also felt exhilarated—not by the contents of the cylinder, but by its implications. Criminal catchers were highly regarded among the aliens.

"Technically speaking, he didn't have much equipment," Fyrrell said. "His hands and feet, a knife, and that gun. No means of detecting the criminal."

"I'm not sure we can draw too many conclusions about their technical ability from that." Neteel gestured toward the cylinder. "Probably it's like some of the entertainments I used to watch—more for enjoyment than edification."

"Well, parts of it looked enjoyable," Fyrrell replied. "What particularly well-shaped breasts the hero's lady friend had."

"I thought they amounted to a deformity," Neteel retorted. "No, make that two deformities. I'm surprised he was able to get close enough to do her any good."

Cord laughed at the repartee and kept silent. He did not think it was the time to point out the complete strangeness of the human society as depicted by the adventure.

The spaceport was located in an area which had been low-lying marsh; the enterprising humans had efficiently drained, filled, and paved it—and made room for more of themselves. The Council had erected a high, molded-stone wall around the complete installation. At the gate, a Council guard asked to see their passes and inspected their vehicle for contraband.

Beyond the wall loomed a black, glassy-looking building like nothing Cord had ever seen or imagined. It was set well back from the Council's barrier, but its sheer size made it loom over them.

From the material which the Council had given them, Cord knew that the domed black monolith contained all the alien enclave's offices and living quarters. It housed almost a thousand humans, yet it occupied only a small area of the port compound. Beyond it was the paved field where the interstellar ships and their shuttles landed: a great gray cicatrix surrounded by service buildings and the apparatus which controlled landings.

They left the rented float car—not new but large, its teardrop shape brightly painted in red and yellow—not far from the port facility's door. The entrance looked virtually impregnable; there were no windows. Cord filed it away as an item of interest.

The door parted at their approach. Within, the first alien Cord had seen stopped them. He greeted them in good Mehiran and requested their passes. This must be a security guard, thought Cord: the human wore some sort of dark-colored uniform with shiny badges.

The human was close to the Mehiran norm in size and features. The most notable differences were his lack of a tail and his round ears, set low and flat against the sides of his head. Cord wondered how acute his hearing could be with such an arrangement.

His emotional output was alien, too, but not as much so as Cord had expected. The man was bored and a little hungry. His emanations were obviously not Mehiran, but they were easy enough to interpret.

Having scrutinized their passes, the Terran instructed them to follow a yellow line inset in the floor, and wished them good trading.

In a room richly furnished with carpets, cushions, tables, and heavily padded seats and benches, another human met them. He was older than the guard, dark-complected and stocky. His clothing looked nothing like the guard's, but perhaps it was a uniform too, since other badges were affixed to it.

The human spoke what the aliens called Multi-Lang, with which Fyrrell, Neteel, and Cord were now reasonably comfortable.

"My name is Stev Greffard," he said. "I'm a specialist in technology trade. We've been informed that you are licensed to offer us law-enforcement technology. What do you have that we might be interested in?"

Terrans certainly got straight to the point. It was difficult to concentrate on a new language and on the man's emotional state at the same time, so Cord opted for the latter. His mother and father would be responsible for the trading; he was there as a backup, to observe.

The Terran was curious but not eager, hopeful but not expectant. It was, Cord analyzed, simply another potential business transaction. There was no novelty in it for Stev Greffard. He was much like any shopkeeper on Mehira. As a contact with the alien mind, it was disappointing. Cord transferred his attention back to the conversation.

Stev Greffard invited them to sit, and he sank down in an uncomfortable-appearing cross-legged position. Fyrrell, Neteel, and Cord squatted among the pillows, bracing themselves slightly with their tails.

"We have small pursuit mechanisms for trailing. In places where a person would be seen, a robot no larger than this" —Fyrrell pantomimed with thumb and forefinger barely apart— "can pass unnoticed."

"We also have robot shadows," Stev Greffard said.

"Do you have sensors which detect a lawbreaker in a crowd by his body odor?"

Cord caught a flash of interest in Stev Greffard's mind, followed by caution.

"No," the human replied slowly. "But would it work with those not of your race? There are dozens of humanoid species. Surely metabolic differences would render your detector useless."

"With adjustment," Neteel answered, "I am certain it would function with any humanoid. Granted, you would have to establish criteria for each species you wished to check, but the principle should be the same in all cases. With nonhumanoids, I could not say whether it would work. I don't know enough—yet.''

"You are very confident," the Terran observed wryly.

Which only proved that the aliens were incapable of detecting emotion.

They discussed several other devices; most of them elicited a positive response from the trader—emotionally if not verbally.

"Can you return tomorrow with some of your devices and demonstrate them?" Stev Greffard asked.

"Yes, we can arrange to do so. Though our schedule is tight," Fyrrell added.

Cord and Neteel experienced amusement. Fyrrell was not going to sound too anxious.

Their host rose. "Thank you for your time," he said. "Perhaps you will take a tour of our port facilities—we would like you to have a better idea of what we have to offer. And perhaps by learning about us, you will think of things we might wish to buy from you."

His mother accepted promptly—Cord could feel that she was fascinated by the humans' technology.

Greffard summoned another human, a female, this time.

"This is Julia McKay," he said. "She has been conducting the tours, since she has no regularly assigned work." He bowed to the Mehirans. "I will expect you tomorrow at the fifth hour."

"That is agreeable to us."

Cord studied their guide with interest. She was about his own age, he thought, possibly a little older, although with an alien it might be difficult to interpret age. She was as slim as Bird, but her skin was pale—whitish rather than golden or leathery brown like Greffard's. Her coppery hair was severely tied back and lay at the base of her neck in a roll. While she did not appear to wear a uniform, she did have a single, large emblem pinned to her white tunic—a cross with arms of equal length inside a rayed circle. The plain garment did not do justice to her slim elegance, Cord thought. She reminded him of the blade of some well-wrought, perfectly honed knife.

"What shall we call you, Julia McKay?" Neteel inquired, still puzzled by the use of two names.

"Just Julia, if you please," the human woman replied. "We are not formal here. We'll skip the office section," she continued, leading them down a corridor to a door marked "Trans Tube." A panel slid open and a small cubicle lay beyond. The seats were designed for humans, with no accommodation for tails, so Cord's family stood as the tube shot up. Cord gave up trying to calculate how many levels the building contained, and how fast the trans tube was rising.

The complex was a self-contained city, as it needed to be, isolated from the world on which it was located. The tour took them through storerooms, entertainment areas, housing for transients, laboratories, a hospital, even a shrine of some sort. But it contained no ancestral relics, so Cord could not understand how it could be meaningful. Of course, it was new: Perhaps in a few years, when it had acquired some mementos . . .

His father was surreptitiously scratching at a wall made of the same black material that formed the exterior of the port buildings. The attempt was apparently futile.

"This place is a fortress," he observed to Cord, sotto voce, while Neteel asked their guide about the system of transport used in the complex. The trans tube intrigued her.

"They use this stuff to separate sections. Probably they could seal off any one from the others, and that area would be impenetrable. That's what I think," Fyrrell qualified. "Did you notice what an odd texture it has?"

"Do they anticipate trouble?"

"The Council did," his father replied dryly. "Why not these?"

Next were the recreational facilities: rooms in which to play games, a pool for swimming (imagine doing that for pleasure! Well, bathing is enjoyable) and a large hall where a handful of humans were lifting weighted objects, and—

Two males were grappling. Cord tensed and felt his parents do likewise, ready to leap in and separate the aliens. But Fyrrell signaled to hold back.

No one else seemed to have noticed the combatants. Cord opened his mind to impressions. With strangers, unless they were experiencing some strong emotion, it was necessary to concentrate on sensing them.

There was no anger in the men. Competitiveness, yes, more than Mehirans thought proper, and excitement, but it was not a fight as Cord understood it. His mother and father

seemed to have reached the same conclusion and to have
dismissed any thought of intervention.

They *are* different, Cord realized, shaken. They play at
fighting, they take actual violence for granted, they admire
those who use force. . . . To them, my parents and I would
be heroes.

It was a heady thought. He almost wished he'd been born a
human.

He reached out with his empath's sense to Julia, wanting a
human contact for reassurance.

There was nothing there. Startled, he unwittingly transmitted his surprise to Neteel and Fyrrell. His mother glanced at
him inquiringly. With the code of body signals his family
used when working together on a case, he indicated that it
was nothing of importance.

Cord tried again. The absence of emotion in Julia McKay
was different from the way a shielded mind felt. This, he
decided, was what he expected an alien to be. But why did
she differ so much from the other three or four humans whose
emotions he had touched? He wanted to ask her about herself
and her background, but one could hardly pry.

"I would like to see more of your buildings," Neteel said,
"but we don't wish to monopolize your time or keep you
from your other duties."

"I don't have any other duties," Julia responded. "I am
here to meet Mehirans and to learn about them." She led
them out of the recreational area and into another corridor.

"Are you a scientist, then?" Neteel, coming from a scien-
tific family, regarded that branch of study highly. "We understood this was a commercial enterprise."

Julia laughed. "I'm a missionary: I have no commercial
value. But most of the worlds on which a trading company
might incorporate require such enterprises to carry out other
functions. Trading companies have to file planetological reports with the Allied Systems Survey, for example, to increase our knowledge of the galaxy. And if a trader wants a
branch on my world, he must agree to carry a missionary if
asked to do so."

"What is a missionary?" Fyrrell inquired.

A flash of surprise crossed Julia's face, but she recovered
quickly. "A missionary's function is to impart knowledge of
his or her religion, so that others will recognize its truth and

efficacy, and adopt it as their own." She touched the emblem on her tunic and added, "When I was sent to Mehira with this expedition, no one anticipated that access to your people would be so limited. The Church assumed—everyone assumed—that we'd be able to travel freely. However, though I see only a few Mehirans this way, I am able to know them better than I could if I saw hundreds every day."

"I see. Thank you for your explanation," Fyrrell responded.

"Perhaps you will tell us about your religion sometime," Neteel said politely. "Unfortunately, if we are to return tomorrow with samples of our equipment, we must go home to check them over and pack them."

"Of course," the alien woman agreed. "I shall look forward to meeting you again." With a serene smile and a nod, she led them to the end of the hallway and opened a door, gesturing them to go through. Then she locked the glossy black door behind Cord's family.

They had learned to interpret the colored lines in the corridors. By following the green strip, they found the exit with ease. The guard at the door made a note that they had left, and at what time. Security seemed tight enough, Cord noted.

As they drove back to the city, Neteel observed thoughtfully, "Finola is right. Those humans are wealthy, and they're interested in what we have to sell them."

His parents wre unusually silent for the rest of the trip. Cord himself had things to think about. It had not even crossed the minds of the humans they'd met (except Julia; he didn't know about Julia) that Cord's family were investigators. At least, they had not reacted to the knowledge, as Mehirans always did, unless they were close friends. Why should they react? Cord asked himself. The humans' own emotions and pastimes branded them as hardly better than Mehiran criminals and degenerates. Certainly they were no better than Cord and his family. Worse, if anything, he concluded. Would he want to be a "hero" among such people?

They parked their rented vehicle and walked to their door, where a Council messenger was waiting for them.

"You should leave word when you're going to be out all day," he complained.

"We were at the alien spaceport, trading," Fyrrell said smartly. That was cause for pride. "Come in."

The messenger shook his head.

"It must be urgent then," Neteel observed.

"Let us say that the Council gives it high priority. A case of deviant behavior in the Council itself," the man murmured, handing over the authorization.

"Oh . . ." Fyrrell said, reading it over, his fine features grave and intent.

Cord felt revulsion at the word "deviant." It was used to cover so many things now. When he was a child, deviancy meant killing or hurting for pleasure, but now it seemed to be applied to conduct that once would only have been considered eccentric. Or even, he added to himself, to disagreement with the Council.

"Well, do you accept?" the messenger asked sharply, making no effort to conceal his feeling of irritation.

"Yes, of course." Fyrrell signed the receipt and handed it back to the man. Neteel, who had been waiting by the door, clearly impatient for him to leave, shut it firmly behind him and secured it.

"Bad news, Fyr?" Fyrrell's emanations of distress were unmistakable.

"I wish we could have turned this one down," he muttered.

They almost never refused an assignment. They could not afford to, and when the Council was the client, it was unwise to do so. Cord recalled that they'd last declined an assignment two wet seasons ago, when his mother was ill with the dry-lung infection.

"We are to secure evidence of crime, so that the object of the investigation can be charged."

"But don't they know whether he's committed one?" Cord asked. Usually they were called in when there was a known crime and an unknown perpetrator. This case seemed backward.

"The Council feels it likely the subject is engaged in criminal activity, in view of his . . . ah . . . 'deviant' behavior."

"Which is?" Neteel prompted.

"He has no lovers, as far as is known, has turned down invitations to have sex, and keeps his feelings to himself."

"Discourteous to refuse an offer, certainly," Cord's mother remarked, "especially if he should be so clumsy about it as to give offense. But that's not a crime."

"Who is our subject?" Cord asked, with growing apprehension.

Fyrrell raised his golden-brown eyes from the authorization and report to Cord's face.

"I'm sorry, Cord. It's the Speaker for the Third District."

Neteel looked stricken, but Cord did not feel much surprise. He'd thought for a long time that his friendship with Bird was too good to last.

His parents felt sorry for him. To make them feel better, he said, "Well, it isn't as though they knew he'd done something. Maybe there won't be any evidence to gather."

Fyrrell and Neteel were not noticeably cheered. Cord knew what that meant: the Council—even if they did not say so explicitly—wanted results. Still, one could not fabricate proof of crime. If the Speaker was doing nothing wrong, all the Council could do would be to expose his allegedly deviant habits, which might well be enough to remove him from the Council. But if that was all they desired, why not do it, instead of hiring investigators?

"We needn't all go to the spaceport," he replied. "You must, because you invented most of our tools. If the humans have technical questions, you must be there to answer them."

Cord saw the difficulty at once. Someone had to initiate the Council assignment tomorrow. His mother could not go to the spaceport alone; some of the devices required two to operate, or two to carry, at least. He, Cord, could accompany her, but he'd been assisting in investigations for only about three years—some of that part-time, while he finished his specialist courses. His father was the one who should go to the spaceport with Neteel.

"I can watch the Speaker," Cord said. "It doesn't sound like a very complicated case. The day after tomorrow, if I haven't made any progress, we can talk it over and see what I'm doing wrong. But I think I can handle it. All I'll need is an audiovisual shadow."

"I wish you didn't have to, Cord. It will be hard enough for you if Bird finds out that your family is involved. But you understand how it is. We can't afford to miss this chance at the spaceport, and we can't risk the Council's displeasure."

"I know, Father."

# Chapter 3

In the very early morning, Neteel and Fyrrell began packing up the equipment they intended to demonstrate to the humans. No one said anything further about the assignment given them by the Council.

Cord, feeling unusually serious, took their best mechanical shadow. The second-best was really good only for night work, as it was bulkier.

"We'd better be starting," he told his parents. "I can place the shadow and be back before the Speaker leaves home, and then monitor it from here."

It was not difficult. His parents dropped him off within walking distance of Bird's home. Cord knew where the Speaker's vehicle—a sign of his importance and wealth—was kept. There were some advantages to investigating acquaintances, he thought bitterly. At the back of the house, in a service courtyard not overlooked by windows, Cord could do his work with no likelihood of being spotted. Setting the mechanism took only moments.

Then he sprinted for the public transport station. He wished now that he'd gone out the previous night to place the tracking device, but he'd been tired then and upset at the prospect of investigating Bird's father. Well, no point in worrying about that now; and it was still early. People like the Speaker did not rise as early as Cord's family did. If only this did not prove to be the morning he'd make an exception!

Cord was breathing more rapidly than usual when he reached the station, but his mind was calm. There had been no indication from the audio transmitter yet. The coach came, and Cord made himself comfortable, regulated his breathing, and watched the city go by: first the pink and yellow homes of the well-to-do, with the phalluslike towers of the hillside mansions in the distance. The hillside was the most desirable section of town, as the riverside was the poorest. Fine houses, mauve and pale green, a park, businesses ranging from genteel to merely necessary, then dingy white multi-residences.

The day's being gray and chill worked to his advantage in two ways. Few were out yet, so the public vehicles were running on schedule and without too many stops. Also, such cool, damp weather guaranteed that the Speaker would be wearing bulky clothing—trousers, perhaps, and surely a mantle.

By the time he reached the station nearest his home, he was less apprehensive. Evidently today would be no different from any other for the Speaker. It had been Cord's chief fear that Bird's father would alter his routine and leave earlier than usual, which would have destroyed Cord's chances of watching him for the day. Entering his parents' unit, he went straight to the monitor. It was recording and transmitting a good picture, which relieved another anxiety. Sometimes it was unreliable. Fortunately all it showed was the underside of the Speaker's vehicle and a restricted view of the courtyard's paving. If the Speaker had left before Cord got back to the monitor, the shadow's microphone would have picked up the sound of the engine—but that would have been little use, if he was not back at the monitor.

Well, here he was, and now he had to wait.

Invisible footsteps, eerily clear in the receiver, clipped in his ear. Dress shoes, lacing halfway up the calf, came into view—though from the shadow's vantage point, Cord could see no higher than the ankles.

Now, he thought, quickly. The Speaker was sliding open the door. Cord manipulated the controls. The shadow detached itself from the vehicle, hovered, and moved out toward the Speaker's feet. This was the tricky part. If the Speaker glanced down, or felt the shadow when it attached itself . . .

It moved quietly and without disturbing the air in its passage. Forward, rise, elevate lens . . .

Cord made a quick decision. He wouldn't attach it until the Speaker left the vehicle. But when the Speaker slid the door shut, the shadow was in the car with him.

The Speaker's car did not travel far. Cord estimated that the direction was west, which would mean toward the hillside section. It came to a halt, and Cord heard stirrings as the Speaker prepared to get out. The painstaking work was ahead. Cord searched until the Speaker was in the viewscreen.

Then he detached the pursuit capsule from the main unit. The entire assembly was too large to use in daylight without cover; certainly it would not be possible for it to follow the Speaker through the streets or into a building. The capsule by itself might pass unnoticed, but it did not have the range to send its data back to the monitor. Instead, it transmitted to its carrier, which would remain with the Speaker's vehicle, and the carrier would relay the signal back to the monitor. It was not an ideal arrangement, since if the Speaker moved beyond the capsule's limited range, Cord would lose contact until the Speaker returned to his vehicle—and the carrier unit.

The capsule, hardly larger than an insect (in fact, it was disguised to look much like one of the larger insect species), attached itself to the Speaker's mantle. The garment's fullness and rich embroidery reflected its wearer's position in society—and provided concealment for the surveillance device. Once the Speaker was inside, it should be possible to manipulate the capsule to get a visual broadcast as well as sound.

From the glance Cord caught of the area in which the Speaker had parked, he was sure that it was the wealthy section. He had no time to study the scene in detail, as his attention was taken up with maneuvering the bug. Its tiny grips opened and closed upon the fabric until it had a stronger hold. Then he had a few minutes in which to untense his muscles, and to consider possible courses of action. There was a moment's anxiety when the Speaker removed the mantle, letting it fall into disarray on the floor. Cord guided the shadow out of the enshrouding cloth, bringing it to a halt under the edge of the material. Working blind, it was a delicate operation. But it resulted in his being able to see again, as well as hear.

Swiveling the camera, Cord focused on the Speaker and his hostess—a person Cord did not recognize—who were crouching before a refreshment table.

If the Council could make anything of a conversation revolving around fisheries and the production of fish jelly, Cord thought, they were welcome to do so.

"I hope you will consider petitioning the Upper Council for more trade with the humans," the Speaker said. "While you may not sell much to them directly, you will profit from others' trade. People from all over Mehira will come to transact business with the offworlders, and virtually everyone in my district will prosper in some way. The visitors will buy fish, the residents will have more money, so they will buy more fish—and your business will grow.''

"The prospect is beguiling," the woman admitted. "That was why I asked you here to discuss your views on the alien trade. Still, there is some risk, is there not? And my profits have always been adequate."

"And they are no bigger than your parents' profits were when you were an infant. The aliens travel from star to star more easily than we go around Mehira. They did not gain interstellar travel by living in a static system. We are more civilized, yet less advanced. If we wish to equal and exceed their accomplishments, we must break out of our period of stagnation. Besides," he added with a slight smile, "at present the trade is benefiting only a few persons—those chosen by the Upper Council."

The businesswoman muttered agreement, evidently impressed by the last point. There was no further conversation for some moments. The Speaker sampled a dried fish roll filled with vegetable paste, and the fisheries owner sipped from a bowl. Sweetened fruit vinegar and water, Cord guessed; that would be the appropriate beverage for a morning business conference. Then she picked up a ripe, succulent berry and rolled it between well-manicured fingers, bruising its flesh, before a moist, pink tongue tasted it. The act of eating the fruit was decidedly sensual.

"I have heard a rumor that the Council has restricted contact because the humans are savages." She smiled slyly. Though the shadow could not transmit emotions, Cord was sure savage lovemaking appealed to her.

"There are always rumors of some some sort," replied the Speaker. "The Council is overcautious and naturally does not wish to upset the status quo. I have met the aliens, and I do not believe they desire anything beyond expanded trade opportunities and profit. As what reasonable person does not?"

The woman agreed with a laugh. Setting her cup carefully on the table, she rested her hand on the Speaker's arm and said, so softly that Cord almost did not catch the words:

"I did not ask you to come here only to discuss business. Life does not revolve around work alone. I have admired you for a long time, although we have not known each other well. Please consider me your friend."

"I am honored," the Speaker said. He sounded more apprehensive than flattered. Common courtesy forced him to add, "Please consider me your friend."

Cord was conscious of a feeling of embarrassment for the Speaker. He could see where the conversation was leading.

"Then let us seal our friendship," the woman breathed. "We won't be disturbed here."

Cord sat up straighter. He had been to parties with other young people, of course, at which no one worried too much about being observed in sex. But everyone doing it together was different from spying on someone in the act—particularly when the someone was much older and an honored leader. Cord hoped the Speaker could find some way to excuse himself from a duty which he seemed unlikely to desire, but doubted he could do it. It would be so very rude.

"I am sorry," the Speaker replied after a noticeable hesitation. "For many years I have been incapable in that way."

"Are you certain it isn't for lack of trying? I'm very good."

The fisheries owner's gown slid down on her shoulders to pool around hips. Although she was older than Neteel, Cord thought she was still extremely desirable. She had large, well-shaped breasts and inviting, firm flesh; her arousal was evident. Cord sympathized with the Speaker. There was really no way now that he could extricate himself . . . but no normal person would want to turn down such an attractive offer anyway. Certainly the Speaker had been maneuvered into this position so that he could not withdraw without insulting his hostess—and losing her political support.

But with a smile which was clearly forced, the Speaker said: "I am sure you are delightful. And if I were able to respond, I would certainly sample all the pleasures you offer. Unfortunately that is not possible. Thank you for your hospitality. I must leave now."

The Speaker stood up with dignity. His hostess gathered her garment around herself and rose also, her tail lashing angrily. After an exchange of restrained courtesies, the Speaker picked up his cloak and departed.

By then, the golden red sun had broken through the clouds, so he did not bother to put on his mantle; the surveillance device remained concealed in it. The Speaker then went to the Lower Council building, where surveillance was not necessary—indeed, the Council forbade the making of record-ings in the chambers, except during public sessions. Even in the course of an investigation for the Council, the discovery of a shadow there would have been embarrassing for Cord's family. However, since the Speaker left the mantle in his vehicle, the problem did not arise. When he came out at sunset, he returned to his home, and Cord left the monitor unattended, only switching the panel to "Alert." If the Speaker went out again, later in the evening, a tone would sound, to claim Cord's attention—or perhaps Fyrrell's or Neteel's.

Cord was very tired, so tired that he was not even hungry, but when his parents arrived at dark, their obvious happiness revived him.

"We bought something at a cookshop," Neteel said, set-ting a stack of leaf-baskets on the bench. "To celebrate," she explained, since such an extravagance was rare for them.

"We're selling the Terrans plans to one or two things," Fyrrell said, carrying in the cases containing their demonstra-tor models and samples.

"One or two things!" Neteel laughed delightedly. "Say five or six."

"And they will pay us so much for every one they manufacture. It's a very small amount of money for each— but Greffard was speaking of selling hundreds of thousands of them."

"And that would make our . . . royalties very great." Neteel used the human word; Mehiran lacked a term for it.

As they took their places around the low table, Neteel asked, "How was your surveillance today?"

"I don't think I got anything the Council will be able to use. Most of the day the Speaker was in the Lower Council. This morning he talked to someone about expanding trade with the aliens. It's not very interesting. No sign of anything you'd call an illegal activity." During the day, following the Speaker's movements, Cord had been able to regard him as simply another subject for investigation. Now he found him-self feeling slightly defensive about Bird's father.

"That, of course, is for the Council to decide," Fyrrell gruffly told him. Cord knew that. And he was definitely uncomfortable about that monitored meeting without knowing why.

"Did you recognize the person he met?" Cord's mother inquired, helping herself to minced vegetables.

"No, but she should be identifiable from the recordings. She seemed to have widespread fishing interests."

"Perhaps, after dinner, you should take the recordings to the Council. They expect regular reports, whether there is anything to report on or not. You know where to take them?"

"Yes. I've made deliveries to the Council before."

"So you have. Sorry, Cord, I keep forgetting. Don't worry about following up tomorrow—your mother and I will keep an eye on the monitor while you catch up on your sleep. One of us would go tonight with the recordings, but we've got some work to do before our next meeting at the spaceport."

# Chapter 4

There were few people in the streets so late, but when he came to the Council's administrative building, Cord saw that three of its six wings were still fully lit. Someone was always on duty in case the Council had to be summoned to deal with an emergency. Cord knew his parents had often come to the Council representative here at night with case reports or for instructions. Usually the attendant in the entrance hall was alone. Tonight, several Council guards and half a dozen men and women of obvious importance (though they were wearing plain mantles or hooded cloaks) were waiting there. Cord glanced around, his nerves raw. Six wings radiated from the domed entrance hall, their dim, green marble corridors echoing. By comparison, the lobby seemed a haven of light and safety.

"Your business?" the attendant demanded.

"I have an investigative report for the Council," Cord replied. He kept his empathic sense shielded. He did not want to know what all those respected and powerful people thought of his work.

The attendant beckoned to a guard.

"Take him to the Council representative."

Cord followed his escort, looking to neither side. He had the uncomfortable feeling that he had involved himself in something large and complex. The guard led him to an upstairs room, not one of the usual rooms where ordinary Mehirans with ordinary business would be admitted. A stiff-backed Council representative sat waiting—and Cord quickly dampened his startled reaction.

A representative was usually in the prime of life, holding the position as a prelude to a career of public service. Bird's father had been a representative when he was young, Cord understood. But the man seated among many cushions before him was old. His scalplock had darkened almost to brown,

45

and his skin was yellowish, but his back was still straight and his thinness only increased his dignity. Perhaps he was someone of prestige, resuming his old role temporarily. That happened, sometimes, in a time of unrest or danger. Cord wondered uneasily what was wrong.

"You may sit," he instructed Cord.

Cord did so. It was an honor.

"You have recordings of your surveillance of the Speaker of the Third District?"

"Yes, respected one." Cord passed the box to him.

"It will take some time to study these. In the meantime I want a brief report from you." The representative pressed a button in the control panel beside him, and a woman in Council dress entered almost at once. Cord wondered if she'd been waiting in the corridor.

The old one gave her the recordings, she left, and he turned his attention back to Cord.

"Why are you withholding your emotions?" he asked unexpectedly. "Open your mind."

Reluctantly, Cord let down his defenses.

"In my family," he said, "it is often necessary. How could we trap criminals if they could feel our impulses?"

"Very sensible, but don't do it here. In the future when you are with decent people you had better permit your emotions to be known."

"May I ask why, sir?" Cord realized he was presuming upon the Councilman's good humor, but he was curious.

"Anyone whose feelings are not open to inspection by all must be hiding something: thoughts of violence or dishonesty. To withhold yourself is a form of deviancy which will not be tolerated much longer."

Cord said nothing. He was puzzled and a little frightened of the powerful man before him. He'd never been particularly afraid even of the most savage criminals he helped trap, only excited and tense. This was different. There was no excitement, only apprehension. And it was not good to come to the attention of the great—not in his parents' experience. For others, it was all right—an artist, a craftsman, or a cook might find himself with a wealthy patron. But no one took notice of investigators except to be offended by the brutality of their behavior and profession.

"Tell me about the Speaker of the Third District," the councilman said.

Cord obeyed. Condensed, it seemed little enough—but Cord could feel that his interrogator was pleased. He hoped he would be dismissed soon.

Without prelude, the woman who had come in earlier reentered. There was an aura of suppressed excitement about her, and the representative turned toward her.

"Yes?" The man's face, seen in three-quarter profile, finally triggered a memory. Cord realized that the official was a former Council head who had left office long before.

"I have cycled the recording," she announced, placing a sheaf of papers before the onetime Council leader. "The relevant sections are marked."

Cord understood. By playing it at far greater than normal speed, a computer could print it out in minutes—a fraction of the time it would take to listen to it at regular speed.

"Thank you." The official had been noted for his courtesy, Cord remembered.

She took it as a dismissal. The official turned back to Cord. "You've done very well.

"There is one other little matter you might handle for the Council," the old one said, as Cord began to bow in farewell. "It does not take precedence over your investigation of the Speaker, but it is a matter which interests the Council because it occurred near—very near—the spaceport. A solution will be rewarded at the usual rate for a . . . murder."

The word was tinged with distaste, understandable but perplexing. The Council paid for the solving of crimes only if they concerned the Council in some way. Otherwise the relatives and friends of a victim paid for the capture of his killer. The only exception would be in the case of an infamous crime or crimes which threatened to disrupt society.

"May I ask for details now, respected one?" Cord requested cautiously. The other might not care to discuss it.

"It is late to begin now. However, I will tell you what is known and the remains will be kept in stasis until you or your parents are able to examine them. No witnesses were present. The body was discovered by those on duty at the checkpoint outside the spaceport—where the wall encircles it."

The old one summed up concisely. A lifetime in the Council's service had taught him that skill. He went on.

"Indications were that he intended to attempt to enter the spaceport without authority."

"He was killed in the commission of a crime, then?"

"So it must be supposed. We wish to know who killed him, however. If the aliens did it, they must have come out of the spaceport, and that is a violation of the treaty. If a Mehiran was responsible, then a very vicious murderer is at large."

Cord raised his eyebrows questioningly.

The old one inclined his head deferentially toward Cord and said, a shade sarcastically, "We are not experts in the methods of death, but there were bruises on the throat and the neck was broken. And—and there was one peculiar circumstance," the Councilman finally said. A fleeting expression of extreme distaste crossed the wrinkled face, and a shudder rippled the air between them.

"Yes, sir?"

"Parts of the victim had been eaten. It was obvious to anyone who saw the remains, but the Council physician confirmed our suspicions."

"Eaten—but not by scavengers?"

"Scavengers had begun to feast, but it was no night prowler that broke open the skull and devoured sections of the brain. And then replaced the top of the skull very neatly. It fell off when the body was moved."

Disgust boiled up in Cord, then curiosity, then resolve.

"Good," said the old man. "You seem likely to have a long and successful career before you."

Cord felt the radiation of his approval—a rare sensation for a Catcher. The other's psychic emission shifted to one of command.

"Since you are intelligent and perceptive, I am sure you will not speak of anything that you have heard or seen here."

"Not even to my father and mother, sir?"

"You may tell them, on the understanding that they will hold it in confidence also. No doubt they will understand: they have often served the Council. Besides, your mother comes of an honorable family, and your father is a man of discretion."

Cord bowed his head to signify agreement and comprehension.

"Have you further instructions for the surveillance?" he asked.

"Continue it. You may report again tomorrow evening, if you have not received other orders in the interim."

"May I go, then?"

"You may."

As Cord rose to leave, the old Council chief picked up the printed report and studied it intently. It began to appear that Bird's father had given serious offense to the Council.

Cord trudged home, his thoughts as black as the night. The public transport had ceased its evening operation, and a warm rain was falling. His clothing was soon saturated, but being thin, did not inconvenience him.

He felt guilty about the Speaker of the Third District. Or about his own feelings about the Speaker, which was not the same thing. While he was operating the monitor, he forgot that the subject of the investigation was the father of his love-friend. Now he was glad to have earned the Council official's praise—perhaps it would mean a large gift as well. But it would mean the end of Bird's love and friendship.

He wished his work were regarded as highly on Mehira as it seemed to be among the humans. Cord spun himself a brief fantasy of life on exotic worlds, admired, richly rewarded—and fulfilled.

When he arrived at home, his father was up. Or still up, Cord did not know which. All of them were accustomed to unusual hours. Fyrrell was making a list of electronic components.

"You ought to sleep," he remarked, glancing up at Cord's wet clothing and slicked-down scalplock. "You were long at the Council."

"Yes. Something was going on there, I think—it was unusually busy. And a retired Council leader was there; he spoke with me about this case—and a new one they want to assign us."

Fyrrell stopped writing. "I see."

"That's more than I do, Father. He swore me to silence, and told me to warn you and Mother. Is she asleep?" he asked.

"No, she went to spend the night with her love-friend, Lanim. She wanted to share our good news."

Lanim had been his mother's friend for as long as Cord could remember. When Neteel had been recuperating from her illness two years before, he'd even taken her to stay in a better climate for four hands of days. Good friends, especially for Catchers, were rare.

"Good friends," Cord said aloud, thinking of Lanim and Finola, and of Bird, who might not be his friend much longer, if she learned of his Council assignment.

His father seemed to follow his thoughts. "I think, if it is a matter of such delicacy, that I had better take over tomorrow. It's nearly dawn, and you've had no sleep, but I napped earlier. If we both sleep now, I can wake in time to watch the Speaker."

"What about trading with the humans?"

"In that, Neteel is the important one. Besides, we are not due to go back to the spaceport for several days. In the morning you must go and get these." Fyrrell tapped the list. "It may be expensive, but we've decided to sacrifice our surplus. Neteel is certain that the special invention we've been working on will greatly interest the humans. And with money coming from them for the other devices, and what we'll receive from the Council, we can afford to gamble."

"And the new case?"

"It will have to wait its turn."

# Chapter 5

"Today you are free to do as you like," Neteel announced as they passed through the portal into the alien building. The humans had given them identification badges, so the one on duty merely waved them through without the formalities of the first visit.

"Is it permitted?" Cord asked.

"They don't mind," she replied. "They are as open in their conduct as in their minds. I am to speak with scientists this morning: Stev Greffard knows only a little practical science, himself."

"Shall I meet you here at a certain time?"

"No, it may take me longer than I guess. When I am finished, I will have them page you. Then come."

Cord marveled at his mother's composure in such a foreign environment. This was his second visit, and he still felt awkward. He went with Neteel as far as the office where they had first met Stev Greffard. The alien greeted her with every sign of respect. Cord, deciding he had done his duty, went looking for the amusement area.

He found it without difficulty: the complex of buildings was well-marked with maps. Once there, however, he wandered aimlessly, watching the humans at their sports and entertainments, but too shy to join in without an invitation. Well, he did not want to wrestle or practice hand-to-hand combat—their martial arts were too different, and none of those Cord practiced was meant for anything but killing or disabling. After all, if he had to subdue a criminal physically, the situation was too desperate for half-measures.

But he would have liked to try some of the games of chance, if he'd known the rules. The cubicles where one could view recorded entertainments interested him, too, although it was strange to think of seeing and hearing a drama without feeling the characters' emotions.

"Hello," a human voice said behind him. "You are called Cord, aren't you? We met once before."

Abruptly turning around, Cord saw the woman with coppery hair. It was still pulled back in a severe bun.

"Yes," he concurred. "Your name is Julia McKay." He stumbled over the first sounds, it was so un-Mehiran. The second name was closer to what he knew.

"Were you looking for someone?" she inquired.

"No. Is it permissible for me to be here? Neteel was occupied with technical matters and did not require my presence. We thought it was acceptable to observe."

"It's perfectly all right," Julia McKay assured him. "You looked as though you might be lost, so I thought I'd see if you needed directions."

"Only a friend," Cord responded candidly.

"I am available." She smiled. "Would you like something to eat or drink? The restaurant is quiet, and we could talk there, perhaps learn more about each other's culture. Will you be my guest?"

"Thank you. I am in your debt. Perhaps you will tell me about your 'religion.' "

Cord used the word hesitantly. No Mehiran spoke of religion, but if he understood the concept, it was similar to the reverence and affection one felt for one's ancestors. One spoke of them—Mother's fathers's father, who designed the Inlet Bridge, or Father's father, who was given an armful of golden bracelets for finding the kidnapped child of a great merchant. One spoke of their successes, of the good actions they'd performed, even of the clever things they'd said or done. And when one needed help, sometimes they would give it. Fyrrell always invoked his most illustrious criminal catcher ancestors before beginning a hazardous operation. And heirlooms and mementos of the deceased were important, preserved carefully as aids to remembrance.

Still smiling, Julia led him to a quiet, small room filled with empty tables and chairs. There were a few other patrons— Cord gathered it was the wrong time of day for the humans to congregate there. He sat carefully in a chair, his tail dangling out its open back. None of the items listed in the shiny tabletop (a sort of viewer, he decided, set level with the surface) meant anything to him, but his escort seemed willing to make the decisions.

By the time their order came, Cord felt very comfortable with the woman. Also, he thought he was becoming more familiar with the language, which would be of assistance.

They sipped their tangy beverages and nibbled on an assortment of tidbits until Cord finally said, "You still have not told me about your religion. Are you having any success spreading it?"

She laughed. "Not a bit, though on first acquaintance with your world, I would have thought it would prove very compatible here. We believe that true happiness and virtue are attained through subduing the passions and desires. You can't be happy or successful if you are at war with yourself."

To Cord, that sounded like good sense.

"A wish to do others good will fight with the urge to accumulate wealth, for instance. Our appetites for food, sex, possessions, and 'happiness'—in the worldly sense—usually prevent us from being truly good. But if we have no physical desires, there is nothing to prevent us from doing what we ought to do. In addition, we enjoy peace of mind unblemished by doubt, fear, shame, and longing."

Cord wished he could say the same of himself. He ate another crisp-fried appetizer and waited with an attitude of expectancy. When Julia did not continue, he asked, "How do you attain such peace of mind?"

"First," she said, regaining her stride, "one must not pollute the body. Most of the people who come here"—she indicated the room around them—"come to drink intoxicating beverages. Neither does my religion permit one to ingest any mood-changing substance, in any form. We eat simply, and only the quantity needed to maintain the body."

Cord noticed that she had indeed eaten only two or three of the tidbits.

"Nor do we engage in sex for its own sake."

"Do you abstain totally?" Cord asked, appalled. No wonder she'd made no Mehiran converts.

"Oh, not totally. Within the bonds of marriage or to procreate, it is acceptable. Sometimes it is appropriate with a good friend, when celibacy becomes a burden and lust threatens the integrity of the mind."

"I think you will not be successful here," he told her

frankly. Better she should understand now than be disappointed later. "No Mehiran, no normal Mehiran anyway, would agree even to partial abstinence. Why, it would be almost like cutting oneself off from . . . from life." Must not mention empathy. "Sex makes people happy, relaxes them, is an antidote to violent emotion. I've seen it often in my work: violent criminals usually don't have normal sexual relationships."

"Well," Julia replied, after a pause, "if you're right, and you must know better than I, then I may be doomed to fail. But the Missionary Society paid for my passage and board here, so I must keep trying."

Her emotional aura was unchanged: Cord could detect it no more than he'd been able to do last time. Now he knew why: she had disciplined her mind to absolute serenity. He shut off contact.

"Many of your other ideas impress me and would probably seem attractive to many of my people. But, Julia, do you really believe that sexual contact is not beneficial?"

"It is the doctrine of my religion. I know nothing of the matter from personal experience," she said forthrightly.

A tall human passing through the lounge detoured to stop at their table.

"Making any converts, Julia?" the man asked pleasantly, and added to Cord in good Mehiran, "We are pleased to have you visit us. I hope your trade prospers."

"I am sure it will, to our mutual benefit," Cord replied.

"Ham, this is Cord"—Julia gave the shortened form of his name—"a practitioner of police science. Cord, this is Hamilton K, Trade Agent for Ten Suns Enterprises."

The humans were evidently a diverse lot. Hamilton K's skull was shaven—or else he was bald—and a green K ornamented the middle of his forehead. His features were well shaped, however. Cord saw that the belt over his silky black tunic and trousers bore a K-shaped buckle, too, enameled green.

Perhaps this was the master of the human complex, Cord thought. So far, K was only the second human Cord had met who spoke Mehiran—no doubt learned as Cord had learned Multi-Lang. A pleasing gesture and most courteous. A few more polite exchanges, and the Trade Agent passed on.

"Why does he wear a letter on his forehead? Why don't the others here also?" Cord asked, bewildered.

"It is his last name as well as a letter of our alphabet. Hamilton's world dispensed with ordinary last names when it was colonized. Instead, they substituted letters to signify certain broad genetic groups. Many traders come from his planet."

"Why?—I'm sorry, Julia, I should not ask so many questions."

"Why not? This is all new to you. How else would you learn? The people who settled K's world, to answer your question, were pragmatists. They brought up their children to be pragmatists, which is a useful trait for a Trade Agent: they make a profit and abide by the rules, and as long as they do, no company will ask many questions about their methods."

"Here, the Council regulates some aspects of trade," Cord said slowly. The Council would act against someone who sold unwholesome food or lied to sell his goods.

"The galaxy is a very big place. Some parts of it have not been explored yet. Each civilized world makes its own rules, which govern its ships and its offworld enclaves, like this one. Spaceport Mehira operates under the laws and regulations of Andar VII. Ships registered on Andar VII observe its laws, too. A trading enterprise from Terra would operate under that world's laws."

"But then if two groups of traders from different worlds disagreed . . ."

"They'd fight it out, most likely."

Cord shuddered inwardly, half revolted and half excited by so casual a mention of violence. Yet what opportunities there might be!

"How is criminal catching carried out, with so many inhabited worlds?" Cord did not bother to apologize for speaking of a subject which would disgust most Mehirans. It was obvious that humans were hardened to violence. And, of course, not being empathic, they did not suffer the mental results of violence, so it must seem like a less important matter to them than to Mehirans.

Julia seemed quite content to answer his questions.

"Some worlds have treaties with others—mostly those with similar cultures and legal systems—which permit extradition. The majority don't, feeling that if a criminal gets offworld and stays there, it's not worth pursuing him. The ports are watched, so that if a criminal tries to come back to a world where he's wanted, he'll be caught.''

Cord believed he was open-minded, but he was a little shocked.

"You must not think any crook is safe if he gets offworld,'' Julia hurried on. "Some criminals a planetary government will think it worthwhile to pursue. That varies from world to world. And a victim, or his friends, or a special-interest group may raise the money to hire a bounty hunter.''

"Perhaps that is not very different from Mehira.''

More humans were drifting into the lounge, Cord noticed. The level of noise was rising, as well as the cacophony of emotions.

"You've asked me questions, Cord,'' Julia was saying. "Now you must tell me about Mehira. I conclude that there are similarities between your police work and bounty hunting.''

"If I understand the term 'bounty hunter,' there probably are many parallels,'' he agreed. "Sometimes we are hired by individuals to find stolen goods or missing persons, or to guard something of value. Or if we catch a violent criminal, we are rewarded by the Council.''

"You are very young to have taken up such a profession,'' Julia remarked, not unkindly. "I have met bounty hunters occasionally, and they are usually older and . . . rougher. They are predators. You do not seem like that.''

"My family has practiced criminal science for generations,'' Cord said indignantly, "ever since my father's five-times-great-grandfather was advised by the voices of his ancestors to find a certain murderer. He did, when everyone else had failed, because he knew the ways of the high mountains, so he guessed where the killer was hiding. We have been hunters of criminals ever since.''

Julia looked thoughtful. Cord fidgeted. The increasing noise was making him uncomfortable; humans in groups talked more loudly than Mehirans, and their emotional pitch ran much higher. He was not deliberately receiving their signals, but in a large group, the sheer volume of emotions made a clamor almost impossible to ignore. With practice and concentration, one could tune out all signals, of course. Most Mehirans never bothered to discipline their minds to that degree. After all, among Mehirans, such defenses were seldom needed: few were rude enough to broadcast unpleasant feelings. Occasional embarrassment or discomfort, perhaps, which let your companion know he had offended, and therefore gave him an opportunity to rectify his error, but not . . .

. . . humiliation . . .

. . . anger . . .

. . . speculation . . .

. . . amatory interest . . .

. . . pain . . .

. . . boredom . . .

. . . anticipation . . .

. . . rejection . . .

The waves of emotion beat in on Cord. In comparison, Julia's cool, antiseptic mind was a relief.

"Is something wrong?" the human woman asked.

Briefly, Cord caught an emotional stirring in her, but it was gone before he could analyze it, no more than a darting insect seen out of the corner of the eye or the elusive twinkling of a faint star.

"I think I'd better leave." Cord stood up. "It's getting late."

"Will you be coming back again?" When Cord nodded, she said, "Come and see me when you do. If you ask for me at the entrance, they'll tell you where to find me."

Suddenly her strangely colored eyes were full of promise. Cord felt a strong desire to see her again, somewhere quiet and private, where he would not be distracted by the psychic impact of others. It would be good to discuss her peculiar notions about sex, and convince her that she was mistaken about it. And to find out how a Terran woman differed from Bird. . . .

With a start, Cord realized that he was still staring into those disturbing green and gold-flecked eyes, and that they and her lips and shoulders and thighs seemed to be promising greater delights than any he'd known. It was a good thing that he was used to keeping his emotions to himself, he thought guiltily. If he'd been broadcasting, every Mehiran in the human compound would have gotten a pretty powerful dose of lust.

"I'd better go," he repeated. He turned away abruptly. If he stayed any longer . . .

At the door of the lounge, he looked back. Julia McKay

was still sitting there, smiling slightly, an island of calm in a stormy sea.

He returned to the lobby, feeling as if he'd put in a hard day. Human emotions were so exhausting. Except for Julia's, he added to himself. He looked at the displays on the walls—three-dimensional pictures of products the humans would trade, samples of other worlds' goods, alien artwork. It would be interesting to visit other planets, he thought. The culture which had created that great silver breastplate studded with cabochon gems must be exotic.

"Oh, Cord," Neteel's voice called. "I was going to ask the humans to page you. Did you find something to do while you waited?"

"Yes, Mother. I spoke with the 'missionary' who was our guide the first time we came. You were successful, weren't you?"

It did not require mind-touch to deduce as much. Cord's parents were still in their prime, and today Neteel was glowing with vigor and excitement.

"I can't tell you about it here," she said, lowering her voice a little. "Let's go home, so I can tell you and Fyr about it at once. If I don't, I'll burst."

# Chapter 6

Cord followed her out to their borrowed vehicle, wondering a little at her tension. However, she would not divulge her news. Instead she talked amusingly of her experiences with the humans. Cord was fascinated, having had little opportunity to talk with her in the last few days.

"They're such interesting people," Neteel remarked. "I had a wonderful chat with one of their engineers this afternoon, and I think I've picked up a couple of insights. . . . I'd love to see the control room of one of their ships. But I suppose it would make me feel like a backward child. In so many ways, we're far behind them. Then again, we are ahead in other ways. Maybe their tendency to have wars holds them back. There are still illnesses and wounds they can't heal. Imagine that."

Cord couldn't. Short of a catastrophic accident that killed instantly, Mehirans died only of old age. Even the dry-lung infection, the most serious disease they knew, had not been fatal in two centuries or more. It required many days of rest, following lung-tissue regeneration, but it was no longer regarded as dangerous, merely inconvenient.

"And I've had compliments," his mother continued. "It makes me feel young again."

Cord twitched his ears satirically. She might be his mother, but a woman with three lovers besides her husband was hardly sunken in age.

"What was the compliment?" he asked, knowing she looked forward to sharing it.

"The chief merchant—what do they call it? The Trade Agent—invited me to visit his rooms. His name was Hamilton K—have you met him? I was tempted, because he is very attractive, almost like one of us."

"I hope you didn't refuse just because I was waiting," Cord said, amused.

"No, I knew you wouldn't mind my being a bit late for such a good reason, but I felt that he was more interested in cementing a trade relationship than in sex. Still, I would have liked to find out how humans manage without tails," Neteel remarked meditatively.

"I have met this Hamilton K," Cord said as she guided the car from the highway into the building-lined streets near the river. "Julia said he was a pragmatist, and that was what made him a good trader. But I wonder if his practicality will be a match for your inventiveness."

His mother laughed delightedly.

The setting sun cast lavender-pink-carmine on the walls of the small common room Cord's family shared. He lay sprawled across a large floor cushion to one side of the low table while his mother, excitement still sparkling in her eyes, sat on the low, soft couch. His father brought out a metal tray with vermilion-tinted delicacies and glasses of sunset-colored nectar.

"You know I went to speak with some of their scientists today," Neteel said as she leaned forward to pluck a morsel from the tray. "My avowed purpose was to discuss some details of the devices we're trading to them, and to ask in return for some materials that are rare here."

Cord suspected that his father already knew all of this. To him it was new, though.

"My real intention was to pick up some hints about their science." Excitement burst from her once more. "I did, Fyr. I know exactly what to do now, to make it work as it ought to do."

"To make what work?" Cord asked, as he rose to take a glass of nectar.

"The . . . thing we've been experimenting with," Neteel responded with a return to caution. Cord knew his mother was working on a special but secret invention. She never wanted to speak of her devices until she was sure they would work.

"When it's finished," Fyrrell began slowly, "do you think they'll buy it?"

"Oh, yes. There's no question about it, if I'm any judge of people—even if they are aliens. They'll buy it."

Fyrrell looked worried. "But is it wise to sell it to them?"

Neteel made an unhappy little gesture. "I don't know. I'm less and less sure as I'm sure the instrument will function."

"If it should be used against us . . . ," Fyrrell said reluctantly.

Neteel laughed. "That possibility is the least of my worries. There's a counterdevice, naturally. I started work on it as soon as I began to see how this one would operate. And remember, the device itself is short-range: you'd have to be virtually touching the other person."

"Mmmm . . ." Fyrrell frowned, eyeing the dinner he'd barely touched, while he radiated concern, suspicion, and a tinge of fear.

Cord and his mother exchanged glances. "Why don't you go for a walk? You need the exercise," she suggested pointedly. "Have you seen Bird lately?"

Cord was startled, then briefly angry at his mother's change of mood. He gulped down the rest of his drink and picked up a handful of the tidbits. Broadcasting reproach, Cord left.

There was a large park east of the river, forming a barrier between the commercial sections and the expensive suburbs. It was a place where all classes of Mehirans could mingle, and it was here that he'd first met Bird. Their favorite place was a shady grove of sea-green trees and cascading vines with tiny white starflowers. A small brook ran through the grove, flowing over a special stone bed in a miniature mountain torrent. There the spray made the tiny rock faces glow green with a mossy night growth that shone softly in the night. In the daytime, the spray formed rainbows in the sun.

By the time he arrived in that western section of the park, it was well into the night. The phosphorus-yellow streetlamps stood like giant matchsticks along the path. He passed only a few strollers, mostly arm-in-arm couples. It made him long for Bird.

There was only one person sitting by the waterfall, gently bathed in the light of the green-glow moss. It was a woman, sitting in profile, wearing a beautiful and expensive shimmering shift. Was it Bird? His heart leaped at the stab of love such a thought brought him. He could not control the feeling, and the woman turned, startled, as the emotion touched her.

Yes, it was Bird! She had been sitting on a boulder scooped out to form a comfortable bench. When she sighted him coming up the path, she jumped up and ran to meet him.

"Cord," she breathed in his ear, throwing her arms around his broad shoulders and neck. "It's good to see you—you've been busy for so long!" she exclaimed.

"You know how it is," he said lamely. "I've missed you."

"I've missed you, too." She reached up to rub him behind the ears, stroking the downy fur that covered them.

They walked back to the bench, arms around each other. Bird's body was soft and warm; it made him long for its familiar and inviting recesses.

They talked and joked, exchanged gossip and plans for future excursions. By a silent but mutual understanding, they avoided Cord's profession, the Speaker's unstated disapproval, and how their relationship could work in the future. There was enough to talk about for quite a while, but when they had run out of words the conversation faltered and died: they were well attuned to each other. One of Bird's hands rested on his thigh. It tensed and slid upward.

"It's been too long," she breathed.

Cord suddenly realized that it had, indeed, been too long. Filled with a quick heat, he pulled her closer yet, his hands touching her everywhere.

"Not many here at this hour," Bird whispered. "But— maybe we'd be more private under the trees."

How they got there, Cord could not remember later. Screened from the open spaces by low-hanging branches and leafy shrubs, Cord ran his hands up under her short, loose gown. He felt himself responding to the pressure of her hips and the sweet scent of her perfume. This time, neither of them bothered to undress. Bird's thin tunic, pulled up over her downy stomach, gave Cord easy access. He positioned himself between her thighs as Bird thrust up her hips to meet him. Cord's tail slipped underneath her buttocks to tease her.

He tongued her neck and shoulders, her breasts and nipples, holding back as long as he could, feeling her mind empty of all but pleasure. When he exploded far up inside her, their mutual ecstasy was all he knew.

They lay in each other's arms, unspeaking, until Bird giggled and suggested a new position she'd just heard about. The second time was slower, the edge having been polished off their desire, and longer, as Cord's contorted body fulfilled every expectation of the new posture she'd demanded. When it was over, they lay exhausted, watching the stars come out.

"It's getting late, Cord. We'd better get ourselves together."

"You're right," he said, releasing her and sitting up. Bird rose, brushed herself off, and shook out her gown.

"Those are pretty bracelets," Cord observed. He had not noticed them earlier—but he'd been thinking of other things. Everyone wore bracelets sometimes, and Bird wore them often, but these were unusual enough to be memorable. They were broad, silvery bands set with a design of unfaceted gems in several colors. In the light, they flashed like tiny rainbows. Surely he'd seen a similar design recently. . . .

"Aren't they? My father brought them from the spaceport. They would be beautiful no matter who made them, but their having come from another world makes them even more intriguing."

"How did he get them?" Cord asked curiously. The humans usually offered rare metals or practical goods in trade. According to the Council, the humans were supposed to supply materials which would aid Mehira's development.

"He was given them," Bird replied, checking her braid for bits of twig and leaf.

"I see," he said, untruthfully. Still, he couldn't claim to be an expert on the humans' behavior. He could not imagine Hamilton K or Stev Greffard giving anything away unless they expected something in return. But there were other humans he had not met at all, and so could not judge. Too, Cord's parents were there to trade; they were top professionals, but not persons of importance and dignity like Bird's father. Perhaps the Terrans gave gifts to curry favor.

As they walked down the path, Bird frowned. "You know, Cord, I wish my father had a love-friend. He's missing so much"—she linked her arm through his and snuggled closer—"being close, having someone to talk and laugh with, even having someone to share worries with."

"Maybe he hasn't met anyone he really likes," Cord suggested.

"It's been six years since my mother died. That should be long enough to meet someone. After all, he wouldn't have to live with her, but at least he would have someone to relax with once in a while. No, I think the fact is, Mother's death hurt him so much he doesn't want to open up to anyone again."

"And that worries you," Cord said. He understood—he was shy of revealing himself to strangers, too. He caught an echo of Bird's concern and squeezed her hand in silent reassurance.

"Well, it doesn't seem natural. And if he had a love-friend, I could talk to her. She could help me watch out for him."

"Your father seems self-contained. Besides, what if you didn't like the friend he chose?" Cord asked, hoping to tease her out of her anxiety.

"At least I wouldn't feel that I was the only one taking care of him. I don't *mind* doing it—but what will he do when I establish my own career? He'll be so lonely."

"Perhaps he's self-sufficient and doesn't need anyone. Not like me. . . ." Cord stopped as they reached the edge of the park and caressed Bird's deliciously curved body. His fingers brushed lightly over the straining tips of her breasts; she took his hand in hers and kissed his fingers, smiling.

"I must go home," she said. "My father is waiting."

"I will see you again." It was more of a statement than a question.

She tweaked his ear and ran off, to her side of the river. Cord watched her disappear in the darkness, then he trudged off, to his own part of the city.

A feeling of expectancy mixed with joy touched Cord as he passed the door of the dwelling unit. His mood lightened immediately, responding to the irresistible emotional power.

Fyrrell and Neteel emerged from the workroom. Even if he had been deaf to their psychic emissions, their expressions would have prepared him for the news.

"It works," Neteel said without preamble. Her golden-brown eyes shone.

"I knew it would," Fyrrell added. "Your mother is the foremost inventor on Mehira, and if she had devoted her time to medical devices, she would have been famous as such long ago."

"But if I had, I might not have known you," she pointed out.

"I only wish you had not had to give up so much, 'Teel."

"It's been worth it, Fyr."

The warmth of their mutual affection enveloped him for a moment, making Cord hope that there would be someone who would feel the same way about him after twenty years of marriage.

He asked, to cover his wistful thought and because he was curious, "Now that it works, may I know what it does?"

Neteel and Fyrrell exchanged delighted looks, and Neteel laughed.

"Basically, the instrument registers, interprets, and translates into the code of one's own brain."

"Basically," Fyrell corrected, "your mother means it reads minds."

"It actually reads minds? The way people read emotion? Telepathy?" Cord was astounded. The possibility had been speculated upon by various natural philosophers who suggested that by training the mind in certain ways or by using certain drugs, one would be able to feel thoughts as readily as emotions. No one had proved successful in the attempt, although a few had claimed partial success. The idea of using a machine to achieve the purpose was new.

"It really does," his mother assured him. Her pride was evident, but she remained honest. "It's necessary to be in physical contact with the other, however. In time, I expect to overcome that problem."

Cord's tail swished in excitement. What an advantage it would give them! And when Neteel perfected it—he felt no doubt in the matter—they could even walk through a crowd and pick out those who were merely contemplating theft or violence. One point occurred to him.

"Is it portable?"

"Come and see." Neteel beckoned him into the workroom.

Sitting on the bench was a small spheroid; it reminded Cord of a miniature moon with peaks and craters. It was about the size of a fist, with uneven projections and what looked like indentations for fingers. Cord noted the signs of his mother's workmanship: the use of objects which could be bought cheaply or found in scrap bins. It gave the device a rough, unfinished look.

Neteel positioned her fingertips in the depressions, then reached out to touch Cord's arm.

". . . first Bird and now this. We'll be rich and the Speaker won't object . . . looks like a toy from the trash . . . in trouble with the Council . . . Bird unhappy and me too . . . this is real . . . it works . . . I don't—one, two, three, four, but the walls are brown and it's so hard to concentrate on one thing when you're trying to—"

Cord took a hasty step back, breaking the contact. Abruptly, Neteel's calm voice stopped announcing his thoughts.

"See how it works?" she asked, after a pause.

"Ancestors! I didn't realize it would be like that."

"It's frightening," Fyrrell admitted. "When she told me what I was thinking, I was embarrassed, then angry and afraid—and I was prepared for it!"

"Here, you try it." Neteel held out her hand. Reluctantly Cord took the device and fitted his fingers into the depressions while his mother still held it. Their fingers touched.

Thoughts ran through Cord's brain, and they were not his own.

They were only partly verbal, but they were clear enough: *. . . greater efficiency with money to give Fyr a rest he needs one we all do want the best for Cord being poor bad enough but to see Fyrrell treated like dirt because he does the dirty work . . .* Then a string of mathematical equations Cord knew he could solve, but they were gone in the rush of thought. It was going to take some getting used to, this rush of mindflow. The kaleidoscope tumble and jumble ended as though cut off by a knifeblade. Cord became aware that his mother was no longer touching his hand.

"Amazing," he said, awed not only by his mother's invention but by its myriad possibilities.

Fyrrell plucked the spheroid from his hand. "Let's celebrate with a modest banquet from the cookshop. Fried melon seeds, fish dumplings, melon in aspic, bean cakes, and some kind of soup, I think. Also blue-root wine. It won't be commensurate with your abilities, 'Teel, but it's all we can afford."

She laughed delightedly at Fyr's obvious preoccupation with food and flashed him a mental reproach.

"I'm starved," he explained. Neteel gave him a quick, affectionate hug.

"If we're going to eat like that," said Cord, "then let's go out. There's a feast house by the north end of the gardens—we could sit on the terrace and watch the stars."

"And leave this alone?" Neteel took the device and held it protectively to her chest. "Now that it works, it's not leaving my keeping until I've sold it to the humans."

"I guess you couldn't carry it around," Cord concurred.

"Besides, dining out takes time, and I have one or two

things to do this evening. And I would like you to arrange a demonstration at the spaceport for . . . say, tomorrow or the next day. It's a nuisance, your having to go to the port to communicate with the aliens, but I'd like to get this over with as soon as possible.''

Cord understood. They were all eager to reap the first benefits of trade with the offworlders. It would have been convenient to have had radio contact with the spaceport, but the Council did not permit it. They felt it would be too easy for the humans to learn more of Mehiran life than was safe for Mehira.

"It's early for dinner. Perhaps Cord could bring the meal on his way home.''

Fyrrell's suggestion was accepted. Cord could rent a skim—a one-person vehicle which provided rapid if not luxurious transportation.

"Before you go,'' Fyrrell said, "we should thank our ancestors.''

They gathered before the tiny shrine in the main room. It contained the relics of sixteen of Cord's ancestors on his father's side and of three on his mother's. The main mementos of Neteel's people had remained with her parents, brother, and sister. All she had were those of her deceased grandparents. These were particularly important to her, Cord knew, because she had known her parents' parents. She had made small, beautifully knotted ancestor bags to hold their oddments: Grandmother Kattan's hair ornament, a poem carved on a wood plaque by Grandfather Tanit, and a well-worn bracelet of Grandmother Neteel, for whom she had been named.

Fyrrell's ancestral inheritances went farther back, but although their bags and the hangings around the shrine detailed their lives' achievements and their most cherished traits, there was no knowing now why a certain great-grandfather was commemorated by a smooth piece of petrified wood or why a great-great-grandmother's memory should be kept alive by a bracelet of braided hair in several shades and textures.

"I think the different hairs were from her love-friends,'' Fyrrell had once said. It was as likely an explanation as any.

Gratitude offered to his forebears, Cord left the unit. As he went out into the street he could not refrain from imagining how the tale of the telepathy machine would be handed down to his own descendants.

# Chapter 7

This time Cord entered the spaceport complex proudly and without shyness, tail flicking. He asked for Greffard, and was directed to him without delay: Neteel's name seemed to be a talisman.

Greffard listened politely while Cord explained that his parents wished to give a demonstration of an important new invention as soon as possible. His mother preferred to have one major meeting which included human scientists rather than repeat herself many times for piecemeal gatherings.

"What's the nature of the invention?" Stev Greffard asked.

"It is a mind-reading machine." Cord observed with satisfaction that his statement had surprised the human.

"And it works?" The words were tinged with incredulity.

"Yes."

"You're sure? How much has it been tested?" The disbelief had turned to excitement.

"My mother, my father, and I have all tried it. It works."

"That's not much of a sampling." Greffard's emotions were now colored with disappointment. "Perhaps Neteel should test it further—"

"If you are not interested in my mother's invention, which will revolutionize crimefighting, we will not press you. She will find a ready market, if not so large a one, here on Mehira."

"Please do not misunderstand, Cord. We are interested in your parents' devices, but it is difficult to believe in a mind reader."

Greffard's level of excitement was again high, but his face was now impassive. "Many have attempted it but none has succeeded."

"That is why I am here to arrange a demonstration," Cord

68

said with careful patience. "When you have experienced it, you will believe."

"Well, why not?" Greffard shrugged. "I have seen some strange things from your mother's lab. But you understand, one of my functions here is to screen trade offers so the experts can devote their time to the ones with real commercial potential."

Cord bowed his head in courteous acceptance of the semi-apology. Inwardly he smiled at Stev Greffard's attempts to conceal his desire—and greed—for the device.

"What will you need for the demonstration?" Greffard asked.

"A room large enough to hold those who wish to attend. If you will arrange for the presence of whoever might be interested, that will be all that is required. Can you set a time now?"

"Yes, it should be easy enough to get the necessary group together. Would the day after tomorrow be all right? At the"—Greffard paused, seeming to count to himself—"at the fifth hour? Oh, will Neteel need extra time to set up the device?"

"No, it will be ready when it arrives. The fifth hour will be acceptable. Thank you." Cord rose to leave, then thought to ask, "Do you know where I might locate Julia McKay, the missionary?"

"You know Julia? Ah—yes, she was your guide once. Her quarters are on the sixth level—section Sigma, room S-600."

"Thank you," Cord said again.

"Is she a friend of yours?" For some reason, Greffard seemed mildly surprised.

"I regard her as a friend, although we do not know each other well." Yet, Cord added mentally.

"Then perhaps you would not object if I asked her to help make the arrangements? There's a lot to be done before the demonstration: advising various departments, inviting a few Council representatives . . . it has been made very clear to us that the Council expects to be kept advised of our trading activities."

"Will it be necessary to mention the nature of the device?" Cord inquired, suddenly uncertain. The thought of such news going out while the telepathy machine was still in their possession filled him with unease. Not that he mistrusted anyone . . . well, spirits of his ancestors, he did! He did not want the Council to know about it until it was safe in the Terran compound. He could not remember if the Council had ever suppressed an invention or confiscated one, but there was no law to prevent its doing so. Once the sale was accomplished, the Council would do nothing, he was sure. In the meantime it would be best if it knew nothing about it.

"No, it won't do any harm for it to come as a surprise. Besides, it will make a better publicity release if those attending are startled. Ten Suns Enterprises likes to record its history-making moments. Your family won't object to that, I hope, Cord?"

"No." It could make no difference.

"Good. It's set, then. I'll see you all the day after tomorrow."

Their interview might be over to Stev Greffard's way of thinking, but there was still one point to be settled.

"And what sort of payment can my family expect?" He should not have to ask. Among Mehirans, the reward would have been named when the service to be performed was stated. Matters seemed both more and less complicated among humans with their marked preference for bargaining.

"If it works, we will pay ten measures of gold and five of whatever other element you specify."

"I think," said Cord speculatively, "that a thought-reading machine would be worth more than that to our own Council."

"Well, we won't argue about it now. After the demonstration we can discuss the details."

Cord was satisfied with the response. The humans wanted it, all right. Neteel and Fyrrell could probably name their own price.

He found his way to Julia McKay's door without much difficulty. Clearly he was in the residential section of the complex—two or three humans he met in the corridors reacted with surprise.

When Julia came to the door, Cord almost forgot what he had intended to say. Her hair hung loose in a cloud that almost brushed her shoulders, and her robe was a diaphanous gray webbed with silver. Promising hints of a fully curved and feminine body showed in the swells of material. Surprise flared briefly in her green-gold eyes, but not in the serene aura she maintained.

"Come in." She said it calmly, as though she'd been expecting him. But he was sure she was glad to see him.

He stepped inside and curiously looked around. The room was small, no larger than the common area in his parents' unit, but it was bright and airy. The walls and ceiling were a pale, pale yellow, while the bed, set level with the floor, was covered in purple. It was simple, yet exotic and strangely enticing. Somehow it was the perfect setting for the human woman, who outshone her surroundings.

The one chair was not meant for someone with a tail, so Cord sank to the floor to be comfortable. Julia did the same, though she knelt rather than crouched. The gray fabric swirled about her in a way that made Cord pleasurably aware of the organ in his pouch.

"I came to make an appointment for my mother and father to demonstrate their newest invention," he told her. "Since I was here, I thought . . . I wanted to see you again."

He knew he was being as awkward as a boy making his first assignation. Worse, he could not recall being so inept when he'd asked Bird to be his love-friend. But Bird and he had grown up with the same conventions and moral code.

"I'm happy you did. Can you stay for dinner? The kitchens can produce a few Mehiran dishes as well as those of a number of our own worlds."

"You are kind, but my parents expect me back soon. I must not linger."

"Then I won't detain you." But neither of them moved.

"I think Stev Greffard will ask you to aid him in arranging the demonstration," Cord said.

"Good!" Julia smiled. "It will give me something useful to do. But why is he asking me?"

"The device my mother invented is very special," Cord explained. "Perhaps the first of its kind. I trust you to help gather the appropriate humans—and not to reveal the nature of the device."

Julia plucked at the folds of her garment, pulling the material above her knees and revealing creamy flesh. Cord stared at the smooth pale skin. He had never touched a human, really, and longed to caress Julia's skin, to run his hands slowly along her milky inner thighs, to discover the sweet delights beyond.

"What is this special device?" Julia asked, seemingly oblivious to Cord's stare.

Cord tore himself away from the erotic pleasures he was imagining. "It is a machine that reads minds." If Julia could read his mind now, would the human woman be shocked or would she be willing to share his lustful curiosity? Suddenly he was desperate to explore the physical differences between them.

"Thank you for telling me. It is an honor to receive your trust." She learned forward and squeezed his forearm—a human gesture of reassurance?—and said, "I regard you as a good friend."

Cord captured her hand in his own. "One trusts one's good friends. I wish you felt the same way about me."

"I do, Cord." She placed her free hand over his; a pulsing current passed through him at this, burning his already heated body.

"Among Mehirans," he said slowly, "if two people are friends—as we are—and find each other attractive . . . You are very beautiful in my eyes, but perhaps I am not to your taste."

Julia pulled her hands free. "If I understand you, Cord, you are inviting me to have sex with you."

"Yes. I don't wish to offend you, but I hope since we are friends you won't be offended." *Oh, Cord*, he addressed himself, *you sound like a fool.*

"I am flattered." She lowered the lids over her eyes. "But you know my religion is very important to me, and I have already explained this to you."

The faint odor of her body came to Cord like an intoxication, stealing over his senses. Cord placed his hands on her thighs. Desire rose in him like a tide of lava. It was almost like the excitement of the chase.

"Don't," Julia cried. She tried to push him away, but he was too strong. "The truth is that I'm afraid. I've given myself to God, but I'm afraid I'll give myself to you any way you want, as often as you want!"

The pupils of her eyes were dilated, and Cord could feel her arousal, though it was like none he had ever felt in a woman. And her words confused him: who was this "God"?

If she had given herself to a human male, then why would she be afraid of sex with Cord?

"I'll go," he said finally, his own emotions painfully churning. "But I hope your ancestors will give you a satisfactory enlightenment in this matter."

Julia rose gracefully.

"I hope so, too," she said, her voice husky. Her nipples were standing up hard against the flimsy material of her gown. With an obvious effort to regain control, she added, "I will study the holy books carefully."

"Will you give me your answer at the demonstration?"

Passion flared in her eyes once more.

"If I can."

Cord, standing in the hallway outside her closed door, was baffled at the feelings she aroused in him. He found himself almost able to understand why some deviates forced themselves upon an unwilling partner. His overwhelming desire for Julia had nearly made him lose control, and now his hunger was turning to shame and disgust.

But he still wanted the alien woman.

# Chapter 8

Bird, flying home from a party, savored the cool night air. It seemed to caress her body, just like . . . she laughed to herself, remembering. A pleasant evening, she thought, with several interesting young men. She'd drunk too much aphrodisiac, though: her clitoris began to feel hot and large as she enumerated the men who'd pleasured her—or wanted to. Her thighs tingled at imaginary touches and her breasts ached. She smiled and sighed. It was too bad Cord refused to accompany her to passion parties; he would be such an asset. And she would have liked others to learn how exciting and virile her love-friend was, to sample the strength of his muscular body.

The sight of the Council building, fully illuminated as it was when a session was in progress, distracted her. Bird slowed her skim and stared at the massive structure. Resumption of a Council meeting in the evening was a sign of serious trouble.

*I should go in. Father will be there and he may need me.* Strange he had not mentioned an evening continuation when she'd left the house late in the afternoon. Maybe something had arisen suddenly.

No, there was no point in her going in. It was very late, and they would certainly adjourn soon. Father would tell her to go home anyway. Also, the scent of passion was heavy around her, and it was in poor taste to distract those who were working. Certainly she was too tired for any more lovemaking, and she wanted to look her best for tomorrow. Her father had been invited to attend an affair at the spaceport the following afternoon. Bird was to go with him, and she wanted to be fresh, because it was in honor of some machine Cord's mother had built.

Having made her decision, Bird passed the government

complex and headed toward the suburbs. She put the skim away and went up to bed immediately, leaving the house lights on for her father's return. Usually after so much sexual activity she rested well. Tonight, however, her dreams were chaotic and troubling.

Waking to the morning sun, Bird felt neither rested nor easy in mind. It was unusual for her to be upset by nightmares. After washing and dressing slowly, she went downstairs, to find that the lights she'd left on last night still glowed. Could the Council have remained in session all night? He must have come home, she decided, and she simply had not heard him. Perhaps he was tired and worried.

She crept up to her father's suite of rooms as softly as she could. The door to his office was not quite closed. It looked familiar and comforting in the sun that shone in the great round window. Austere, everything in its place—except for a scroll, half-written, on the Speaker's low desk. Bird smiled and crossed the room to roll it up and slip it into a holder until he should care to continue it. She never completed the gesture—her own name loomed large and foreboding. . . .

"Bird, I wish I could do this differently, to spare you the anguish you are about to experience, as well as the inconvenience and embarrassment. However, no practical alternative exists. Thank all the ancestors, on both our behalves, that you were gone tonight.

"Bird, in my life I have made several major mistakes, but until this last one, I have been the only one to suffer thereby. The first one was cutting myself off from emotional contact with others after your mother died. No one could replace her, and I let no one try. That was foolish, but this is worse: I began to give myself airs of nobility for the deprivation. I let myself believe that it was somehow ignoble to indulge in palliative affairs, when sexual and emotional contact would have kept me from brooding, from turning inward.

"You know, naturally, that I have not been in the habit of letting others see my feelings. What no one knows is that for years I have not been receptive to others' feelings either. It may have been a brain dysfunction; I don't know. But I welcomed it. The joys, sorrows, and needs of the rest of the world were too painful after Tareel joined her ancestors.

"This was my last mistake: having ceased to listen to the feelings of everyone else, I let the aliens deceive me. I believed what they told me without the precaution of sensing their emotions. Having done so, I promoted trade with them against the Council's judgment, which was based on empathic sense as well as on reason. I know now this was foolish—and arrogant—to the point of insanity. I must have been mad to ignore common sense to such a degree.

"Tonight I was called before the Council. They charged me with willfully ignoring a Council directive, which was true but would not ordinarily be a matter of importance. They accused me of acting as an agent for the humans in return for gifts. It is possible that the humans intended those beautiful bracelets as bribes. I don't know. If I had listened to their souls as well as to their speech . . .

"Finally, my 'deviancy' was denounced, my lack of emotional sharing, as if that were a crime. Someone actually suggested that I must be a pervert because I have no love-friends.

"The Council demanded my resignation, and I have complied. It may look like an admission of guilt, but you know as well as I do that if I refused, they would find some other way of removing me.

"I am afraid I know why your friend Cord has not visited you lately. His delicacy of feeling does him some credit; his family was engaged to gather the evidence which was brought against me.

"Bird, if I resigned to live in retirement, I would be disgraced and you would be disgraced because of your connection with me. Therefore I am going to kill myself. It may save you from ostracization. Others will pity you, and maybe they will give you a chance. Lovely one, farewell."

There was no signature; none was necessary. Bird, with a sick sensation in the pit of her stomach, ran to the door of her father's bedroom, still clutching the scroll in one hand.

The Speaker was lying on the bed platform. One glance at the drawn, colorless face was enough. Beside him was an open box. Bird recognized it as a medication container, in which her father had kept lozenges to help him sleep. It was empty.

She stood there for a space. Then, shivering, she turned away, to make the necessary arrangements.

She spent most of the morning reporting her father's death to the Council clerk in charge of death registry, and in arranging for his cremation. Finally, having written short messages to their relatives, Bird found herself alone in the house. She felt stunned and abandoned at first—then she began to be angry. Not at the Council so much as at their tools and at those who had made the Speaker their tool.

And she remembered the invitation and her pass to the spaceport.

# Chapter 9

Contrary to Cord's apprehensions, nothing occurred to complicate their preparations. His father rented a vehicle without difficulty; the telepathy machine continued to work; no one attempted to hijack it. They left for the spaceport much earlier than necessary; none of them wished to be late because of some mishap enroute. Cord was amused to see that his mother had knotted an ancestor bag for the device, by way of disguise. To conceal the main object of their visit further, she had brought along several other tools.

"Here, you carry it," she said to Cord, as they got into the ground car. He took it and suspended the pouch from his belt. It would arouse no curiosity; many people carried ancestral mementoes with them. Running a finger over the pattern of knots, Cord deciphered the meaning: Fyrrell—Neteel—Cord: 3228 Year of Council: 205 year of family—Gifts and Good Fortune from the Sky. His mother's idea of humor, he thought.

The road to the spaceport had become familiar, so Fyrrell pushed the vehicle along at near its top speed, although they had plenty of time.

Stev Greffard seemed to be waiting for them, in spite of their early arrival.

"The room is ready," he told them. "There's been considerable interest, so I expect a crowd. This is the first major gathering we've held, and Julia McKay's announcement piqued their curiosity. She studied persuasion and logic at her seminary. And, of course, there's been a great deal of speculation about the nature of your invention." He smiled slyly at Neteel.

She smiled in reply. The fulfillment of years of work was in sight.

The human offered them beverages and morsels of food, all exotic but quite tasty. Cord decided that the pickled vegetables were the aliens' most outstanding accomplishment.

Julia joined them in Greffard's office. She greeted them, maintaining a slight formality with Cord which he found charming.

"Is everything you need here?" she asked, glancing at the pile of gadgets Neteel and Fyrrell had placed on Greffard's desk. The ancestor bag, however, remained on Cord's belt. "May I arrange for it to be taken into the conference room?"

"Yes," Neteel answered. "Yes to both questions. Thank you."

They had not informed even Greffard that the real demonstration piece was still with them. Let their prospective customers wonder.

"Everything is ready," Greffard reported soon afterward. "It's almost time. If you've finished your refreshments, I'll escort you to the room we've scheduled for you."

"We are prepared," Fyrrell said. An electric current of excitement passed between the three. They followed Stev Greffard down the corridor, with Julia close behind.

The room assigned was surprisingly large and already full. Most of the crowd were human, but many Mehirans were present as well; it looked as though every Mehiran who had a pass to the spaceport had attended. Cord thought he had never seen such a collection of notables in one place. The most honored members of the Council, both Upper and Lower, were well to the front—not in the first rows of seats, which would have been vulgarly pushy, but in the forward middle section, as their dignity demanded. He hoped the Speaker for the Third District was there to witness their triumph.

A long table at the front of the room held the gadgets Neteel had brought along. It was flanked by a pair of tough-looking guards carrying guns. A broad expanse of polished floor separated the table from the spectators' chairs. No one could say that Greffard wasn't giving Neteel full honors.

A knot of people around the door—those who lacked the prestige to gain seats—stirred as someone pushed through behind them.

"I didn't expect so many," Neteel remarked, obviously pleased.

"Shall we go down to the table now?" Fyrrell asked Greffard. "Or would you rather we stayed here? We seem to be in the way."

"As my father was in the Council's way?" a voice inquired, sharp-edged.

Bird had come through the crowd around them. Her face was set and colorless; worse, uncontrolled and scorching anger flowed from her.

"Yes, I'm here," she said, her voice dripping venom. "But my father isn't. He'll never be anywhere again. He's dead."

"Dead?" Cord repeated blankly. "What happened? When?"

"*They* killed him." She was looking at his parents, anger and tears fighting in her eyes. "The Council wanted him eliminated, so they hired Fyrrell and Neteel to find a way. Once the Council had disgraced him, he thought it would be better to die—for my sake. Maybe my father made mistakes, but he never deliberately did anyone harm. But you're the Council's tools. You've made it dangerous to have a difference of opinion with them." Her voice had risen shrilly; now it fell to a whisper. "You . . . you should have told me, Cord. You owed me that much."

Cord dropped his defenses to let Bird feel his concern and surprise. In the background he sensed his parents' embarrassment and alarm. Others' reactions came through also: concern, irritation, confusion, and faintly, as though from a great distance, an immense need, a gnawing hunger. . . .

Before Cord had time to wonder about it, Hamilton K appeared with an escort of security guards. They surrounded Bird as if cornering a vicious animal.

"She should never have been permitted inside," a Mehiran voice observed. "Under the circumstances . . ."

K said, "We were not aware of the 'circumstances,' whatever they are. She has a pass. Needless to say, it will now be suspended. Get her out of here."

"No," Cord snapped.

Hamilton K looked at him. Cord was glad he did not work for this alien, cold man.

"Is she a friend of yours?" he asked.

"Yes," Fyrrell replied. "We will deal with the matter." To Bird, he added, "I'm sorry. I did not know what they intended to do with my report. We've often worked for the Council, even gathering material about its members. Nothing ever came of it, before. Nothing we've been aware of, at least. And I would have sworn in the names of my ancestors that there was nothing in your father's life to give the Council so much power over him.''

Bird's chin had been trembling. Two or three tears slid down her cheeks. The sight wrenched at Cord's heart. He moved forward to take her into his arms, but Bird motioned him away.

''I'm sorry, too. But it doesn't do any good, does it? My father is still dead, and you're still alive and profiting by it. And you, Cord—you may not have helped drive him to suicide, but you didn't do anything to prevent it, did you? You might have warned me, if you did not care enough to speak to him.'' Her eyes brimmed with tears.

''Is this affair settled yet?'' K demanded. ''If this young woman is going to make further scenes, I must insist on having her expelled.''

''Yes, let's get started, if Madame Neteel agrees,'' Greffard suggested.

Bird wiped her eyes quickly with the back of her hand, then said clearly, though there was still a tremor in her voice, ''I have said what I came here to say. It isn't necessary to put me out.''

Neteel took over with her customary efficiency and made one deft change in the program.

''Cord, you stay here with Bird. Fyrrell and I can manage without you.''

He gave Neteel a grateful smile. She was always thoughtful. Bird needed someone with her right now: he did not mind giving up his share of the limelight (a small one, anyway) to offer her what comfort he could.

''Thank you, Lady,'' K said softly.

Cord was momentarily surprised that it should matter to the Trade Agent, then realized that the man's gratitude was for the resolution of an awkward situation.

Neteel smiled, and her ears twitched toward Hamilton K in salute. She might yet find out how human males coped without tails.

''I'll introduce you first and then leave you to your demonstration,'' Greffard said.

''Thank you.'' Fyrrell spoke stiffly, painstakingly polite.

''Cord, I'll take my bag now,'' his mother said casually.

He slipped its loops free of his belt and passed it to her. Then she followed Greffard and Fyrrell up the aisle, carrying their future as easily as though it had been a personal pouch for trinkets.

"Cord, I want to apologize," Bird said. "I liked your parents, the times I met them. They wouldn't intentionally push my father to kill himself—I was half insane with sorrow and anger. Completely insane. When I felt your father's emotions, I knew I was wrong. Do you think they'll be able to forgive me?"

"They understand, Bird. So do I. After this is over . . ."

At the other end of the hall, Greffard waved away the guards by the table. Cord's parents took their places behind it.

"Most respected ones," Greffard began, the Mehiran honorific sounding odd when translated into the human language. A metallic voice repeated his words in Mehiran for those who spoke no Multi-Lang. "You have come here today to see the dawning of a new age. The most respected Neteel and Fyrrell . . ."

Neteel pulled open the mouth of the bag, then placed it, still swathed in the ancestor pouch, on the table.

That sight was frozen forever in Cord's memory, because it terminated in twin explosions.

If there was a sound, Cord did not hear it. A flash of light blinded him, followed by a breath of heat. Cord's bones seemed to vibrate with the force of the physical blast. But that was not the worst. It was the almost simultaneous psychic storm that deprived him of the ability to think or move. The horror and helpless despair of the dying reverberated through every Mehiran mind and were amplified until the world around Cord dissolved in a maelstrom of emotion.

As reason returned, he realized his parents were dead. The explosion had killed them in a single flash. Even now, after what seemed an eternity, debris was still falling on him. Someone, a human—Greffard, Cord thought—had been mortally wounded and was still lingering. What was left of his body convulsed in pain.

With an iron effort of will, Cord closed his bruised mind to the human's death agony. He found that he was clinging to Bird and that there was confusion around them. Bird was limp in his arms, sobbing softly. The other Mehirans were no better; many were unconscious. There was something to be said for the callousness he had acquired as a Catcher.

Through the psychic haze surrounding him, he heard a voice and identified it as Hamilton K's.

"Get him out! Quick, while they're still . . . medical team, here . . ."

Cord opened his eyes. Where the demonstration table had been was a tattered ruin, red and wet-looking. On the floor, beyond the ragged thing that had been Greffard, were lumps of flesh. . . .

His mind turned automatically to the litany of his ancestors' names, blocking out the sight. He felt someone pull Bird out of his grasp.

"Bird!" he called, trying to follow. He stood up, swaying, and found his feet were leaden.

"Not that one," an alien voice said. "She's our number-one suspect. Lock her up and get the rest out."

A human dragged Bird away. She was not struggling; probably she was so deep in shock that she did not realize what was happening. Other Mehirans were being pushed toward the entrance, some of them bruised or cut. Caught in an emotional storm, some struck out blindly.

Someone took him by the shoulder and spun him around: Hamilton K. At any other time, Cord would have reacted by going into a defensive stance.

"Are you all right?" the human asked, then rushed on, not waiting for a reply. "Your mother's device—can it be set to work on other races?" Then Hamilton K muttered to himself, "Stupid question—she wouldn't have offered it otherwise."

Cord stared at him mutely. K apparently thought that the device was responsible for rendering the Mehirans in the audience helpless. Of course, he did not know their empathic ability—or that the invention was for telepathy.

"Well, we'll talk about it later." K shrugged. "Joniss! Help this one out—gently: he's our inventor's son."

Strong hands propelled him out of the room and into the the lobby. Cord dimly recalled seeing Julia McKay leaning against a wall.

Down the road, at the Council's checkpoint, Cord could see two Mehiran guards on duty leaning against their vehicle. The pair looked agitated and disturbed. They must have felt the psychic blasts but were far enough away not to be prostrated by them.

In the distance, alarms sounded. Up the road, carriers sped into view, and soon half a dozen Council carriers were halted before the slick black facade of the spaceport. They'd been efficient. One vehicle was equipped for medical care: its staff began treatment of those in shock. The worst cases were placed in cots in the van. Those recovering on their own were helped into a personnel carrier.

"How many is that?" someone asked.

"Twenty-three, respected one. According to checkpoint records, we're missing three."

"I suppose we won't be able to identify them until the rest are able to speak," the first voice observed.

Cord looked around and saw a Mehiran wearing the Council's insignia.

"Respected one," Cord addressed him, "Fyrrell and Neteel, the Catchers . . . my parents . . . are dead." He fought down his sorrow and anxiety. "And the humans are holding Bird, the Third District Speaker's daughter."

"The late Speaker," the Council representative automatically corrected. "Are they, now? Why?"

The man was ten or fifteen years older than Cord, and had the look of all those whom the Council appointed to carry out its instructions. Efficient, pragmatic, used to giving orders and having them obeyed.

"I heard the Trade Agent say she was suspected of having . . . having caused the explosion." Cord briefly sketched the afternoon's events for him.

"The Council will want to question you," the Council agent said. He looked at Cord again. "Fyrrell was your father? And you are also a Catcher?"

"Yes, respected one."

"You have some experience of violence." He made no apology for his blunt speaking. The Council never did apologize. "I will relay your report to my superiors. You had better get into the carrier now." He turned away to give instructions to a group of Council guards.

Dully, Cord did as he was told. Slumped in a seat in the carrier, he felt empty of emotion for the first time in his life.

# Chapter 10

The carrier delivered them to the Council buildings, where members of the staff took charge of most—the majority of attendees had had Council affiliations of one sort or another. No one took any notice of Cord. He began to trudge toward home, moving by rote.

Activity and distance from the tragedy cleared his mind. He could not think about his parents, not yet. But other matters occurred to him. Reviewing the afternoon, as Fyrrell had taught him to do, Cord came to several conclusions.

The humans accused Bird. It was true she had been distraught over her father's death, but she had not set the bomb, nor did she have the technical background to construct one. More to the point, there had been no murder in her mind.

He was inclined to eliminate all the Mehirans present on similar grounds. Even if someone there had been a psychopath, would any Mehiran have had an opportunity to put an explosive in place? Cord doubted it.

The humans and only the humans had had the opportunity to plant a bomb in their own complex. But why? The humans wanted Neteel's inventions. Why kill their source?

It made no sense—but murders never did.

Cord found himself at his own door. He had come through the streets like an automaton. He let himself in and remained leaning against the door for some moments, thinking.

There was one way to find out. He must go back to the spaceport, using the promise—or threat—of the telepathy device as bait.

If the guilty one believed that Cord had or could build another device with which to detect the murderer, he might attempt to kill Cord, as well. Cord had no fear that such an attempt might succeed. After all, he was forewarned. The murder of his parents would not have been successful if they had not been sure they were safe there. Now that he was prepared, the killer was in far more danger than he.

Cord activated the lights—to his surprise, it had grown dim. The sun was down, leaving little more than a golden afterglow—gold, like Bird's skin, so soft, so sweet. His loins tightened in reflex and his tail twitched.

With the ache still in him, he went into the workroom and tried to concentrate. The bench itself was tidy, but the walls were festooned with tools, completed equipment, and material which might be useful for some future project. This would be the difficult part. Neteel might have left a complete blueprint of the telepathic receiver, or she might not. Sometimes his mother had jotted notes to herself or made drawings of sections she was having trouble with, but sometimes she made no formal plans until after perfecting the thing. Cord could remember parts of the mechanism, but not all of it.

All of her notes and plans were stored in a jumble in a compartment under the bench. Cord took everything out and sat down to sort through them. His blunted emotions slowly sharpened as his mind cleared. He worked with a cold and calculating purpose, his feelings now dominated by a new desire: revenge.

Cord rented a skim to return to the spaceport, beyond worrying about the expense. Strapped to its back was a case containing the most useful—and salable—of his parents' inventions.

He had no illusions about his chances of being admitted to the spaceport. Oh, the aliens wouldn't stop him, but the Council might. A detachment of Council guards were on duty at the entrance, and it certainly wasn't to keep the aliens in. If a fighting force came out of the port, the Council militia would not be able to stop it. Cord doubted the guards had ever had occasion to fire upon any being. Ordinarily they carried no weapons.

But he wanted to get inside, and he knew Hamilton K would be willing to trade once he did. When the skim was far out into the marshes, with the city out of sight behind, and the Council gate not yet visible ahead, Cord halted the vehicle. He donned a helmet that had rested on the seat beside him and flipped a switch. Objects beyond the skim went slightly out of focus.

Then he turned the skim off the road and moved off across

the marsh at an angle. The camouflage field would not absolutely conceal him, but it would deceive anyone who glanced casually at the marsh. The onlooker would seem to see nothing but reeds and spindling foliage stirring in the breeze. If the marsh had been barren, with only moss-covered hummocks, Cord would have had to abandon the skim and crawl. The field could not disguise any height which was out of keeping with the surroundings. Neither would it work at close range; although it still deflected the eye, the distortion it produced was evident. Anyone who saw it straight on at, say, five or six meters would be conscious of a shimmering—a miragelike quality.

For that reason he kept a safe distance from the guard post. He moved the skim slowly until the post came into view—and then he gasped.

It was not the action at the gate, however, that drew a reaction from him. Up to that time, he had not worried too much about Bird. The humans were certain to discover she was innocent, even without the aid of empathy or telepathy. They were not likely to harm her, not if they still wanted to trade with Mehira. And from his experience of them, he suspected that little was permitted to stand in the way of their trading.

But with the first wave of horror and pain, Cord lost his comfortable certainty of Bird's safety. The force with which she was sending astonished him. Their relationship made them especially sensitive to each other's emotional output, naturally, but even so, he should not have been able to "hear" her at such a distance. He noticed that the Council guards, too, had felt something. They had withdrawn up the road as far as they could without completely disassociating themselves from their post. Thus distracted, they hadn't noticed him.

Dismayed by what he sensed, he pushed the skim's speed up to its maximum for such terrain until the Council's roughly built wall was near. He veered to parallel it, leaving the checkpoint far behind.

Cord intended to attempt entrance to the spaceport as far from the main building as was feasible. He landed the skim next to the wall and removed his equipment, working with practiced efficiency. Using a long-bladed knife, he cut a large rectangle in the thick-growing moss and pulled it up. The skim, laid on its side with the moss blanket replaced, should remain undiscovered if anyone happened to pass by. Not that it seemed a likely contingency. Cord marked a corner of the cache with a pair of twigs which would mean nothing to anyone else.

At last he took a multipronged climbing hook from the case, unfolded it, and locked it open. He stood back to throw it; the hook caught on the first try. Cord had spent a great deal of time practicing the art. Without hurry, he transferred the equipment case to his back; it was heavy but left his hands free. Finally, with an experimental tug at the rope, he began to climb.

At the top of the wall he shifted the hook to the other side, while hunching low. Though he trusted to distance and the camouflage field to make him inconspicuous, he did not take the risk of sitting up straight. The descent was easy. At the bottom, he gave the rope a brisk twitch to detach the hook. Gathering it up, he refolded it and stowed it in the chest.

With his back to the Mehiran wall, Cord studied the next obstacle. Ahead was the massive alien-built wall. The broad expanse between the two walls was covered with a gray-white gritty material, not quite sand but too small for gravel. With no cover, the camouflage field would not be convincing. There was nothing to do but mutter an oath to his ancestors and run across.

Cord reached the shining black wall. Nothing happened. But he did not expect to get over this wall so easily. It was an enormous number of hands high, and its surface was too smooth to give his boots any purchase. He stretched out a hand cautiously and pulled back. If the wall had some protective field which would electrocute or vaporize him . . .

Tail curling at its tip, Cord knelt by his case and considered the options.

On some smooth surfaces, he would have glued hand and foot holds, using a special adhesive. Once set, which it did in a short time, it would support heavy weights. Cord was not optimistic about its properties on this wall. Nevertheless he took out the glue gun and daubed on a lump of the sticky substance as a test. It wasn't vaporized, but the blob of glue not only did not stick, it slid down the obsidian-slick wall, leaving no trace at all. Cord was not surprised. The alien material's inertness and its frictionlessness would be properties as vital as its density.

He pulled out a compact telescoping ladder and the climbing hook. The ladder, opened to its full extent, was about half the wall's height. He propped it up, sinking its foot in the sandy soil after extending the spikes which would increase its stability—he hoped. The wall might be so friction-free that the ladder would not remain against it. He hefted the climbing hook and calculated his throw. It might be his only one. if he missed and it flew over the wall . . .

It spun up and up and came down—engaged! The rope hung past the top rung of the ladder and no farther. Cord was more relieved than he would have cared to admit.

His last action before beginning was to find a length of cord and make a loop in one end. Once more he shouldered the case and fastened its straps around his broad shoulders.

The climbing went slowly. With the ladder so insecurely balanced, and his weight greatly increased by his burden, all his concentration and strength were needed. He preferred not to remember that the ladder, collapsed, was less than the length of his arm and far less in diameter.

When he had climbed as high as he could, he halted. One-handed, he took out the cord and slipped the loop over his belt. The other end he tied to the last rung of the ladder.

Carefully, he gripped the climbing rope and started up, pulling the ladder along with him. He could not brace his feet against the wall—it was too slippery—so he had to use the handholds for his feet as well. It was not easy to get toeholds in the loops, sliding against the ladder swinging free beneath him. There was no way he could fold the ladder now, and the weight of a double burden taxed his muscles unbearably.

He was getting tired, and he feared he would be seen, so high up against the gleaming black. The camouflage generator could not cover both the rope and the ladder, which dangled beneath him like some fantastically oversized sexual organ.

Muscles bulging under the strain, Cord neared the top, which was in sight. Suddenly, he nearly lost his hold—brutally assaulted by a new rush of feeling from Bird.

Pain . . . unendurable . . . unending . . .

Ancestors! For the space of a breath, Cord wondered if he was dying. The rope slip-slid out of his moist hands, but his forearms came to rest up his thighs; his feet still kept their toeholds while his tail wrapped around the rope too. His body doubled over as the torrent of raw emotion pounded him. He fought to shield his mind to his utmost ability.

Bird's emotional outpouring muted—then ceased. Her signal had not stopped entirely, but she was sending at a normal level, no longer in pain. Fear and despair were now dominant.

He pulled himself up and started for the top again. By the time he reached it, he was winded and drained. Wrapping himself around the rope, he untied the ladder and swung it up, across the broad ledge of the top. He pulled himself alongside and lay there, panting.

From his vantage point, he surveyed the spaceport. In the distance, the main building loomed, towering higher than the wall, windowless on the outward-facing side and windowless entirely until the upper floors. Cord doubted he could reach it directly. However, there were outlying maintenance buildings perfect for his purposes. Adjoining the wall and lower than it were those buildings utilized only when a trading ship was in port. Far out on the field, several small spacecraft were parked. Relying on what he'd seen and heard previously, he felt that such landing area crews were not on continuous duty.

Against the wall, not too far from Cord's perch, was a small shed. Estimating, Cord thought that the climbing rope would reach its roof—or very nearly, he reflected grimly. It should at least bring him close enough to drop off the rope's end safely.

With the climbing hook looped over one wrist and the now-folded ladder still suspended from his belt, Cord crept along the wall. His progress was neither fast nor graceful, but Cord was indifferent to appearances—as long as there was no one to see him.

At last he was over the service building. He let the rope down; it fell a scant half body length short of the roof. Cord grinned and breathed praise to his ancestors—now including his father and mother—as he eased down.

He moved silently across the roof, wondering whether the humans realized how easily their compound could be breached, even with comparatively primitive equipment. Would it be as simple to get into the main building?

The rope served to lower him from the roof to the ground.

Then, pressed close to the wall, he made his way toward his main objective.

In the lower level of the building there were great doors: the loading dock where cargo was brought in from the ships, and from which Mehiran cargo was transferred to outbound vessels. Several huge freight-handling machines stood in front of the closed doors. The lack of activity was a fortunate thing. When a freighter was in port, this area might be busy all day and all night, too, making it impossible to slip inside. If no better opportunity offered itself (he had a sudden fantasy of opportunity personified by a lavishly breasted woman with friendly thighs), he would wait until dark and cut his way through the doors, which apparently were not of the black substance—merely metal. But it troubled him to think of what Bird might have to endure in the hours until dark.

There was a small door beside the machine doors. Cord wondered whether it was left unlocked. The humans seemed to place such confidence in their first line of defense. If no unauthorized person could get into the spaceport, why bother to secure the doors inside? Faulty logic, since it was based on an incorrect premise.

Cord was debating whether to take a chance and try it, as there was no one in sight outside, when a faint whirring warned him back. Pressed close to the treads of a freight handler, he peered out at the field.

A small vehicle, similar to a skim but wheeled, was rolling toward the loading dock. It had evidently come from a shed opposite Cord's hiding place. It stopped near the small door with a "wheeesh!" and its driver jumped down and trotted to the entrance. At his approach it opened automatically, giving Cord a glimpse of warehouse. Faintly a voice reached him:

"Hey, hurry up. Everybody's already gone to the cafeteria."

The closing of the door cut off any further sounds of conversation. Cord took it as an omen. He counted one hundred, then ran for the door.

It opened for him, too, suggesting that the aliens weren't as sophisticated in some ways as one might expect. If his family had designed the facility, they'd have fixed it so that only those workers assigned to the area could activate the door.

No one was inside. Cord breathed deeply and again gave silent thanks to his ancestors. In a corner behind some crates he paused to stow the unneeded climbing tackle and ladder in his case and take out his anesthetic gun. He did not depend on the noon meal to keep the corridors clear. The gun was fully charged, though he could not expect to bring down more than twenty to thirty beings with it. The complex was very large. If he had to search it room by room to find Bird . . .

Bird had become his main goal. He could think about trading with the humans once he had established that Bird was safe. How to find her was his problem at present. He needed a base of operations.

He thought of Julia McKay. Perhaps she would help him. She seemed sympathetic, and a missionary's purpose was to do good, wasn't it? She had said something like that. So he would go to her quarters—if he could get there.

What worried him was the trans tube in the busier sections. He was going to be very conspicuous.

A memory came to him of Julia, saying to his mother during their tour:

"Under some circumstances the power might fail, in which case it would still be possible to move from level to level. The stationary corridors you've seen—they're used because the speedwalks aren't always convenient for short distances. But even in a power failure, we could still go from floor to floor by the stairs. They are located at several places throughout the building. I'd hate to have to climb all the way from ground level to my residence level, but it would be possible."

Cord grinned. This was like a challenging criminal-catching expedition. He moved swiftly past stacks of goods and crates, the paraphernalia common to all warehouses. He slipped out into the corridor and glanced both ways. Here he was very close to one end of the building, and here, as he expected, were the emergency stairs. No good to him, unfortunately. He needed to come out as near Julia's door as possible. Cord turned away from the first set of stairs.

The next area in the lower level was the custodial, but it, too, was empty. If anyone's plumbing went out of order, it was going to have to wait until the midday break was over.

Next, storerooms.

Then—the second set of stairs. Now he drew his gun from his belt. He expected no menace beyond the metal door, but his training made him cautious. He threw the door wide and scanned the stairwell. Nothing. Cord began to climb, keeping the gun at ready. The many blind turns made him jumpy.

At intervals he came to exits, each marked with the level number. Third level. Fourth. Past the fifth, Cord paused to steel himself for the dangerous foray into the corridor. Up the last few steps. He hesitated at the door leading to the sixth level. It was solid and tight-fitting, offering no physical way of checking for the presence of humans beyond. Fortunately, another sense was available to him. He opened himself completely to psychic impressions, leaning against the doorframe.

Far off, he felt human emotions, but none of them were near. Good. He had also caught a trace of Bird, but she seemed distant, as though she might be in a troubled sleep.

Gun in hand, he stepped into the hall. Empty—as his empathic sense had told him. He noted the color coding of walls and floor; he was closer to Julia's room than he had expected. It should be to the left, then down a transverse passage. He reached out to sense her impulse. The odd, almost nonexistent trace of her was present. If he had not been seeking her, he might not have noticed it at all, although he was now at her door. Cord touched the plate set in the wall beside it.

She opened the door; her eyes widened but she spoke quietly.

"Hello, Cord."

He pressed in past her and shut the door.

"I need your help, Julia," he began. He had no time to waste on polite exchanges. Cord noted, reassured, that there was no alteration in her psychic currents. Julia McKay was still almost unreachable, still cool and detached. The only change he noticed was that today she was clad in a form-fitting brown overall that molded her generous breasts and hips. Perceiving no need for further empathic contact, he broke it.

"What can I do?" She led him into the main room and seated herself on the edge of the cushioned area that served as a bed. She beckoned him to sit beside her.

Unstrapping his gear, Cord dropped it in a corner where it was out of the way but still near at hand. He dropped wearily onto the bed next to her. He was glad she was so . . . collected. No demands for explanations, no cries of surprise. Merely, "What can I do?"

"My friend—Bird—is being detained here," he explained. "I think she may have been accused of murdering my parents and the others who died.'' Was it yesterday? It seemed a long time ago.

"Yes," Julia agreed. "She was charged with the murders. The security department has been interrogating her all morning."

Cord's stomach contracted.

"They are hurting her?" He made a question, since there was no way he could reveal his knowledge, even to Julia.

"Yes," she said again. "They want her to confess. Then they could execute her as an example, you see, and no one could deny them the right."

The idea of forcing someone to confess was so alien that Cord could scarcely comprehend what the woman was saying. Among Mehirans, where one's own emotions would betray one, a confession was superfluous. Still, humans, with no empathic sense, would be handicapped when it came to proving guilt. The important thing was to get Bird away. He said so.

"All right. How shall we do it?"

"You will help me, Julia?"

"I said I would, Cord. Tell me what to do."

"Can you find out where Bird is being held? Exactly? It would help if I knew how many are with her, but I suppose that would be harder to learn."

"Not at all. I was with her this morning. Besides myself, there was the security chief and a technician." Julia recited the level, section, and room number of Bird's prison.

"How . . . how did you happen to be there?"

"I wanted to be there." She went on, "You are a friend of mine, and she is a friend of yours. And also, if I am to be a missionary, I must be willing to share suffering with those I am trying to help." For a single heartbeat, Julia's emotional aura seemed to blaze up so that Cord could feel it without trying. He had known the phenomenon to occur with Mehirans who spoke of ideals to which they were devoted, but it wasn't common. It was a sign of dedication or of passionate interest.

Cord regarded the human with some awe, but he could think of nothing to say, except, "Thank you, Julia. That was kind of you." Even allowing for the humans' lack of empathic contact, it could not have been pleasant to witness such horror. He turned his mind from that thought. "We will have to plan this carefully, so no one suspects you, and to make escape as easy as possible for Bird. How badly is she injured?''

"She is not physically impaired. Theoretically, one can undergo direct brain stimulation indefinitely without harm,'' Julia told him. "Indefinitely . . .'' Her eyes were very wide, the pupils dilated.

Cord thought that if he gazed into them long enough, he would begin to fall into their depths. How beautiful she was, in her alien way, and how kind!

"Try not to think about it'' was all he could find to say. Grasping her hand in reassurance, his fingers brushed her leg and the old longing rose in him.

She seemed not to notice.

"I can supply you with clothing from a dispenser. Your tail''—she caressed that member, which was resting beside Cord's leg—"would fit into a pair of loose trousers, wouldn't it? That would conceal your most noticeable difference. If you wear a cap or a cowl, that will conceal your ears. Your skin color is close enough to some of Ten Suns' employees that no one will pay attention to it.''

"Julia, if you think it will work, I will take your advice. But how can you get clothes to fit me without attracting attention to yourself?''

"It is only a question of putting credit coins in the machine rather than my debit card.'' She shrugged. "And no one is likely to be at the dispenser now. If someone is, I will not make my selection until he is gone. But I will need to know your size.'' She smiled.

"Can you measure me? Or guess?''

Her hands bracketed his shoulders, then fell to his hips.

"I never leave anything to chance. You are very lean,'' she added. "Tall, too. I think I can fit you.''

Cord did not know whether to be glad she was empathically deaf or to wish that she were an empath, so she would realize she was rousing desires in him which he could not satisfy. If she were Mehiran, if she shared his feelings, he would take her in his arms, press her down on the bed, and begin peeling that tight garment off her. . . .

Perhaps Julia McKay was experiencing similar sensations: her slim fingers skimmed over his groin and came to rest in his crotch.

The gentle pressure made Cord gasp.

"Julia," he said, concentrating very hard, "I'd like to discuss this with you, but there's no time. I've got to get to Bird before they start hurting her again." His ancestors grant that he get another chance like this when he had an opportunity to pursue it!

"Don't worry," Julia said. "The head of security is a Kamean. They always rest after the noon meal. She won't be ready to resume for some while. And she will call me first, because I asked her to, and she promised to do so. She did not want to, but I argued and argued, and now, having given her word, she will keep it." Julia's fingers continued to roam.

"I see." Distractedly he wondered what a Kamean was.

"We have time," Julia said, stroking his tail again. "I want to find out what it's like, Cord. Since I left my own world, there's been no one I wanted. Mmmh," she murmured as Cord pulled her down on the bed.

Shyly, Julia traced the seam in the front of her overall, and the fabric parted.

Cord did not speak. He ran his hands under the open edge of her jacket, easing her out of it, so it slid down, exposing her shoulders, arms, and breasts. Then it was down around her hips and thighs. There was surprisingly long hair between her thighs, veiling her secret place, where a Mehiran woman would have only short, velvety fur. Gently he explored her with his fingers while her breathing became rapid. She moaned in pleasure and in anticipation of greater pleasure to come. In its pouch his organ throbbed and grew, pushing against its protective cave.

Julia plucked at his clothing, trying to find unfamiliar fastenings. Quickly he pulled off his own suit and saw her eyes widen at the sight of his pouch parting to reveal the tip of the organ within. Slowly it snaked out.

She licked her lips—fear or anticipation? Cord didn't know which. He'd shut down his mind out of deference to Julia's humanness.

"You are so slender," she finally said. "I'm afraid I'll hardly feel you."

Cord knew she was too kind and too innocent to mean it as a taunt, but her words stung him anyway. He did not want to hurt her—but he did want to prove she would feel it. He plunged into her and came down hard. He could feel the softness of her breasts and the way her hips rolled under his. The muscles inside her squeezed him, urging him on. Cord thrust again and again, feeling her back arch, feeling her muscles squeeze convulsively. He held back. He wanted her to cry out, to writhe more. Slowly he raised himself upright and hooked his knees around her thighs. He was almost out of her now, remaining only a fingerbreadth inside her warmth. Cord rotated his hips so that the tip of his organ tantalized her.

Julia ran her tongue over her lips. The sight stirred Cord so much that he came close to filling her cup too soon, oh, far too soon. With an effort he controlled himself. He let his tail travel up under her buttocks in search of another orifice.

When he penetrated her the second time, her whole body heaved in ecstasy.

She laughed softly and raised her head. Her tongue flicked across his nipples. The moistness of her lips inflamed him.

So she wanted to make him come before she did? It had become a contest between them, one which Cord meant to win. He renewed his efforts. She seemed to like it best when he paid no attention to her comfort, so Cord cast off the last of his scruples. The joy of subduing her blocked out every impulse to be gentle and considerate. It was easy not to care with shields up. He tried several variations: thrusting with both organ and tail simultaneously, thrusting and slightly withdrawing first one, then the other . . .

"This is called the Horns," he whispered. "Feel how you are impaled. The Horns go deeper and deeper . . ."

With volcanic force, Julia's slim body arched and she cried out. Cord, looking down at her, felt a rush of triumph hot as an eruption of semen. But he continued to plunge until she lay supine and panting. Only then he permitted himself to let go, to release the pressure that was growing unbearable.

When he collapsed beside her, Cord was aware only of his shame.

"I'm sorry. Please believe me, I'm sorry. I don't know what came over me." He drew her closer, hoping he had not harmed her.

She rested her head against his shoulder drowsily.

"I didn't intend it to be like that," he began again.

"I know," she replied.

Opening his shields, Cord detected nothing in her mind but her normal self-contained, almost imperceptible signal. He wasn't even sure she felt there was anything to forgive. He was not satisfied, however. He knew his behavior had been disgusting, shameful, and brutal. Maybe he was as bad as his people said Catchers were. Ancestors, maybe he was as bad as the humans!

"I think," Julia remarked, disengaging herself from Cord's embrace and sitting up, "I ought to go and get you some clothes."

She kicked off her shoes and the overall, which Cord had not succeeded in stripping all the way off, and walked into the next room. Moments later she emerged, looking and smelling fresh, and did something to one wall of the room. Drawers and a closet appeared. She took out a garment and began to dress.

"If you wish to clean up, there are facilities for washing in there." She nodded toward the door from which she'd come. "Red for warmer, blue for cold, and green when you want to dry off."

He did as she said. The cubicle filled with a warm, damp mist, but it must have been something more than mist, too, because it seemed to float sweat and dirt away, and to leave him refreshed. Touching the green control caused the mist to vanish. Cord wondered whether to expect warm air or a heat lamp. There was neither. Instead, he simply found that he was no longer damp.

Emerging into the main room, he found Julia ready to leave.

"I'll be right back," she told him briskly.

Cord paced the room in restless anxiety. She could betray him so easily. Even if she didn't, he still had to rescue Bird, and he was beginning to feel that would be no small accomplishment.

# Chapter 11

Julia McKay returned with a bundle.

"These should fit. Put them on. I brought something else too. It occurred to me that you have that big box—I suppose you want to take it with you."

"Yes, I'll need it." The problem had been worrying Cord. Always before, he and his parents had known what they were likely to need in a chase, so it had not been necessary to carry everything. Now he could not afford to leave any of it behind. Some might be useful if he needed goods or money—having failed to trade with the humans, it was likely he would—while others might be vital to his and Bird's survival.

"In that case, my efforts were not wasted." Julia produced a small boxlike object with sliding grippers evidently meant to hold a crate firmly. Attached to it was a wire lead.

"We'll have to get this under your box. Can you tilt it? Oh, thanks. The slides will contract to hold it. Now push the button on the handgrip."

The equipment case floated gently to about Cord's waist level and hung there.

"You'll have more mobility this way."

"Yes, I see. Thank you, Julia. But won't someone notice it's missing?"

'It's kept in an unlocked closet for use by anyone who needs to move something large or heavy. Its not being there won't be thought suspicious. What will cause people to wonder is how you will know where to find your friend. So I'll take you there, and we will pretend that you came to me—since we are known to be acquainted—and forced me to take you to the security department."

"Will your people believe such a story?" Cord asked skeptically.

"They are traders. They have no very high opinion of

missionaries. They will think I was easily frightened. It is true that I am very timid."

"I don't think so. I don't think I've ever met anyone like you."

"Perhaps not," she responded. "Anyway, when you've got Bird, you can leave me—push me to one side; I'll seem to be stunned. But please don't let yourself be captured. Under questioning, you won't be able to keep from revealing who helped you."

"I won't be caught. I can't. I have a responsibility to Bird."

"Even if it means killing?"

"With any luck at all, it won't come to that," Cord said, thinking of his anesthetic gun.

Julia looked unconvinced. She had noticed the weapon, of course, but he had not mentioned it was nonlethal.

"We should start," she said. "Can you break through locked doors?"

"It may depend upon the lock."

"They will all be like this one." She indicated the lock on her own door. "A burn ray would probably deactivate it in a second."

"I have something which should work, but won't there be more complicated security devices where we are going? If it is used for prisoners . . ."

"With a dangerous prisoner, they would use extra precautions. They did not bother in your friend's case. She is in restraints, after all, and as a rule that is enough. She can't free herself, and no one else would. Everyone in a trading port like this is psych-screened before assignment."

Cord was stowing the cutter gun from his equipment chest in one of the pockets of his tunic. It had a loose cowl, which he pulled over his head.

"Let's go," he said. Now that action was imminent, he was calm. Why not? He had been trained all his life for similar situations.

They left Julia's room and proceeded to the nearest trans tube, Julia walking slightly in front of Cord. He casually held his right hand in his pocket. If anyone remembered seeing them afterward, it would seem that Julia had been his prisoner.

Four levels down, they left the tube. Julia turned right and indicated to Cord that they would take the speedwalk. It rushed them along faster than they could have walked: so fast that Cord, glancing from side to side, could not take in their surroundings. When Julia led Cord off the walk, it appeared to Cord that they had traveled all the way to the far end of the building.

The color of the walls and floor shifted to a bright orange-red, and ahead of them the hallway ended in a cul-de-sac.

"This door." Julia spoke for the first time since leaving her room.

Cord gave a quick glance around him. This was not a busy section. No one was in sight, none of the doors stood open. He tried the one before him experimentally. It was locked.

"Hurry," Julia breathed.

Cord withdrew the cutter and motioned Julia to stand aside. With the ray at its narrowest setting, he gave the trigger a brief squeeze. When he tried the door a second time it gave way.

He slid it open and entered, cutter gun in hand. Julia, following him, slid the door shut.

"In the next room," she told him.

The outer room in which they stood was nothing more than an office. Cord passed through it in three strides. The next room was bare by contrast: just a large machine in one corner, and a metal table on which Bird lay. Heavy straps bound her wrists and ankles. She was pallid, and there were shadows beneath her golden eyes. She stared toward the door, cringing. Cord remembered too late that she could not have felt this approach, with his mind shielded as it so often was. Immediately he poured out reassurance.

At the sight of him, Bird gasped.

"It's all right," he said, working to free her hands. Julia struggled with the straps at Bird's ankles.

"It's all right," he said again as he helped her sit up. Bird was shaking. She clung to him. Her hair had come loose from its braid, and she was unable to keep her voice steady enough to utter more than a word or two. Her emotions were a cascade of fear, apprehension, loathing. Cord had never known her to be so distraught, physically or mentally.

"You'd better hurry," Julia said. She remained calm.

"Can you walk?" he asked Bird.

She continued to tremble but replied, "Yes."

"Good, Bird. We'll be out of here in no time at all." He turned to Julia. "I don't know how to thank you. I couldn't have gotten this far without your help. Why don't you change places with Bird? When you're found it will be obvious that I forced you to bring me here, then left you bound."

"I have a better idea: I'll go with you as a 'hostage.' If anybody notices you and Bird at all, he'll probably hold his fire with me there."

"Probably . . . ?"

Julia smiled faintly. "One must take some chances." On a more practical note she added, "Of course, very often people don't notice at all. Perhaps if we all simply walk to the entrance, everyone will assume you've got a right to go out."

"We'll find out." Cord was not optimistic—but who would have believed he'd get this far without challenge?

"How soon is the security chief due back?" he whispered as they approached the speedwalk. They would get to the trans tube nearest the entrance, then hope they could make it to the door.

"Very soon now, I think. But she will be coming from a different direction—we won't meet her in the tube. I ought to have thought to bring clothing for Bird," Julia continued. "If I had, you could stroll out without a second thought."

They entered the speedwalk, Julia first, followed by Bird, with Cord close behind. Bird held the lead to the antigravity device. A woman bringing a crate through the halls might be inconspicuous enough. As protective coloration, Julia had combed Bird's scalplock, parting it in the middle, so the hair fell to either side of her head. Bird's ears had posed a problem until she herself had solved it by laying them back along her head. With her hair over them, they were invisible. She had also doubled her tail under the short gown she was wearing.

Cord prayed to his ancestors that she would be taken by any who saw her as another member of the trading party, if an unfamiliar one.

Their transfer from the speedwalk to the trans tube went unnoticed. A few humans were passing. They all seemed to have places to go and things to think about; no one did more than glance at them.

"We're almost there," Julia said softly.

They were in the concourse, with the entrance before them

like a hope of future bliss. Only an expanse of empty floor separated them from it.

"Hey!"

At the shout, Bird gave a little cry, almost inaudible. Opening his mind, Cord caught her panic and, as strong but opposite in character, the suspicion and doubt of the one who had shouted.

They had all frozen. Cord turned an inquiring face to him as he came toward them. Julia, he noticed with approval, was remembering to play her hostage role. She appeared tense and held a fine line between seeming nervous enough to attract attention and being so relaxed that she might later be accused of aiding the Mehirans. Cord thought they might be able to talk themselves out.

"Where are you going?"

"Out," Cord replied. Maybe he should come up with some explanation, but he did not know enough about the port's operation to sound convincing.

"Got your passes?"

"Passes?"

"To go out, of course. Don't you know we're under Condition Yellow? Nobody goes out without . . . I don't recognize you. Name and department?" The man's mild distrust sharpened.

Cord fired the anesthetic gun though the pocket of his tunic. It was a thin, high-pressure stream and the distance was short; Cord reckoned the intervening fabric would not dissipate it too much.

"What the hell . . . ?"

The human looked down at the wetness on his jacket. He should have been stretched on the floor by now, oblivious to them. Either the drug did not work on the human metabolism or else its passage through the layers of material—his own pocket and the human's clothing—had cut its efficacy.

The human was sending out impulses of anger. One hand went to a stud on his belt. Cord did not know what it was, but that it was a menace he did not doubt. By reflex, he simultaneously threw up his shield and drew the cutter gun left-handed and fired.

The hole in the man's chest was quite small, but red frothed from it. Through his shield Cord was still rocked by a brief flare of surprise and pain. The human folded in on himself very slowly, and began to fall.

"The alarm," Julia said, low-voiced. That was what . . ."

"I wasn't fast enough, it would seem," Cord answered, sweeping back and forth with the cutter in search of possible attackers. "Move toward the door, Bird," he ordered.

Bird staggered at the mental output of the dying human. It was distressing, but not as much as the idea of remaining a prisoner at the humans' mercy. She obeyed his command without hesitation.

Cries of surprise and fear came from the far end of the great lobby, as a small group of humans became aware that something was terribly wrong. They threw themselves flat on the floor and tried to seek cover. The rapidity of their reactions argued a certain familiarity with violence. Julia had already hit the floor and rolled under a bench, away from the two Mehirans.

Cord's mind was open now for early warning of attack. And so he heard the mental energy of the two guards even before they reached the concourse. He could determine the direction from which they were coming—a door to his right. He waited, receptive to their emotions . . .

And raked the cutter's ray across the door. The beam itself was almost invisible except for a faint opalescence, but its track could be followed in the damage it inflicted. It passed through doorframe and door as though they were paper and also through the bodies on the other side; the door remained in place with only a hair-thin slit across it. His shielded mind was assaulted by the psychic protest of a pair of dying human brains. He gasped but steeled himself against it, hoping that Bird was too numbed to feel.

He began to back toward the entrance, careful to watch and feel for the coming of more humans. Behind him, Bird uttered a soft cry. Her output was a haze of fear and anxiety, but she said, "The door guard, Cord!"

By the time she spoke his name he had swung around to face the new peril.

The human on duty at the entrance had left his post in response to the alarm. He was raising his own gun when Cord snapped off a shot at him, missing by a handbreadth as the guard leaped for shelter behind a tapered obelisk mounted on a rough stone base. It offered adequate cover—the base was man-height, the stele half again as tall. Its faces bore elaborate carvings and what might be script.

A tan hand holding a pistol darted out from the base and fired. Cord flung himself down a fraction of an instant before the projectile passed through the point in space where his stomach had been. He heard the dart explode against the wall. *Ugly*, he thought. If he hadn't ducked in time or if the human had been able to aim more accurately . . .

"On the floor, Bird," he called. "Let the carrier settle and crouch behind it."

There was a moment's lull. The human did not care to risk showing himself, and unless he did, he could not expect to hit Cord. And neither could Cord hit him. But the human needed to do nothing. As long as he stayed there, whether he fired or not, Cord and Bird could not get past him to the door. Meanwhile there were surely more guards coming.

Cord slithered over to join Bird behind the equipment case. With an eye always on the obelisk, Cord inverted the cutter and adjusted the setting. The wider beam would not cut as quickly, but it would cut a broader swathe. It might work, he thought, as he trained the tool's sight on the point where the great metal slab met its base. Or it might be a waste of time and of the cutter's power pack. He needed skill and blind luck and the aid of his ancestors, and all of them together might not be enough. He fired, holding the firing stud down to maintain a continuous beam.

Cord, with his extra sense alert, felt a surge of apprehension from the guard behind the block. So the human guessed what was happening! So much the better.

The ray was disintegrating stone and metal with steady efficiency. Cord estimated that the pillar was eaten away halfway through its thickness.

The panicked human fired three rapid shots. Twice he missed (though not by much); the third shot detonated against the equipment box. Bird caught her breath sharply. Cord felt her trembling throughout his body, they were lying so close behind the scant cover. Cord wished he could reach out with arms and mind to comfort her, but there was no opportunity now.

"Cord, if . . . if we aren't going to make it, please kill me."

"Bird!" He was dismayed at the request, but his aim on the obelisk did not waver.

"I mean it. You don't know what they're like. I can't go back, I can't, I can't." Her voice broke.

Cord thought she was weeping in silence. He could no spare the time to look.

"If it comes to that, Bird, I'll kill both of us. I promise." *Our ancestors grant it will not be necessary*, he added to himself.

A groaning sound came from the stele. The whole weight of the monolith was supported now by a pillar no thicker than Cord's wrist. Perhaps the metal sang in protest at the strain. With desperate haste, Cord switched the setting back to narrow beam and continued to cut it away.

The pillar tottered on its new, shaky foundation. With a suddenness that made Cord flinch, the human darted out. He dashed headlong for the cover offered by a heavy bench near one wall, well beyond the arc of the obelisk. Cord's shot cut him in half. Bird screamed in unison with the human; Cord doubled over in pain. The sound was lost in a greater one as the metal monolith finally toppled. It hit the floor with a roar.

Stumbling to his feet, he pulled Bird up with him. He groped for the antigravity control and succeeded in floating the box. Still watching for attack, Cord pushed Bird toward the door.

The humans in the lobby seemed stunned—and they were not armed. Still no sign of more guards.

Bird moved ahead of him readily, pushing open the entrance; they emerged into the golden light of late afternoon. He ran toward the nearest ground car, but Bird caught his arm.

"Aircar!" she cried.

They veered off and with one mind, they ran toward it. Bird might be exhausted by her ordeal, but she was not hampered by the equipment case, which dragged at the lead looped around Cord's wrist. Bird reached the aircar first and climbed behind the controls. Cord shoved the case into the back of the car and cut the antigravity. The box dropped to the floor, and Cord clambered in after it.

Bird was already throwing the switches; the reassuring hum of a Mehiran aircar in good maintenance and ready to ascend filled Cord's ears. He gave Bird full credit for reacting so well in a situation she could never have anticipated. There was still distress in her signals, but it was overlaid by her determination and efficiency. With Bird at the controls they were already moving and gaining speed.

With a lurch, they were airborne. The machine was a powerful model, good for a flight halfway around the globe. Below, shrinking to toy size, humans were running out of the port building to stand gazing after them.

The humans' anger and hate dwindled to nothingness, leaving them touched only by a cool wind of relief. They stared ahead blindly, and said not a word.

# Chapter 12

"Where are we going?" Bird finally asked.

The question brought Cord back to reality. To cover it, he struggled into the front passenger seat from his crowded position in the storage compartment. His planning had gone no further than getting them out of the building and into a vehicle. At that, he'd been expecting to use a ground car. This was better: it eliminated the need to run the Mehiran blockade of the port. The Council would not be pleased if he damaged their vans.

"The Council?" he wondered.

"Are you insane?" Bird's normally soothing voice was ragged with emotion.

Cord let himself receive her impressions and found them full of incredulity and horror. "What's the matter?"

"Have you forgotten that you *killed* back there?" She pronounced the word as though it were an indelicacy, which it was. "Oh, Cord . . ."

He experienced her misery and pity in all their vividness. Ancestors, she was right. He had destroyed four living beings without a second thought—with hardly a first thought. And here he sat as calmly as if he had spent the day weeding a garden, with the sweat of decent labor on him.

"When you killed, you didn't feel anything, did you?" she accused.

"Of course I did," he retorted. But it didn't stop him from killing again and again. The enormity of his actions finally began to dawn on him. Bird could feel his revulsion.

Neither of them had anything else to say. She had spoken the truth, and sooner or later it must be faced.

Their heading, he saw, was south. Ahead was the Yellow Desert. He remembered going there once with his parents. Not on vacation, of course. No one went into the desert for fun. Someone they'd been hunting took refuge there. When they found him, he'd been dead four days. The body was well on its way to mummification where it had not been gnawed away by the few creatures who inhabited the waste.

"Why not land in the desert?" he asked. "We both need rest and peace, and we'll get it there. In the morning we can decide what's best."

"There's no 'best' anymore." But she guided the craft toward the heart of the drylands.

"The mountains, then," Cord said.

"What mountains?" snapped Bird irritably.

"The Spine of Arzet—it's easy to get lost in them, and camouflaged, the aircar will be indistinguishable from the boulders. But you're right, it's only a ridge of rock—a kind of spine running east and west."

Beneath, the marshland had turned to dry flats covered with coarser growth than that found near the port. Then the vegetation below grew sparse and the dusty ground took on a dun cast. Eventually they could see sand.

They flew on as the shadows were lengthening.

"If we don't come to Arzet shortly, we'd better set down. The light will soon be gone." Cord wished his memories of the Yellow Desert's geography were less vague. His only visit was several years past, and they'd approached from a different direction.

"There!"

The line of tumbled rock was a more welcome sight than any Cord had seen. He did not know what geologic upheaval had raised the stony mass above the sand, but its dull-black sides, cut with cracks and scattered with huge blocks broken off the main body, promised shelter.

Bird banked the aircar to begin the descent. She made a neat landing, paralleling the ridge, then taxied in close to a pile of rock.

"I suppose these won't come down on us?"

"No reason to think so," Cord assured her. "They've been here hundreds of years."

"As long as they stay put for another day. What do we do now?"

"I'll unload my gear and do a little more to hide the car. Come on out—you'll find it more bearable in the shade. And once the sun goes down, it will get much cooler."

She crouched by the rocks while Cord took his case from the aircar. He removed the camouflage-field generator and placed it on top of the vehicle. From the air, it would resemble another pile of rock. Unless the Council sent another Catcher after them, they were quite safe.

At least as far as other people were concerned. There was still the matter of survival here in the desert. Cord thought they would need a fire, but except for a few weeds growing among the rocks, for practical purposes there was nothing to burn. His kit contained a small tent which would become warm with their body heat. He hoped it would be sufficient: the nighttime temperature in the desert fell abruptly.

At the moment it was still warm; while the light lasted he had a more urgent task. Cord took a large, impermeable sheet meant to keep supplies and equipment dry in the field, and set it aside. Then he improvised a digging tool and began to excavate a hole.

He dug it waist-deep and twice as wide. To his surprise, when he was finished he found that Bird had gathered the rocks he would need.

"You described this technique to me once," she explained. "It helps to have something to do."

He gave her a quick hug to show his appreciation, before fetching a storage container for the bottom of the pit. Bird helped him spread the tarpaulin over the hole and weight it with the stones. Finally Cord placed a handful of pebbles in the center so that the sheet sagged over the container.

"There will be water in the morning," he said. "Not much, maybe, but enough. By then . . ."

"By then we'll have decided what to do," Bird finished.

Together they unpacked the tent. The frame went up in moments. Then Cord slipped the cover over the skeleton and tightened it. Bird and he carried it to a sheltered place among the boulders as the last light was fading along the horizon.

They had shelter and a source of water; they would not even go hungry, thanks to the supply of emergency rations in the equipment chest. They crouched outside the tent and Cord handed Bird a cake of the dense, chewy stuff. She unwrapped it and nibbled at a corner.

"Cord," she said slowly, with evident reluctance, "what will you do? You can't go back now."

Their people would never forgive him, even if he escaped

execution. Perhaps the Council would agree he was justified in killing the humans in view of Bird's imprisonment and the humans' hostile action. Nevertheless he would be tainted, far more than he had been as a Catcher. Most would regard his actions as murder, different from the work of a Catcher operating against a criminal on Council orders. Most likely, the Council would have him killed as a potential danger—a Catcher gone mad, liable to run berserk at any provocation.

"I don't know yet what I'm going to do except get some sleep tonight. Tomorrow I'll petition my ancestors for guidance," Cord said. "Maybe they'll tell me."

"Oh," Bird murmured doubtfully.

People often spoke to their ancestors, though one did not expect a verbal reply or physical aid. But the ancestors could give advice or instruction if it was needed enough. History was full of stories of those who had obeyed the spirits' injunctions and been saved in spite of dreadful odds. There were also tales of those who petitioned and failed to take the offered advice. Their endings were never good. Most never had cause to ask their ancestral spirits for real help, because it was something done only for the gravest cause. And of those who asked, few were answered. Tradition said that if you could help yourself, your ancestors would not.

Bird's response did not surprise Cord at all. What he proposed was a very serious matter. Considering his recent activities, neither of them would be astonished if his ancestors struck him blind or paralyzed him for his presumption.

"Well," she said after a long pause, "I guess you haven't much choice. I hope the spirits will aid you." Her forlorn voice matched her listless aura, but Cord felt both resigned and committed. There was nowhere to go but onward. He was more worried about Bird than about himself.

"Bird, are *you* going to be all right?"

She was so slow in answering that Cord wondered if she had heard. At last she spoke.

"For a while, I wasn't sure—but now I believe I'll get over it. It may take a few visits to a mind healer to erase some of the memories or at least to make them less vivid. It was worse than feeling someone die, Cord. The first time I thought I was dying myself. The other times, I hoped I was or that I'd go mad. You don't understand," she concluded sadly.

"I'm sorry. I knew you were suffering, but I still don't know what happened to you. I can't imagine anything that would make you despair." She was the one who always believed things would work out for the best, the one who was so sure the world was constituted as it ought to be.

"The humans have a machine . . . it makes you believe a dream is reality. And they control the dream—or nightmare," she corrected. "They'd start the machine again and again and I would find myself living through another horror. Burning alive, perhaps, feeling my skin crisping and my eyes melting—" She broke off, face an unhealthy yellow. "But I still wouldn't confess—I couldn't tell the humans what they wanted to hear."

"Put your head down. There, now, don't think about it. Don't think about anything." Cord poured out sympathy and love. It was the best he could do under the circumstances.

"I'll be all right now, Cord, I promise. For a second it all came back to me."

"Julia told me the humans wanted your confession. It seemed ridiculous to me. Even allowing for their ignorance about us, I don't see how they could think you did it. You wouldn't have had the opportunity."

Bird laughed a little, shakily.

"Always the Catcher. All the same, I might have confessed so they would stop. Your friend Julia gave me strength and courage; her serenity was like cool water damping the fires of hatred. The other woman—my torturer—wanted me to confess and yet she wanted me not to, so she could go on hurting me. Probably I imagined this, because I was so hurt and terrified, but it was as though the room were filled with something black and hungry. Something that was feeding. The humans are beasts. Except for Julia. She was kind."

Bird's description made Cord shiver. "It's getting chilly. Maybe we'd better get into the tent and sleep."

Bird wriggled into the tent—meant for one person rather than two, but they'd be warmer that way—and Cord followed, closing the entrance against anything which might prowl the night.

With the thin emergency cover over them, they were pleasantly snug. Bird curled close beside him, apparently content. Cord tried to relax and sleep.

Bird had other plans. She slid one arm across him and

began to caress his chest, working tantalizingly downward. Her need washed over him, sparking an answering flame in his own loins.

Bird rolled on top of him, fully clothed. The tip of her tail boldly explored inner recesses, but was thwarted in its exploration. If he had worn his usual clothing, he would have had her at once. With Bird astride him, he could not reach the fastening of the alien trousers. Fitting as they did, his organ could not even emerge from its pouch. The stimulation and its frustration fed his lust.

Bird guessed the difficulty and shifted her weight. Cord tore the closure open and felt his tool swell and blossom in record time. Then his hands sought Bird's hips as she settled onto him with a moan of delight.

It was good, of course. Bird was a sensitive and practiced partner who prolonged the pleasure until there was nothing for either of them beyond their own sweat-slick bodies. Yet Cord found himself imagining other women: how they would smell and how they would feel as he entered them. And he wanted Julia again.

Then Bird's hands and thighs and moist warmth brought him back to the present: she was losing control; her muscles sucked at Cord, drawing him in farther and farther, as deep as he could go. He came in a gush, still thinking of Julia.

Bird slipped off. She had shielded her mind, but not quickly enough to conceal from Cord her lack of fulfillment. He wouldn't leave her like that.

"Not so fast," he murmured, embracing her from the back. It was only a question of summoning the reserves to do her again as she ought to be done. But with his tail still trapped in the Terran pants, he'd have to be more inventive.

He remembered a conversation he'd heard between his father and another Catcher:

"Working with your family, you don't get the opportunities we loners do, Fyrrell. Of course, you got a woman already, but for the rest of us, we take it where we can get it. And sometimes the taking is pretty good. That poisoner last year—now, she was good. I caught her in six days, brought her back in nine. Must of had her eighteen different ways. I think she thought I'd let her go if she performed right. . . ."

Fyrrell had been contemptuous of the other, Cord knew.

But the thought of catching a woman and lying with her was intriguing. Inflaming . . .

Cord pushed Bird's tail aside. His organ was at the ready once again. As he slid it in, he felt the stickiness on the insides of Bird's thighs. There would be another load of his seed in her tonight—but not too soon.

She was surprised to feel him again. Pleased, too. Her buttocks tightened against his belly.

This time he did not finish until she was sated. Afterward, she turned over and kissed him lingeringly, before cuddling beside him. He felt conscious thought fall away from her almost at once. Smiling, he closed his eyes and floated into darkness.

He came awake fast, a survival trait for one of his trade. The increasing light outside the tent was not what awakened him. It was Bird's stirring.

"What's the matter?"

Bird, extricating herself from the cover, laughed softly.

"Everything is fine, Cord. I'm getting up to look for the privy."

Cord laughed, too.

"I'll stand guard for you. There are no large predators here, but . . ."

"But you leave nothing to chance."

"No. Anyway, the sun is coming up, and I'd like to get started."

At dawn the desert was lovely: golden sand touched with pink and rose and mauve. The sky was dull blue. It might be a good day for many endeavors. Cord took their morning ration from the chest. It occurred to him that possibly he ought to fast—an idea he rejected as contrary to common sense. The old stories did not speak of fasting as a requirement, though in some tales the petitioners had done so. In this situation, Cord decided it would be foolish and perhaps dangerous. If he was going to climb the Spine of Arzet he had better be in top form. A fall from those rocks would be fatal.

They ate their ration cakes and watched the sun rise. Bird was calm, confident, and lighthearted. It was only when he brought up the subject of his climb that he saw the change in her.

"Bird, if something happens to me this morning—if I break my neck or . . . well, whatever—promise you won't do anything silly, like trying to bring my body back for cremation. You get in the aircar and go. Tell the Council anything you like about me. They will probably be glad to be rid of me, the way things are."

He expected her to try to convince him that nothing would happen to him, that the ancestors would aid him, that they'd leave together or not at all. Instead she replied, "Very well. What shall I do with your box?"

"Whatever you wish. If you need money, you could sell it to the Council. There's some useful equipment in it. I won't need it, if I'm dead."

"I have sources of income. I won't need to sell it. I thought if you had some intention for its disposal, I ought to know."

Of course: it constituted his and his parents' whole estate, the only thing of value—besides their lives—that they owned.

"My father's family is all dead. My mother's family would be more likely to feel insulted than flattered if I left it to them."

"I will do as seems best, then, if you don't come back," said Bird.

Cord hugged her, and felt her arms press him in return.

"I expect to be back, Bird. This isn't goodbye."

"I know. But I have to be realistic about it, Cord. I knew my father was going to die someday of old age, an honored member of the Upper Council. I was going to follow the same career. Now that's all gone. I can't make any assumptions or build on anything that may turn to dust."

"Maybe you should try asking your ancestors' help, too."

"Things are bad, but I'm not that desperate yet. You go on, Cord. I'll enjoy the sun and sand down here."

He left her the anesthetic gun for defense—most likely unnecessary—and strode to the base of the ridge. The climb did not look too complicated, Cord reflected. The mass of stone was broken and weathered and by no means vertical. Anyone with four limbs and a tail and in reasonably good health should be able to scramble up. He found a ramp of stone and began to climb.

# Chapter 13

A handful of pebbles rattled down the slope. Cord paused. His reach for the next handhold had dislodged them, but the rock face seemed stable otherwise. He began to move again, carefully. Halfway up, he wedged one foot in a crack. For a moment he faced the prospect of a slow death by thirst and heat prostration. Still he had remained calm and worked the limb free. So near his goal he must not fail.

The ridge rose at a sixty-degree angle. But for the broken, crumbling stone it would scarcely be a challenge. At last he pulled himself up onto the top of the ridge.

The platform of rock was not wide—not as wide as a street—but not so narrow as to be worrisome. And he could see in all directions—an ocean of yellow sand. After the exertion of the climb, the wind felt cold on his skin.

He stood in the cooling wind and tried to compose his mind. Alone with sand, rock, and sky he felt very small— beneath the notice of the Mehiran ancestral spirits, surely.

"Ancestors," he said, the word sounding loud in his ears. "Ancestors, I am Cord, son of Fyrrell and Neteel, who have joined you." He added the names of both sets of grandparents and those of his paternal great-grandparents as well.

"I ask your help." What should he say? He found himself describing the events at the spaceport—though whether the ancestors would understand, if they were listening at all, he did not know.

"I have killed and cut myself off from my people and I don't know what to do. Please help me.

"I know that what I did was wrong," he continued. "Everyone would say so. But what else could I have done?"

The sibilance of wind in his ears rose to a roar—though its force seemed no stronger. Then the rushing resolved itself into the whisper of many voices.

"Being what you are," they said, "you could have done nothing else."

Everyone knew the ancestors spoke sometimes, yet Cord wondered whether the words were of his own imagining. He shook his head to clear it. Why complicate things more? They had spoken, if only to utter a reproach.

"We do not reproach you," the voices said, replying to his thought. "You are what you are, and that is not as others are."

"Am I really so different from everyone else?"

"You are, are, are, are, are," the voices echoed. Here was confirmation of his worst fears. He suspected he possessed certain tendencies, criminal traits. Until now he believed his worry had painted them larger than they were.

"Why? What is wrong with me?"

"All but one of your forebears are among us," they told him. "But that one is very strong in you. Your strangeness springs from that source." Deep/high, soft/loud, distant/near, a thousand thousand separate murmurs.

Blood congealed around Cord's heart. To think of someone so terrible that his spirit was not even accepted among the ancestors whom all—all!—were said to join at death.

Cord's muscles felt stiff, and his eyes ached. The urge to face those who addressed him was overwhelming, but there was no one there, only the breeze.

"What shall I do?" he asked. Why did he bother? What could they tell him, except to kill himself or live apart in the desert until he died?

"You have no future on Mehira" was the sibilant reply.

He almost laughed. That was one way of stating it. The next words were unexpected.

"You must leave this world, Cord."

"What?"

"Leave Mehira. You have become a source of infection. For Mehira's good and your own survival, you must go."

His first reaction was gladness: to see alien worlds and meet others, like Julia, who would not be offended by his background, seemed an undeserved reward. His second thought was of the obstacles.

"To leave, I need the Terrans' help. And you know that I . . . killed some of them."

"So you informed us. Do you think they will not give you transportation off Mehira because of it?"

"The idea occurred to me," Cord said wryly.

"If they were Mehirans, it might be so, though even among our kind many things can be forgiven if it is to someone's advantage. Offer them what they want."

"And what should I do when I am away from Mehira?" he asked.

The multitude laughed softly.

"No doubt a young man of curiosity and enterprise will find something to occupy him. . . ."

Cord smiled, forgetting the past few days in the warming kindness of their amusement.

"There is one thing more," they whispered, and this time their tones were cold as the wind from a northern sea. "There is another source of contagion on Mehira, and that is the one who killed your father and mother. Remove it."

"Yes." He had intended all along to find his parents' killer. To have his ancestors' sanction lightened his heart. It had been uncomfortable to conceal from them a crime he planned to commit. He was only surprised to find the spirits advocating revenge.

Once more, they read his thoughts.

"We are not concerned with revenge. Our interest is Mehira's good. The murderer is a source of danger."

"As I am?"

"There is a difference. You would do harm inadvertently. But there is a hunger for emotion and experience which amounts to lust. It must be removed."

"Who is the killer?" The ancestors often spoke in riddles, Cord knew; that was well known from the old stories.

"We cannot tell you. We can sense the murderer's presence—but not his identity—as we can sense your genetic inheritance. Once you have found the murderer and eliminated the threat, you will take passage offworld."

The voices were silent, so that Cord thought they had finished. Before he could thank them, they spoke again.

"Be warned: among the humans, maintain your emotional shielding as much as possible, or you will be destroyed by their emotions and by the things you must do. We can aid you no further."

"I understand," he said. "I'll do what you say."

"Good fortune attend your faring, then, Cord. Our good-will is with you."

A surge of emotion rolled over him—joy, comfort, affection, pride, every positive feeling magnified. It lasted for the space of a heartbeat. The ancestors had embraced him, in their own way.

"Thank you," Cord called into the wind, but the murmuring had faded away.

The climb down seemed to pass very swiftly. This time Cord's mind was full of plans and possibilities. Once he got back inside the spaceport . . .

Bird stood waiting as he scrambled down the last rocky shoulder onto the desert floor. He seemed to see everything with preternatural clarity. He noted that Bird's face was smudged and anxious but that she had rebraided her hair and rolled it up into a knot for convenience. It would be cooler thus.

"Did you—?"

Cord knew what she meant. Had he heard the spirits?

"They spoke to me." The words sounded prosaic as a description of what he had experienced. Did the ancestors speak to one in a hundred thousand? To no more than that, he was sure.

Bird waited in silence, her eyes wide. One might never meet anyone who had heard the ancestral spirits.

"Let's sit in the shade, Bird, and I'll tell you about it."

Under the ridge's shadow, it was pleasantly dim. After enjoying the coolness for a moment, he began, "I know what I have to do. They told me to leave Mehira."

Bird drew a harsh breath. "How?"

"The Terrans will take me, the spirits say."

"Is there nothing else you can do? Living among *them* will be a cruel punishment."

"Yet if I stay here I may not be permitted to live at all." He had not thought of exile from Mehira as a sentence for crime, yet most would regard it as a terrible fate.

"Cord," Bird asked, "did the ancestors say how the aliens would take you away—or why? What if they take you away only to punish you?"

"It's all right, Bird. The spirits said the Terrans would give me passage in return for my parents' devices. And that's not all. One of them killed my parents, and I am to discover the murder . . ."

He left the statement unfinished. Better not to speak of what would happen next. But Bird had already been touched by his cold thought of revenge before he could throw up a barrier.

"The spirits ordered you to do this?" Doubt was strong in her voice. "It's sacrilegious."

"Bird, I swear to you, I'm not making this up. They told me the murderer was a source of contagion and must be removed."

Bird crossed her arms on her chest and regarded him seriously.

"One of my father's friends has a theory about the spirits. He claims their advice is directed toward the survival of the race, that it isn't kindness or family feeling that leads them to give assistance. He has documented many manifestations, including times they've spoken to someone who didn't ask for help. He says that one way or another, they get rid of anyone who poses a danger to Mehira. But if it's true, your experience makes sense."

"But why haven't I heard of this?" Cord demanded, then answered himself. "Of course, I'm no scholar."

"The Council has not approved its publication yet."

"Ah."

They sat for a time without speaking. Cord saw with surprise that the sun had not yet begun to slide down the sky. He felt he had already lived a long day, but there were plans to be made.

"We'll have to avoid being caught by our own people," Cord said, mostly to himself. "It may be hard getting inside the spaceport again, if the Council is still blockading it."

"Cord, I am not going with you." She spoke with the finality of death.

"They won't touch you again, Bird. That will be part of my bargain with them. Hamilton K wants what I have. He'll agree."

Bird's tail twitched, throwing a miniature shower of sand.

"Perhaps you can guarantee it, but I am not thinking of my safety. What concerns me now is decency. You intend to go back among the aliens and kill another of them. I want no part of it, whether the ancestors approve or not."

He started to protest, and stopped. She was gazing down at the sand, tight-lipped, her ears lying close to her head. Cord reached out to stroke the nearest one.

"I'm sorry, Bird." For what, he did not know. But what she said was true. No normal Mehiran would do what he planned.

"I know. So am I. If you were someone else—but you aren't. You're intelligent and fun and kind . . . and you're a wild animal. You can't help it, and I can't overlook it anymore—or pretend that you're civilized. The ancestors are right to have you leave Mehira. But I'm not going with you."

"Did I ask you to come?"

"No. You assumed I would, though. Didn't you?"

In his turn, Cord lowered his eyes.

"Never mind. Please understand, Cord. You've gotten worse lately. You aren't touching my mind even now, and you've got your own barriers up, as usual. You are willingly becoming deaf and blind. It's like finding the cub of a dangerous beast, taking it home and making a pet of it, then discovering when it's grown that it's still a predator."

Cord winced. He was a "predator." He liked hunting people. When he was engaged in a chase, he found it utterly engrossing. Now he had killed, and it was really no more difficult than the pursuit. He was no longer fit to live in Mehiran society.

"I know," he replied. "It was foolish of me to think of your coming: you wouldn't be happy among the humans. I'm not sure you could even survive the continual onslaught of their emotions."

"And will you find it easy to endure?" she asked.

"I may not like it, but I can bear it. My training helps." So often he had shut himself off from others, because so often they were hostile to him because of his trade.

Bird put her arms around him. "I wish I could help."

"You can't," he replied. "No one can. It's all right, Bird. I think I'll be happier away from Mehira. At least I won't be unhappier, except for missing you. But what can I do to make things right for you?"

"Drop me off near a town on your way back to the spaceport. You won't want to start until dusk, will you? If you could approach unseen it would be best."

Cord, remembering the Council's guard on the alien enclave, agreed.

"Now that's settled, we have the afternoon left," Bird pointed out. "Love me, Cord."

It would be for the last time, he knew, as he began to peel off her clothing.

She was as hot for him as though she had taken an aphrodisiac, and she wound her lithe legs around him to lock him to her. Cord opened his shields to feel her. Her need was compelling. It affected him, triggering an even deeper urge. He wanted to plow her again and again. His organ felt enormous. She was near ecstasy as he penetrated her, so it was easy to maintain a rhythmic pounding while Bird wriggled, nipped him tenderly, and moaned. He rode her until her passion exploded into orgasm and she lay limp beneath him.

"Anyone would think you never expected to have sex again," he murmured to her, after he had withdrawn. "Whereas there will be dozens and dozens of men in the future who'll worm their way into your . . . affections."

She smiled in drowsy satiation. "You didn't come, Cord. I wish you had."

"The afternoon is young. By this evening, you'll be too sore to do anything but go to bed, alone. I swear."

In spite of her contentment, her nipples hardened as soon as he touched them, and her pelvis angled up to meet him.

# Chapter 14

The sun was setting when the aircar lifted with Cord in the pilot's seat. In the distance he could see lights coming on in the towns that edged the waste. Cord kept the aircar over the desert, with the nearest towns off to their left. He began to bear north. Soon the port would be in sight.

"That cluster of lights over there must be Delell," Bird said. "You'd better land here and let me out."

Since takeoff they had kept their speech to the simple exchange of information. There was nothing more to say, unless they spent their last time together in argument.

Cord brought the aircar down on the sand without difficulty. Fortunately it was a fine model, with a full complement of equipment to make it operate safely even with an inattentive pilot. He turned to speak to Bird.

"Goodbye, Cord." She had already opened the door to leave.

He put his hand on her arm to stop her.

"Wait! Bird, what are you going to do? What have you got to go back to?"

She did not look at him. Her eyes were on the town lights ahead.

"I'm going to campaign against easing trade restrictions with the humans. They're too loose already. Eventually, I'll be a Speaker. Maybe I can keep the Council from making more mistakes. Oh, I have work to do. Good luck, Cord. I did love you."

She slipped out, letting the door slip shut behind her. Her pale gown whipped around her legs in the night wind.

Cord watched her walking away, very straight, very purposeful, a woman who knew where she was going.

A woman walking away . . .

He recalled a story about his great-great-grandfather, who

had gone north into the lava-rock wastes to track a bandit. He had failed to catch the robber but he found a woman there, walking all alone. No one ever knew where she came from or why, but she married Cord's ancestor when no one else would, because of his trade. The history of his family, Cord thought, was bracketed by women walking in solitude.

His eyes could no longer make out Bird's form in the darkness. He touched the instruments and felt the aircar swing around in response. Bound northeast, he left the desert behind. His course would take him to the city, not to the spaceport.

He had let Bird suppose that he intended to go directly to the humans. It would have caused her anxiety to know that he was making a little detour first. He could not leave Mehira without gathering the rest of his parents' instruments. He had a premonition that he would need all the leverage he could get.

Cord veered the craft toward the city's northern precinct. Finola lived in an outlying suburb in a small, luxurious house. If it were not for her, and the fact that she lived on the outskirts, he would hesitate to go back. As it was, the foray was dangerous but worth the risk.

He landed on a public airstrip a short walk from her home. There were many advantages to living in a prosperous section. Cord left the vehicle unconcernedly; it would not occur to law-abiding Mehirans that the aircar parked here with half a dozen others might be stolen. In fact, it was possible that no one had yet realized it had been taken from the port's lot.

He found his way to Finola's door without difficulty, having visited her many times with his family. Pausing in the small front garden, Cord hoped she was not entertaining any of her love-friends tonight. Still, it was a risk he had to take, he thought, looking up at the tall, narrow house. He struck the entrance gong and waited.

At last the door opened, and Cord saw Finola's inquiring expression change to gladness. But she did not exclaim at seeing him. Instead she glanced around furtively and pulled him inside.

"One cannot be too careful," she explained. "Now, Cord! Tell me everything. I thought you were . . . gone, like Fyrrell and Neteel. Where have you been?" '

"From the way you greeted me, I think you know," he responded with a wry smile.

She answered in guarded tones, "I know the Council is eager to interview you. Your 'assistance' is 'requested,' according to the bulletins. I am loyal to the Council—naturally! —but when it advertises for a citizen to give it assistance, it is seldom to the citizen's advantage."

At least there was no city-wide hunt in progress for him. When Cord did not speak immediately, Finola asked, "What happened? Maybe I can help."

"To be honest, I hoped you could. There was no one else I could go to."

Her smile made her shrewd, sensible face almost pretty. Cord realized what his father had seen in her: the humor, courage, and loyalty.

"Thank you! I'm glad you felt you could come to me. Now if we can pass the evasions and get down to whatever is bothering you, perhaps I can think of something. And while you're making up a good story to tell me, I'll get you something to eat."

"No, don't bother, Finola. I'm not evading your questions, and I don't want to put you to more trouble."

"Don't be silly. Be comfortable. I'll be right back."

He was hungry, he decided, as well as tired. Settling onto a cushioned platform, he was quite content to wait.

Finola soon returned, bearing a tray with bottles, beakers, and plates of delicacies. She poured them heartening drafts of blue-root wine diluted with fruit juice, and gestured to Cord to help himself to preserved fish, fruit, and other dishes he did not recognize.

He nibbled a bit of dried melon which had been stuffed with a sweet, spicy paste. "It feels like a year since it happened. The aliens put us all out of the spaceport, except for Bird. It was when I was going back to learn who killed Fyrrell and Neteel that I discovered she was a prisoner." He did not want to tell Finola more.

"So you rescued her," Finola interpolated.

"Yes." Cord sought for a way to gloss over his murder of several Terrans. He wondered how much his father had talked about his work to his mistress. If he had spoken of it freely, Finola might not be horrified, not the way Bird was.

"The humans were not willing to surrender your friend

easily, I suppose," Finola said dryly. "So there was trouble. I begin to see why the Council wishes to talk to you."

Cord relaxed. Finola might not commit the indelicacy of referring to violence, but she evidently understood what had occurred.

"You did get her out?" she inquired.

"Oh, yes. We spent last night and most of today in the Yellow Desert. Now Bird is on her way home. It wasn't wise to come back together."

Finola's sapphire-colored eyes seemed to fathom the trouble between Bird and himself, without a word being said. Without even a sharing of emotions, for Cord was too weary of others' condemnation and shock to open himself to anyone.

"I don't think you should answer the Council's summons," she said.

"Nothing was farther from my mind."

"What will you do, then?"

Cord drained his beaker. "I am going back to the spaceport. I am going to execute the murderer. And then I will leave Mehira."

Having expected her to be amazed and to try to dissuade him, Cord was taken aback when Finola remarked, "It appears there is no alternative. Do you need transportation to the spaceport?"

"I've got an aircar parked east of here, thanks. And I don't want to involve you more than necessary. But if you don't mind a little risk, I do need transportation back home. I can't take the aircar into the center of town safely. If you drive me in your ground car, I'll hide in back; when you stop near our building, I can slip in and get what I need. It should be easy enough if you wouldn't mind waiting awhile before we start." He was aware that he seemed to be taking her agreement for granted, and hoped that friendship would excuse the liberty.

"It seems a reasonable plan, provided you let me drop you off outside the port afterward. If you insist on coming back to get your aircar, you'll increase the odds of being seen."

"My equipment . . ."

"We'll pick it up on the way to town. It's settled." She half reclined on the dais, looking so friendly and safe that Cord couldn't help smiling back at her.

"Thank you, Finola. I wish there were some way to thank you."

"There is. Come closer and I'll tell you what it is."

He slid over beside her and felt her lips brush his ear. Instead of whispering, they played over the soft furry tip and around the base. Finola's hands kneaded his back and shoulders. She smelled warm and salty.

"I hope I can please you," he whispered, embarrassed, "but it's been a long day, and . . ." Of course, he could fill in with his tail, if worst came to worst.

"And you've already been with Bird," Finola concluded. "Never mind, I'm sure there's something left for me."

Finola's body was firm and agile beneath her rainbow-colored shift. Cord stripped the garment from her, drawn by her nearness and her scent. Her limbs were sleek, and strong as those of some jungle animal. Cord remembered his father saying that Finola too had come of poor family and had worked hard.

She was working hard now, he reflected, and not without results. It was no wonder: sexual prowess was highly regarded, and Finola had climbed up from obscurity as much by her erotic ability as by her intelligence. She drew responses from Cord that he would not have believed possible. He ached with pleasure. Finola's own buckings and outcries confirmed her ecstasy.

It was late when they left Finola's elegant little house. They met no one on their way to Cord's stolen aircar. Few of the dwellings in the section showed any light; of those that did, most were only dim nightlights. Once they had transferred Cord's gear to Finola's vehicle and turned back toward the city, Finola kept to the sidestreets. She avoided any area where someone might be awake and watchful—the Council buildings, the utility center, a hospital.

She drove the ground car to a parking square down the street from his family's living unit. The square was half filled with modest vehicles, freight haulers, rental skims, and the like in every state of age and repair. Finola's trim three-seater should pass unnoticed.

"Shall I come and help, Cord?"

"No, thank you. There won't be much. If you stay here, you can keep watch. If you see anything that looks like trouble, go home. I'll come to you there. Otherwise, I won't be long."

She bowed agreement.

*　　*　　*

The unit was not home now. The room was close from lack of ventilation, in disarray from his last visit, empty. He would not regret never seeing it again. Quickly he stuffed the diagrams and notes he had left behind into a cloth bag. Next he chose equipment that might be even marginally useful or salable. There was the tray of precision instruments, several sensors, other small things which might be valuable to him once he was offworld. There was nothing else he cared to take.

No. That was not quite true. He paused at the shrine: generation upon generation of ancestors, who perhaps did not care about their descendants at all. He found he still cared about them. Soon no one of his family would remain on Mehira to remember. He removed the ancestral relics from the shrine. He could not leave them behind.

"I don't have a new shrine to take you to," he told them. "For a time you must travel with me. When I can make you a home, I will." And new mementos—for his father and mother.

The task done, he stood for a moment, pondering. Had he forgotten anything? Was there anything which should be destroyed before he left? No, to both questions, he decided. The Council might guess he had been here a second time, but what did it matter? Now the unit might remain undisturbed until it was reassigned.

Strange that the Council had not searched the unit or sealed it. He was willing to swear that if anyone at all besides himself had been in it he would have known. All the signals he and his parents had customarily set were in place—the thread which any unwary person would have dislodged, the faint sprinkling of powder under the window, the little table set close enough to the normal traffic pattern in the main room that anyone unfamiliar with the room would jostle it out of place.

Of course, it might not have occurred to anyone on the Council that he would return. Cord shouldered his pack and let himself out of the unit, striding down the dim corridor toward the exit. His parents had been assigned a ground-floor unit because their work sometimes required them to keep unusual hours. It was convenient now, as it permitted him to come and go without waking the other residents.

A dark figure loomed before him, framed in the arched

doorway. Its right arm moved in a hideously familiar way; Cord did not need to see the dart gun in its hand to know it was there. He threw himself to one side, certain that the unseen finger had contracted against the trigger. He heard a crunch followed by a liquid *plop!* as the dart splattered against the wall.

Before the other could fire again, Cord reacted as he had been trained to do. The knife came to his hand as naturally as if it were part of it. A split second later, the hilt protruded from the attacker's left eyesocket. His attacker's death throes smashed against the barriers of his mind. Like acid, the emotions tried to eat their way into his brain. Despite the mental assault, Cord threw himself down as the Catcher's hand, jerking in death, released the weapon's entire magazine, a potentially fatal ejaculation. Unaimed, it hit the walls and floor harmlessly.

Cord dropped his battered mental barriers and reached out to sense the other. It was a grim chore: he felt the last reverberations of the man's horror and reluctance to die, but he did gain knowledge. The other was dead. Picking himself up, Cord gathered up his bag and retrieved and wiped his knife. He fitted it back into its sheath and composed his mind as he left the building. He did not wish to alarm Finola, but it was too much to hope that she might have missed the Catcher's death anguish.

"Did you get everything you needed?" Finola greeted him. She kept her voice light, but Cord could hear the tension in it.

"Yes."

"You were fast."

Since she seemed to wish to ignore the occurrence, Cord did not allude to it. To aid someone in hiding from the Council, to ignore a painful experience rather than embarrass him—well, he saluted Finola's courage. He wished Bird were more like her.

"There's a road that cuts across the marshes north of the spaceport," Cord said. "If you leave me there, it won't be too long a walk to the boundary."

"Why not simply walk in the front door—if you expect them to welcome you?"

"The problem is getting there," he pointed out. "I'm not

worried about getting in. The problem is getting past the Council blockade.''

"You haven't heard?'' Amazed, Finola turned her head to look at him, and almost drove into the side of a building. "The Council blockade was removed shortly after you and Bird escaped. The aliens made it clear that they would not tolerate the cessation of trade. So it's back to business as usual.''

"Which means a pair of guards during the day and none at night?'' Cord hazarded.

"You've inherited your father's brains as well as his cock,'' said Finola approvingly.

When they turned onto the highway leading to the spaceport, Finola cut the ground car's lights at Cord's suggestion. The road itself was slightly luminous. That and the starlight were enough for keen eyes.

They approached the Council's gate. Finola slowed to a stop. "You won't have any difficulty getting through.'' It was not quite a question.

Cord laughed. An unattended barrier would present no obstacle to him. His equipment contained half a dozen tools for opening doors.

"We're very trusting, aren't we?'' she said. "Even someone like me could climb over if there were no way to manipulate the lock.''

"Yes, but most Mehirans wouldn't. No one has, since the port was built. No one thinks of doing such a thing.''

"Except you, Cord—and me.''

"You're used to my family's way of doing things.'' He smiled. "But you'd never actually enter the spaceport without permission. It's different for me, because I don't fit into 'our orderly society' anymore. You're a good friend, 'Nola. My parents prized your friendship. I do, too.'' He pressed her hand. "I'll . . . I'll make a braiding in your memory.''

He unloaded his box and pack and left them by the gate.

"Good fortune to you, Finola.''

"To you also.'' She saluted him and drove away.

Once she was out of sight, he turned his attention to the gate's locking mechanism. A suction light attached to the gate supplied him with illumination. The lock was a basic mechanical closure. For anyone without tools—or the will to open it—it would be effective enough. The symbol of the Council's ban alone would keep most Mehirans from trespassing.

Visualizing the inner workings, Cord chose a needle-thin probe. He slipped it in and manipulated it deftly until he felt the locking bar spring up. He pulled the gate open, moved his gear inside, and pulled it shut. A little more work with the probe relocked it. Really, it was too easy.

He activated the floater on his equipment case, slung the bag over his shoulder and strode toward the spaceport. It occurred to him that he was leaving Mehira behind him for good.

# Chapter 15

When he approached the portal, Cord was certain he was being observed, but he walked up to it without hesitation. No one was present in the guard's kiosk, but he recalled a signaling device beside the door. Presumably it was for times like this. His hand stretched out to it, but never made contact. The door panels parted—activated by those within, no doubt—and opened very slowly. Perhaps the operator was dubious about letting him in. Which, Cord told himself honestly, was hardly surprising, his last visit considered. He stepped inside and was not startled to see half a dozen armed men in the lobby.

They crouched behind barriers; an assortment of weapons were no doubt aimed at his heart.

Cord strode forward and stopped in front of the nearest human.

"I've come to see Hamilton K. About trading matters," he added.

"And Hamilton K wants to see you," the human replied, standing up. "Come this way, please."

K's first words were: "For sheer effrontery, I don't think I've met your equal."

Cord waited politely.

"Well, what brings you here again?" K asked, when Cord volunteered no information.

"As I told your staff when I arrived, trading matters. I want to make a bargain with you."

"What do you have to offer—and in exchange for what?"

No lowering of shields was necessary to detect the Trade Agent's interest.

"You wanted my mother's inventions. Do you still want them?"

"We might be interested," Hamilton K replied.

"I thought you would be."

"What do you want in return?"

"The person who murdered my parents is in your spaceport. I want his life." Cord expected amazement or at least a token protest.

Hamilton K said only, "Is that all?"

"I may wish to leave Mehira when I am finished."

"That could be arranged."

"Naturally," Cord added, "I will also require money or a suitable equivalent."

"Naturally," said Hamilton K with a wisp of a smile.

"And now I would like to ask you a few questions, since I am here. It will save time to begin my investigation with you."

K laughed. "I seem to have acceded to all your demands so far. Why not?"

"Do you still believe the Speaker's daughter was guilty?" Cord asked. It would not do Bird any good, perhaps, but the record ought to be set straight.

"No. She had the motive, but it now seems unlikely she could have had the opportunity."

"What changed your mind?" Cord asked.

Hamilton K frowned. "When the bomb's fragments were analyzed, it became clear that it was from our own supply. Explosives are often useful on uninhabited worlds; every trade group carries some."

Useful, too, as a weapon on inhabited worlds, if peaceful trading proved impossible.

"It seems unlikely," K continued, "that the girl had access to the storeroom, even if she had known where it was and that the explosive was there. According to the door guard's sign-in sheet, she arrived almost immediately before the demonstration was to begin. Assuming she could get to the table unnoticed by the security team, she might have had time to plant a device, but not to steal it."

"So you now believe someone here was responsible?" Cord inquired.

"I must assume so," K admitted. "Unfortunately, I am not a criminal investigator and neither is anyone on my staff. Frankly, I would have reservations about dealing with you, but you are a professional, and I want your aid. Even more than the devices you can sell me. If there's an unstable personality in this port, he must be found.''

"I'll find him," Cord said. "Now, I will need living quarters. The use of a private laboratory would be convenient, too.''

"Do you know how many of my people you killed when you left here?'' Hamilton inquired.

Cord knew well enough but replied casually, "Three or four."

"And it did occur to you that it might be dangerous for you to come back?''

Cord forced himself to smile.

"You are a pragmatist, Trade Agent K. You want my help and my family's inventions. To secure those things you must deal with me. I think, for the sake of profitable trading, you will overlook our past misunderstandings.''

"As it happens," K said, grinning, "you're right.''

His room assignment was in the same section as Julia McKay's, which gladdened him. It would be good to have a friend nearby, but he didn't want to see Julia right now. He was exhausted, and there were still a few hours left for sleep. That he did not seek her out immediately was something she would understand. Besides, news of his arrival would no doubt spread among the humans, since no Mehiran—especially a rogue one—had stayed at the spaceport before.

The room was sparse: a built-in closet, a square piece of furniture with drawers, a place to sleep, and a hard chair—which Cord could not sit in. Tiredly he stowed away the equipment and then set alarms to ensure the room's security. Then he wrapped himself in a blanket and tried to get some rest.

# Chapter 16

The following morning Cord set up his workroom and requisitioned supplies. To Hamilton K's inquiry he explained that he would need to build prototypes of the devices, as many of the plans would not be intelligible to the spaceport technicians.

"Fine." K shrugged. "It will save my staff work. What do you intend to work on first?"

"My parents died before demonstrating their greatest achievement. As a memorial to them, I will recreate the device." Cord had not intended to offer this bait so soon, but why not? The opportunity was present.

"If I may ask, what was their invention? I had assumed it was some sort of crowd-control mechanism—a confusion generator, perhaps, judging by the reaction of the Mehirans present. But you said just now, 'before demonstrating,' which suggests it may have been something else."

K was smart, Cord gave him full credit. In the future he would remember he was dealing with a first-order intelligence.

"The crowd reaction was an undesired by-product," Cord replied. "The full demonstration had not yet begun. There should be no such problem next time. I believe I know what caused it and how to correct it. The full use of the device was as a mind reader." Cord opened his mental barriers to feel K's reaction. A ripple of disquiet transmuted into strong curiosity. Cord shut himself up again, having learned nothing conclusive.

"Was it? No wonder Greffard felt he'd carried out a coup. No wonder he was so excited and secretive about it. Or that someone thought it worthwhile to suppress it."

Cord objected, "But if you knew what it was . . ."

"I did not say that. Stev Greffard was a man who enjoyed creating mystery for its own sake. If he knew a secret, he

dropped hints about it, to tantalize. I did not know the nature
of the demonstration, but someone else might have. Someone
with something to hide.''

"On your own staff?" Cord asked pointedly.

K shrugged. "It's not possible. My people have all been
screened, but the system's not infallible. Almost anyone here
might murder under certain circumstances, and I wouldn't
swear that none of them are engaged in illicit activity in one
form or an other.''

Reconstructing the blueprint was not going to be easy.
Cord had seen the components and his mother's notes, but he
did not know how to put them together. Not consciously.

In his workroom, Cord sat at a table and forced his muscles
to relax. The room and its contents created a harmonious
whole, down to the arrangement of noteboard and stylus in
front of him. His mind went through the necessary exercises
easily, blocking out the external world and turning inward.
The alien chamber seemed to fade around him, to be replaced
by the small, shabby place where Neteel, Fyrrell, and he had
worked.

. . . His mother bent over the drawing table, laughing.
Fyrrell said something . . . what?

"If this works, 'Teel, maybe we can concentrate on the
hardware aspect.''

Because building security devices was more respectable
than manhunting. It did not matter now, Cord thought.

"It will work," he heard his mother's voice say. Cord
stared at the sheet under Neteel's hand. He did not realize
that he had begun to draw, copying the sketch.

The vision out of his past dimmed. Cord examined the
drawing and clicked his tongue in exasperation. The plan was
good—as far as it went. But one section was incomplete.

Well, his own lack of skill at recall was to blame. His
mother had been able to slip into a trance in moments, to
recapture almost any event. He himself had seldom made use
of the skill. Now, when he needed it, he was handicapped.

He rose and paced around the room to stretch his muscles.
A second or third attempt should fill in the gaps. The chief
thing was not to force recollection and not to worry about it.
Let the memory lie for a day.

In the meantime, he had other projects to work on.

*      *      *

When he left his workroom in early evening, Cord had finished assembling one of his mother's least successful gadgets—among Mehirans, anyway. But among humans, Cord supposed, it might be useful. His family had used it once or twice in subduing extremely violent criminals. In Multi-Lang it might be called a calmator, since it acted upon the target brain to induce calm, lassitude, or sleep, depending upon the tuning. Tomorrow he would see if he could get a few laboratory animals on which to test it.

He strolled through the complex, past labs and offices which were now closed. During the workday, these corridors were busy. After hours, the traffic shifted to the living and entertainment areas. Perhaps he would find Julia there, where the humans ate.

Hearing his own footsteps echoing behind him, Cord thought he had never been in a lonelier place. Ahead he could see the speedwalk in the cross corridor. It was a strangely comforting sight, reminding him of the presence of living beings elsewhere in the building. His pace increased.

Behind him, very near, was a faint shuffling and a footfall. All languor gone, Cord spun, shifting to a fighting stance.

The massive human was an arm's length away, weapon already leveled. Cord kicked the gun from the man's hand, feeling bones crunch. The weapon skidded down the corridor behind them. Ignoring the lost gun, the human grunted and charged at Cord, who sidestepped. His opponent was huge; wrestling with him would be dangerous. But instead of coming back to try again, the human ran down the hall and into a side corridor.

Cord snatched up the fallen gun and gave chase. He rounded the corner wide, weapon ready for use—and stopped short. It was a cul-de-sac, and empty. There were two doors on each side, nothing more. Deliberately, Cord tried first one, then another. All were locked. Yet his quarry had not been out of sight long enough to unlock one. Even if he had, Cord was sure he would have heard a door open and close. He went to the very end of the passage to assure himself that it *was* the end and that there were no disguised doors or panels through which his assailant might have escaped. Leaning against the wall, he resorted to his empathic talent. In the distance he sensed the jumbled emotions of many, but the area around

him was devoid of life. Nevertheless he passed the four doors
very warily on his way back to the main corridor. Not until
he was on the speedwalk did he stuff the weapon inside his
shirt.

Out of the office section, Cord's first action was to locate
Hamilton K. He found the Trade Agent at a secluded table in
a lounge. Cord sat down without being invited.

K looked at him in courteous inquiry.

"Someone attacked me when I left my workplace."

"You surprise me."

"But not very much?" Cord retorted.

Hamilton K. took a long drink of his beverage, which was
pale-green and contained quantities of ice. "It was to be
expected, either because of your family's knowledge or perhaps because of the humans you killed. I confess I did not
anticipate that it would come so soon. Tell me."

Cord outlined the occurrence.

"You've got the gun he used? Good! The security department has nothing like a criminology laboratory but it can
certainly get the fingerprints off it."

"Fingerprints?" There was no one in sight, so Cord drew
the gun out of his shirt and laid it on the table.

"You touched it?" Hamilton K sounded incredulous.

"Yes, why not?"

"Every human—and every Mehiran, too, I'll bet—has
patterns on the skin of his fingers. Everyone's pattern is
different. On all human worlds, records of fingerprints are
kept, so that when prints are found—on a murder weapon, for
instance—a search of the files will reveal who held it. It's an
important factor in criminal investigation, if the criminal isn't
smart enough to wear gloves or wipe off his prints."

Cord squinted at the tips of his own fingers by the dim
light in the alcove where they sat. He did not need to see
clearly in order to believe. On other occasions he had noticed
the whorls in the skin, but it had never occurred to him that
his might be different from anyone else's. To his knowledge,
it had never occurred to any person on his world.

"We have little crime," he said by way of explanation. "I
do not think there has been the incentive to develop such a
study."

"You're a fortunate race, then. Well, perhaps we can

identify the person to whom the gun was issued—if it was obtained properly. I don't imagine you could describe him?''

"Of course I can. He was taller than I by two handspans, and I estimate he weighed half again as much. He was heavily built, yet light on his feet. His hair was brown and gathered into a band at his neck. His hands were large but not strong-looking, as if he did no manual labor. Would it not be simpler if I sketched him? There's a great deal more.''

"Can you?"

"Certainly. It's part of my training.''

Hamilton K drained his glass.

"Let's go back to my office.''

An odd-looking man, Cord mused, studying the drawing he had finished. The features did not seem to belong together. Cord wondered whether the man had been wearing a mask. He was sure he had set down the face exactly as he'd seen it.

Hamilton K picked up the sheet and regarded it. "If this is accurate, he should be easy to find. Strange, I don't recall his face, though.''

"In any case, I broke bones in his right hand. He would have to go to your infirmary to have it fixed. Whatever he looks like, he can't hide such damage.''

"I'll notify sickbay and security. If you go to your quarters and keep the door locked, you should be safe enough. Unless you wish a bodyguard?'' K asked.

"I do not think it is necessary.'' He kept the wry amusement out of his voice. If he, a Catcher, could not take care of himself, his problems were greater than a bodyguard could remedy. He would avoid the office wing outside working hours, however.

Cord took the most heavily traveled route to his living unit, pausing only to get a packaged meal from a dispenser.

He took it back with him, locked himself into his room, and ate in leisurely solitude. He did not turn on the light over the door—he wanted no visitors, not even Julia McKay. He wanted to think and then to sleep, and that was all.

He was afraid. He knew that much, though he was not quite sure who he was. Things were hunting him—his whole attention was given to avoiding them. Something loomed before him, something with fangs and claws. In an eyeblink the danger passed: the fanged being stood over him, sniffed, reached out a paw to touch him—and walked away, grumbling to itself. Its bafflement and irritation, which he sensed psychically, pleased him. When it was out of range, the thing that was Cord slithered away, abandoning its rock-guise.

He hunted, too, but by stealth, using guile to lure larger, better-armed beings to their death. He ate of them, and of prey killed by other predators, and gained power. But he was still afraid. . . .

Cord awoke abruptly to the sound of buzzing. Confused, he struggled off the bed and moved toward the sound—it seemed to be coming from a blank wall. He saw seams in the wall and small indentations, perhaps for fingers. He slid open panels to reveal a large gray screen with knobs and buttons below and mesh-covered openings on the sides.

"Are you there?" a disembodied voice asked. It was Hamilton K.

"Yes. How do I operate this device?"

"Damn," said Hamilton K. "I'm reading your lips. Press the buttons marked A and V."

Cord complied. A light slowly filtered across the screen and eventually resolved itself into Hamilton K's face. Cord supposed his own presented a groggy, unkempt picture. If Hamilton K thought so, he gave no indication. His face was impassive.

"I've received reports from the infirmary and from all departments," he stated. "No one with a broken or bruised hand has been seen. There are a few people who are off duty, but I've had them checked on by their section chiefs."

"Oh," Cord murmured.

"Are you certain you hurt him?"

"Yes. There was no mistaking it."

"Then," said K after a pause, "we seem to have an enigma. There is no one injured, and no one unaccounted for. And no one who resembles your sketch at all."

"I see."

"I wish I could say as much," K retorted. "Security will continue to keep an open file. If anything comes up, it will be investigated. For the present, everything that can be done has been. Let me know if there's anything more you need for your project."

"Can I reach you on this device?"

"This is a com-screen," explained Hamilton K. "One is in every room, every office, every corridor. Opening the panel is partial activation of it—though you can change the controls to blank out the voice too. There should be a slot to the side—pull on the tab and you will see a guide."

"Thank you," said Cord.

In answer, the screen went dark. Cord found the small tab and pulled it toward him. A sheaf of thin, hard sheets came out in his hand. A combination of pictures, diagrams, and Multi-Lang explained the many workings. It was followed by long lists of names and room numbers, including Julia's. He debated calling her but decided against it, wanting to shower and change first, and to eat a decent meal.

# Chapter 17

Cord chose to eat breakfast alone in the cafeteria. The humans there eyed him curiously and gave him a wide berth. He took a small corner table.

He was busy eating when a human woman stopped by his table. Cord recognized the security chief at once from Bird's and Julia's description. Her face and body were sharp angles, her expression angry. She sat down, leaning forward on her elbows, and said, harshly.

"I am O'as Garatua. I just want to say one thing to you. Don't make trouble."

Behind her, tanks of aquatic plants and animals presented an eerie contrast. The woman was solid and hard against the gently moving forms and colors.

"Why? It is not my intention to bother or inconvenience anyone except the murderer of my parents."

"Security's my department, and the last thing I need is someone making false reports that require investigation."

"K did tell me there was no one who answered to the description of my assailant. I can't account for it, but the incident happened."

Cord's attention slipped to the tank behind O'as. Strange—he would have taken an oath that it had contained nothing but sea plants and a few rocks when the security chief sat down. Now there was an unattractive bluish creature floating near the surface.

"We can find the killer without your dubious help," Garatua warned.

"You don't seem very anxious to find the killer," Cord observed. "First you attempted to force a confession from an obviously innocent bystander, and now you want to keep me from learning the truth. What have you got to cover up?" Part of his Multi-Lang vocabulary had been acquired from a study of Terran dramatic presentations dealing with Catching. He was gaining fluency, he congratulated himself.

"Nothing! Stev was a friend of mine, and I want his murderer. But I don't trust you, and I'll be watching you. If you do anything to endanger this installation, I'll make sure Hamilton gets rid of you. Believe me."

She stood up and stalked off without another word or a backward glance.

Cord, watching her walk away, wondered how much of an embarrassment a telepathy machine would be to Garatua. Enough to murder a friend? Or someone she claimed as a friend, which might be a different thing.

His eyes went back to the tanks. The blue creature was no longer there. Cord pushed aside his dishes and went over to stare into the aquarium. It contained nothing now except gravel, sea grass, and a heap of dark rocks. The pile seemed larger than it had originally. Surely the rock resting next to the wall had not been there.

Bending to examine the plaque below the tank, he read:

> Planet of origin:   Harno
> Species:   Shifter
> Diet:   Smaller marine organisms

Cord stopped at a library terminal on the way to his workroom. The humans' ease of access to vast bodies of information fascinated him. One need only key in the subject wanted to draw out general information and references to more specialized data. The terminal would even print out a copy.

"Shifter—Any one of a number of species capable of changing their appearance to mimic their environment or other forms of life. Also called shape shifters and shape changers. These occur on at least eleven worlds in a variety of forms: insect, amphibian, marine, and land-dwelling.

"There are two kinds of shape shifters. The first only takes on the general appearance, perhaps only the coloration, of its background or of some other creature. The chameleon (Terra) is an example. The second changes physically, to be an approximate or exact copy. With the physical characteristics, it may take on the abilities also. Usually the shifter can reproduce only in its true form, although reports (usually thought apocryphal) have occurred of shifters which breed while masquerading.''

A list of the shape changers with pictures and planets of origin followed. Cord found himself amazed at their diversity and at the changes they could make. In some cases, they grew larger or smaller. Some changed only to hide from predators, others to hunt.

Cord went on to his work area, perplexed. He had intended to test the calmator but could not keep his mind on the task. Finally he decided that he needed someone to talk to. He called Julia from the com-screen.

Her thin, composed face was reassuring.

''I wondered when I'd hear from you, Cord,'' she greeted him. ''I half expected you last night.''

''Something detained me last night. I would not have been a satisfactory companion.''

''What happened?''

Her anxiety was reassuring in its way, too: someone still cared what became of him.

He told her briefly, adding, ''He isn't a professional—and he's obviously not skilled in hand-to-hand combat.''

''How can you be so casual about it? You might have died.''

''Oh, it isn't the first time I've been attacked,'' Cord assured her.

''What?'' The color drained from her face.

''When my family and I worked as Catchers, we all were threatened or attacked occasionally.''

Julia nodded shakily. ''I understand. But you are all right now? Would you care to share my room?''

''Thank you, Julia, but no. I can't take a chance with your life. Besides, I don't want to scare the man away. Next time I will catch him. What I need now is advice. Can you think of anyone who might not be what he seems? O'as Garatua occurred to me as a suspect, since she is very resentful, but I think I'd expect more subtlety from her if she really were guilty.''

''Maybe so,'' Julia agreed slowly. ''I don't know, Cord. I am not well acquainted with any of these people. To them, I'm a missionary, someone who's not a Ten Suns employee, and the next worst thing to luggage. I make myself useful, but I'm not confided in.''

Cord nodded. "Well, you've helped me by letting me talk to you. It's a way of ordering my thoughts."

"I'm glad you think I'm useful. Perhaps we can get together tonight and I can show you some of my other good points."

"You've got great points, Julia. And I've got one just thinking about them. I'll call you this evening, all right?"

"Yes." She smiled.


By the end of the afternoon, in a better frame of mind, Cord had finished testing the calmator. This time he took care to leave when the rest left their labs. He brought the calmator with him.

Hamilton K was in his office, unexpectedly relaxed, his feet up on a desk and arms behind his head. He wasn't even disappointed when Cord explained that what he'd brought was not the telepathy machine.

"So this little thing tranquilizes people?" K remarked, turning it over in his hands.

"Yes. It takes effect immediately, so if you are being approached by an attacker—"

"I understand. Well, I don't know that it's an improvement on the systems already in use. Still, it may have some value. What does it do to someone who isn't rampaging?"

"The effect is in direct proportion to the target's emotional state. It will relax a normal person and knock out someone who's out of control."

"Any side effects?"

"A headache in the latter case."

"It wouldn't be addictive?" K pursued.

"No—I don't think so. But—"

"It may or may not be useful for personal defense. However, as a relaxant it might be a genuine breakthrough. The best tranquilizers available at present are either potentially harmful drugs or else require surgical implantation."

The bargaining began. Cord rejected Hamilton's first offer on principle. After considerable haggling, they came to an agreement although Cord knew he could have gotten more. He wanted K to remain in a good mood. Cord watched with interest while K recorded their transaction on a computer terminal and then locked the calmator away in a capacious safe.

"Nothing will happen to it here. And that reminds me," he said. "You had better stay away from the laboratory section for the next four days. During the festivities there will be no one in that wing."

"Festivities?"

"Didn't you know? This is the quarter holiday. Starting this evening there will be parties and special entertainments. Only vital personnel will have shifts. You caught me just as I was planning my personal morale boosting. Why not come to dinner with me? I'll take you to a few of the livelier parties afterward."

"Thank you, but I should call Julia McKay. She is a friend of mind."

"See her after the parties," K advised. "She won't attend any of them—her religion frowns on immoderation. Of course," he added, "there may be a moderate, genteel party somewhere tonight. But I certainly don't know where it would be. Join her when you're ready for some quiet comfort."

Cord did not wish to offend K; in fact, he wanted to secure the Trade Agent as an ally, as far as possible. And it would be useful to have an introduction into the social life of the spaceport. Julia, with her ascetic nature and lowly position, would not be nearly as useful.

The cafeteria was livelier than usual: people were already hanging colored banners on the walls—on the tables too.

"The kitchen is now programmed to supply a few Mehiran dishes," K told him. "Even fish jelly."

"That was kind," Cord said, surprised. As the only Mehiran in permanent residence, he missed the taste of familiar food. At the vend-a-meal, he selected the fish jelly, among other items, not only because it was a treat but also to find out how well the kitchen mechanism did it.

Their trays emerged from the chutes, and K led the way to a table. Hamilton K asked almost as many questions of Cord as he answered. It was like having one's brain sucked dry by a high-powered vacuum pump. However, Cord was adept at keeping his thoughts to himself, so he felt the conversation was mostly to his benefit. He ate the food with relish, finding the robo-chef as efficient as the Terrans' other gadgets.

His host, he discovered, talked entertainingly and intelligently on many subjects: other species, trading ventures, interstellar politics and crime. Occasionally Cord asked a question. There was a point he had wondered about for some time.

"Do all intelligent races but mine have space travel?"

"By no means. Some have interplanetary travel but not interstellar ships. Some worlds that have not developed interstellar travel have bought faster-than-light ships from races that have. Terra invented FTL ships a thousand years ago, but other races had it earlier. And what we really need is the Empire's warp."

The dictionary he had absorbed left something to be desired, Cord thought.

"I know the word 'empire,' " he said, "and 'warp' is a term having to do with weaving, but . . ."

"But they don't make much sense in this context? Of course, you've never heard of the Empire." Hamilton K sat back in his chair and began. "The Empire is what we call the civilization that flourished about a million years ago, throughout much of this part of the galaxy. 'Year,' I might add, means the Terran standard year, which is about three percent longer than Mehira's. The Empire ended—very suddenly, according to the archaeologists. We've found their traces on many worlds. They were more or less humanoid and apparently not much more advanced than we are—except that they traveled between the stars without using ships."

In the pause that followed, Cord finally said, "They used a 'warp' instead?"

"That is what we call it, for the sake of convenience. No one knows what it actually was, but we've never found any indication that they had spaceships—or ground transport, either. Their word for going from one room to another was the same as for going from one end of the galaxy to the other. Also, there are rooms in some of the best-preserved Empire sites which have no entrance. Some scientists believe the Imperials generated their own space warps whenever they wanted to go somewhere. If so, the secret died with them. A warp, theoretically, is a door you can go through to travel from one point to another instantaneously. It's only a theory. Black holes may be warps of a sort, but there is no record of anyone's surviving passage through one. At least, no one has come back to say so, if he has."

Cord nibbled the corner of his block of fish jelly, which he had saved until last. Both texture and color were excellent—

but the strong, salty flavor could not entirely mask a metallic tang. Cord swallowed with difficulty and quickly sipped the wine K had recommended. Well, fish jelly required a deft touch to prepare correctly, and the spaceport kitchen had evidently not mastered the technique. Or—more likely, since it probably had been bought ready-made—it had been stored improperly. Cord left the rest.

A woman in a skin-tight tube dress—bosom to ankle, with nothing but friction to hold it up—undulated over to their table and greeted K. She invited them to a party she was holding in her quarters.

"I would love to see your quarters," Hamilton K told her, grinning. "Preferably alone."

From K's unconcealed admiration of the woman's form, and from her laughter, Cord gathered it was a witticism.

"Would you like to come along with me now, both of you?" she invited. "I've got to stop and pick up something to drink, but then I'm going to my room to set it up. People will start coming almost anytime."

"I could come just watching you in that skinny little dress," K responded. "What about you, Cord—are you game for a party?"

"Yes, thank you. I would enjoy coming."

"I'll see that you do," his hostess-to-be replied with a smile.

Cord was unsure how to dress for a human party. Once out of uniform, the Terrans wore an amazing variety of raiments and adornments. Cord had brought little with him from his parents' dwelling unit, so he finally chose a simple dark tunic belted with leather.

His hostess—the lithe blond woman in the impossible dress—occupied very spacious quarters. Hamilton K informed him that she was a department head, so her quarters had several rooms and a private office. Nearly every room was filled with humans, laughing, drinking, and openly fondling each other. Now *that* made Cord feel right at home—especially when several human women eyed him appreciatively.

Hamilton K introduced Cord to a number of Terrans in rapid succession and then disappeared, leaving Cord to fend for himself. A small dark-haired woman, standing to his right, looked up at him.

"Are all your people tall?" she asked.

"No," he said. "Are all your people short?"

She raised her glass in salute. "Touché."

"Pardon me?" The word meant nothing to Cord.

"It's an old Earther term for getting in the last word. I guess you shouldn't be expected to know all our languages."

Cord lifted a tall drink filled with green liquid from a passing tray; it was carried by a buxom blonde who smiled invitingly at him. He smiled back but turned to the dark-haired woman beside him.

"I've learned quite a bit of Multi-Lang. I'm a quick learner."

"Are you now?" the woman said suggestively. A wet pink tongue ran slowly over her top lip. "By the way, my name's Tanna. And yours?"

"Cord. Well, not exactly, but it's close enough to Mehiran for humans to say."

"Perhaps my tongue can't handle your name, but it can handle other things. . . ." She reached out and touched him, stroking his lightly furred skin. "I heard some interesting things about Mehirans. I was hoping to find them out firsthand."

"I would be more than happy to show you," Cord said politely, with another smile. Despite the babble in the room, he'd let his barriers down slightly and could feel her strong emanation of desire. "I find the difference between our races quite fascinating."

"And the main difference . . . ?" prompted Tanna.

"Tails," said Cord. His own tail was twitching in expectation.

"You mean you use your tail for making—" Her perplexed look was replaced by calculated glee. She instantly set down her drink and grabbed Cord's hand. "This I've got to see!"

"Feel," he corrected.

She dragged him into another room. "Shouldn't we be going somewhere private?" he protested.

"We are." Tanna led him into yet another room, which was dark and empty. This was their hostess's private office. Inside was another built-in closet, spacious enough for them to fit in comfortably. Tanna was wearing a sleeveless blouse, which she quickly removed. Her skirt, held together by an invisible seam, ripped open quickly. He was surprised to see she wore nothing beneath. But then again, neither did he.

He could feel that right now her desire was tempered with curiosity, so he removed his belt and tunic, although it wasn't really necessary.

Her fingers played lightly over his pouch, while he caressed her smooth skin. Her hands roamed over his strong and lightly furred body and then came to rest again between his legs. He could feel his organ stirring in response. Slowly it emerged from the protective pouch.

In the dim light he could see Tanna's eyes widen. "It's quite . . . different," she finally said.

"Yes," agreed Cord, "but it still works in the same way."

Standing up in the closet, Tanna spread her legs. Cord was about to enter her when the door to the office opened. Tanna closed the closet doors. "Don't stop now," she ordered.

Entering her was simple enough; he could feel her varying emotions, so he assured her, "You won't be disappointed. I guarantee it."

As their bodies moved together, his organ grew. Then he probed slowly with his tail. For a moment she stiffened, then relaxed as his tail probed deeper. She was sitting astride his bent legs now, offering no obstacle to any of his thrusts. Though she was already moaning with mounting desire, Cord bent forward and took a brown nipple into his mouth. Then as Tanna writhed with near ecstasy, he alternated thrusting as deep as he could while her muscles contracted in pleasure. She was nearly bucking herself off his legs, so he wrapped his arms around her and continued thrusting until she peaked. Then he came himself.

She slid down his legs, still holding on to him. "Wow" was all she could manage until her breathing returned to normal. They dressed, and Tanna slid open the closet doors. The private office was now filled with more people, all of whom politely ignored their entrance into their midst from a closet.

Cord went into the washroom to clean up. When he rejoined the party, Tanna came back to him leading two of her friends. They were two red-headed women who looked exactly alike.

At his puzzled expression, Tanna said, "These are May and Mary. They're twins." She gave the word an odd emphasis.

Tanna turned and left them alone. The definition of "twin" flashed across his mind, but there didn't seem to be an erotic significance attached to it. He smiled politely at the two women.

"Tanna's just been telling us *all* about you," May said. To distinguish herself from her twin, she wore a green dress; Mary wore the identical dress in red. Both were low-cut in front and had slits up the sides, revealing identical pairs of shapely legs.

"But of course you'd like to find out firsthand," Cord said.

They all laughed. "Are you up to it?" asked Mary.

"Not right now, but I will be."

He followed them into a side room and then into another washroom. They turned on the lights and locked the door. They'd brought their drinks in with them, and carefully put the cups down on a countertop. These drinks were pink-colored, not like the green one he'd drunk earlier. May explained this was an aphrodisiac, so the three of them drained all the glasses before starting. Cord didn't think he needed it, but it couldn't hurt. Unfortunately, the first drink—and perhaps the first bout of lovemaking in a stuffy closet—was affecting him. He hoped the unfamiliar aphrodisiac would make him feel better. And if the drink couldn't, the women would.

He discovered that among humans, making love to twins was considered a special treat. They made love separately, in pairs, and then all together. May and Mary shared everything . . . no body part was left untouched, no orifice left unfilled. And though he summoned every ounce of stamina he possessed, he felt himself flagging well before they finished. His head ached and his stomach was queasy. Even the intense pleasure the excited and energetic women brought him lost its appeal.

When it was over, he decided to leave the party. He passed into the main living area, in search of his hostess. Along the way he had to decline several obliging offers from female guests. Tanna had certainly spread tales of her satisfaction, and no doubt the twins would do the same. In fact, he seemed the only uncomfortable guest at the party. He wanted water, not any of the alcoholic, sweet, and spiced beverages available.

At last he found her, and managed to thank her for inviting

him, and to make his excuses for leaving at such an early hour. It was not the most adroit speech he had ever made, but she accepted it at face value. Perhaps she ascribed its awkwardness to unfamiliarity with Multi-Lang.

He made his escape into the passage and found it no cooler. Cord headed for the nearest tube on foot. Ordinarily he would have used the speedwalk, but he was in no condition to risk a fall, which could be dangerous at even the moderate speeds involved. Threading his way among the people on their way to or from parties or simply standing and talking with chance-met acquaintances, only the thought of his room's peace and quiet kept him going. Once away from the bustle and the pressure of so many uncontrolled minds, he would feel better.

He made it to the trans tube, mercifully empty, and dialed for his floor. Its rapid surge made his stomach lurch. The sensation of heat had given way to chill. Leaning against the elevator's back wall, Cord shivered and wondered if he could have caught some human illness.

On his own level he stumbled blindly along the corridor, more by instinct than by reason. There was no one to notice him, for which he was grateful. His throbbing head and burning stomach drove all thought of caution from him. If anyone had attacked him then, he would have died.

It took several attempts to fit his palm to the door lock. Finally it admitted him. Cord groped his way into the bathroom. His body, at least, knew what was necessary.

When there was nothing left in his stomach, Cord rinsed his mouth and then drank a little water. He dismissed the idea of taking a painkiller for the headache. His digestive system was in no condition to deal with anything at present. He lay down, fully clothed. The fever and chills seemed to have abated.

His mind began to operate at nearer its usual level of efficiency. Before, he had half concluded that it was some alien ailment against which he had no immunity. Now he thought of another explanation, one which might explain the abrupt onset of symptoms and the lingering aftertaste in his mouth.

Poison.

Though his food and drink had come from the automated robo-chef, Cord had no doubt that the food had been tampered with before it reached the table. He would willingly stake his life that no one could succeed in slipping something into his food in front of him. And no one could guarantee that a portion of food in the automated kitchen would be eaten by a particular person—unless it was a dish that only one person would order. The mechanics of his near-murder stood revealed. The murderer's plan was both subtle and obvious.

Cord was the only Mehiran living in the port. For the next few days, while the holiday lasted, there would not even be Mehiran visitors who might stop for a snack. So until the vacation was over, Cord would be the only one likely to sample the recently added Mehiran food on the menu. And the danger to innocent bystanders could be reduced still further: a few humans might sample this world's foods out of curiosity, but none was likely to try the fish jelly. Humans seemed to find robustly flavored foods unpleasant.

The murderer had planned well. How long would he have survived if he'd eaten the entire block of fish jelly? Or if he'd eaten it first? The chances were he'd escaped a quick death only because he had eaten too small an amount of the toxin. And perhaps because his stomach had contained a quantity of harmless food as well.

# Chapter 18

Cord rose and stripped off his sweat-damp clothing. The garments were Dispoz-a-Cloz, so he stuffed them into the disposal unit. After showering, he felt better physically, but another disturbing thought had come to him.

In all the criminal cases he had studied, criminals who committed a series of crimes followed the same pattern—what the humans called a *modus operandi*. This one used no special method Cord could detect. First a bombing, then a simple assault, then a poisoning. What kind of attack could he expect now?

At home, Catching resembled a hunt, with most of the skill and odds on the hunter's side. This was more like an intricate dance, in which either of them might make an error and bring the pattern to a fatal halt.

He must be prepared for the next move. Clad in a blue-and-green tunic and thigh-high boots, Cord slipped a blade into his right boot top—it was long, slender, and needle-sharp. He was ready. He was also utterly calm, he found. The attacks had something cold-blooded about them, something calculating. They were different from what he had encountered as a Catcher, and so he responded to them differently. There was no excitement in this, only determination to find his enemy.

Cord slipped out into the hall as though in leaving his room he was leaving any doubt behind. A flash of movement caught his eye: something disappeared around the corner into the main hall. Someone watching his door and retreating so as not to be seen?

He bounded down the corridor on swift, silent feet, and rounded the turn with blade drawn and murder in his eyes . . .

To see O'as Garatua thoughtfully inspecting the selections in the clothing dispenser. Cord stopped short, poised on the balls of his feet, ready for any hint of attack.

154

"What are you doing here?" he demanded.

She looked at him with incurious black eyes. "I'm picking something to wear. Why? What business is it of yours?"

"Why here?—almost in sight of my door?"

"Where else? I live in this wing. Why *am* I letting *you* threaten me?" She looked at the knife.

Cord relaxed his stance slightly, but kept his knife in his hand.

"You came into the hall"—he jerked his head toward it—"and watched my door, didn't you?"

"I looked at your damned door," the woman said, and laughed brusquely. "I wondered if you were there or at a party, and whether you were taking adequate precautions. Apparently you were."

"Then you believe someone is trying to kill me? You didn't, when we last spoke."

O'as held her identification card to the machine's eye and placed her right palm against the plate. Having registered her account number and verified that she was the person to whom it was assigned, the machine flashed a green light. She pressed a button to signify her choice, and another to obtain the correct size. A neatly folded and packaged garment slid into the bin. Garatua took it out before answering.

"I still think there's something very peculiar about your account of your alleged attack, but Hamilton K thinks you're the greatest thing since FTL travel. He wants every measure taken to ensure you stay alive."

"Why did you try to hide when you saw me open the door?" Apart from that point, her story carried the earmarks of truth.

"If it was you, I didn't think you'd care to have me checking on you," she replied candidly. "If it wasn't you, it would be too late to save you, but there was still time to catch your killer."

It made irritatingly good sense. Sourly Cord sheathed his knife. He neither liked her nor trusted her, but he could not quite imagine that she would try to kill him. He was about to apologize, but she grated, "And if you ever pull a knife on me again I'll break your arm."

With a curt nod, Garatua walked away, bundle under one arm. Her walk was not graceful, but it was assured. She made Cord feel that he'd made a fool of himself.

He waited until the sound of her footsteps died away before going on to Julia's room.

He was disappointed. The notice board on her door read: "In chapel. Now hearing confession."

Cord's first impulse was to return to his room. Then it occurred to him that he could seek Julia in the chapel. It was a place of spiritual healing and meditation, she had told him, and that was what he needed most right now. Muscles taut for trouble, Cord guardedly passed through the halls.

At the port entrance, Cord noted that the obelisk he'd destroyed had been replaced by a statue. The chapel was nearby. It was an undistinguished room, not very large and slightly overdecorated. There were panels of colored glass, various ornaments or symbols on the walls, and plastic that had been colored and molded to look like carved wood. Cord gazed around, taking it all in, until he spotted a panel to his left, marked "Confessional—Unoccupied."

With a caution born of experience, he slid the door open. Julia, seated in a high-backed chair, looked up. Seeing who it was, she jumped to her feet, her book falling to the floor.

"Cord! I didn't expect to see you here."

"I needed to talk to you." He gave her a quick embrace that became a lingering one.

"It's been too long," Julia whispered. Her body molded itself to his.

Cord found himself responding in spite of his earlier adventures. As he stared into her eyes, the world seemed to vanish around him. How could he find any other woman attractive?

"Do you need me?" she asked.

"Yes," he said, holding her tighter.

"Not in that way. Not here." She pushed him away.

Disappointed, he said, "You people forbid so much."

"Would you make love at a religious shrine?" She sat down and primly smoothed her clothes.

"You're right. I apologize." The fact that he was disturbed was no reason to insult her ancestors. When another person entered the chapel, Cord sat down next to Julia, and she closed the panel.

"What you need is to talk to me. Tell me what is happening. You know," she remarked, "your arrival was certainly no secret. But after that bloody escape, I'm surprised they took you back.''

"Hamilton K and I have come to an agreement. I can stay in the spaceport and hunt for my parents' killer. In exchange he can have my mother's inventions—for a price, though.'' Cord, shifting his position, leaned to one side; the humans' chairs wouldn't accommodate his tail.

Julia was surprised. "Including the one that blew up?''

"I think I can reconstruct it. In any case, it's just a means to an end. I mean to find the killer.''

"Unless he finds you. Oh, Cord, this is so dangerous.''

"I've survived two attempts on my life. I intend to survive any more that follow.

"Two?'' she exclaimed. "I heard about one attack. As I said, news spreads quickly here.''

"Julia—do you think Hamilton K would try to kill me?''

"I don't know,'' she said thoughtfully. "Why?''

He described the previous events, editing out his several liaisons at the party and downplaying the seriousness of his illness.

"Hamilton was the one who told me about the cafeteria's having Mehiran dishes,'' Cord concluded. "If I hadn't been with him, I might not have noticed the additions to the menu—I might not have gone to the cafeteria at all. After all, there's perfectly good food in the machines on the dwelling floors.''

"It isn't as though he were the only one who knew about the Mehiran food,'' Julia said. "Quite a lot of people knew about it, probably. I did.''

"Who would have access to the robo-chef?''

"I don't know much about how it works, Cord, but I suppose it's like most parts of the port. Almost anyone could get in if he chose the right time. After all, the personnel at spaceports like this are carefully screened. The trading companies don't want to find they've got a psychopath loose at an isolated trading station.''

"I was afraid it would prove to be something like that.'' Cord sighed. "Well, maybe I'll have to wait until I've finished the machine to find out who's after me. But it won't be long now.''

"Yes, that would clear everything up,'' Julia agreed.

"May I walk you back to your room, or are you staying here for a while?"

"Oh, I'll be here for some time yet, Cord."

"What do you find to do here?"

"Holidays at the port are difficult times for some. Most people are celebrating and having a good time, but those who are unhappy become more so. And then they come to me and talk, and they feel better. Sometimes they ask advice, and I give it. Holidays are a missionary's busiest time at a port."

Cord kissed her one last time and left her to her confessional and her reading.

He had let Julia think it would be over soon, that he'd finish the telepathy device almost at once. She would have worried otherwise. In fact, it would be several days at least—even if he could recall the last details of the plans—since he had no intention of ignoring K's advice. The murderer was growing bold. To go into the deserted office section would be suicidal, Cord suspected. If he could count on a physical attack he might risk it. But his quarry was too fond of booby traps and violence at a distance.

It presented an unusual problem. Virtually anyone in the port might be guilty. If he was alone, his quarry (*No, be honest,* he told himself, *I am the quarry*) might come upon him or arrange a trap. If he surrounded himself with people, his attacker had a better chance of getting close to him. Considering the varied means the killer had used so far, a crowd would provide an opportunity for a poisoned needle or even a knife. Easy enough to slip a stiletto between his ribs while brushing past him. And the corridors were packed with humans partying outside the rooms. In fact, he shouldn't have gone with Hamilton K to that party, or to any party. By the time Cord fell, his attacker might be some distance away.

He was striding down a nearly deserted hall toward the speedwalk when the idea occurred to him. The killer could attack him only if his whereabouts were known. But if Cord hid inside the spaceport, he would be safe. It wouldn't work indefinitely, because it meant sacrificing his mobility. But for the rest of the holiday, hiding would provide an opportunity to finish his plans for the telepathy machine. When work resumed, it should be the task of half a day to complete the device.

And hiding should not be difficult. On each residential

floor there were spare rooms for visitors. That they were locked posed no obstacle. If a Catcher couldn't bypass a lock, who, could? The vacant quarters were provided with all utilities—Cord recalled that when he'd moved in, it had been necessary only to set the palm lock to his hand.

There must be no clue to his location—no hint, even, that he had gone to earth in an empty apartment. At a money changer he used his identification card to obtain credit disks. Then he took a trans tube up half a dozen floors. On that level he used the disks to get packaged meals from a machine. If anyone wondered, he'd gone to get a late meal for a room party. No one asked—in fact, the halls were almost empty. At this hour of the morning, everyone was sleeping or partying more quietly. When he was far from the area where he'd purchased the food, he stopped to use a public com-screen. He placed a call to Hamilton K's quarters, in the certainty that K would not be there. As he expected, it was set on "Record."

"K, it seems wise to me to stay out of sight for a few days. Don't try to get in touch with me. I'll call after the holiday."

Two more floors up and several corridors away, Cord found what he was looking for. An apartment with no nameplate, located at the end of a passage, would suit him perfectly. After a quick glance around to ensure he was not observed, Cord set the meal packs down and began to work on the lock.

It was not very difficult, particularly since he need not set it to respond to his palm print. And once inside, the room proved vacant.

He had food to last the weekend, and since he had paid cash, there was no record of where he had purchased it. His only worry was that someone possessed master keys to all the rooms. He'd brought a small alarm with him, which he attached to the door.

With the door locked, Cord settled down to the best sleep he'd had for some time.

# Chapter 19

Cord stretched cramped muscles and stood up. For an hour or more, since waking, he had been in a trance. No use to try to remember more, he decided. He could go into recall without effort now, the result of three days' practice.

This was the fourth morning. Today the spaceport was settling down to work again. And he knew how to complete the mind-reading machine.

He heated a meal and ate it mechanically. It would be wise to time his departure from his temporary hideaway carefully. The corridors should be neither empty nor crowded. A trickle of humans going on shift would be best.

When the rush had thinned out, Cord left the apartment. He had removed all traces of his presence. Even if someone searched all the vacant units, he would never guess Cord had been there. Which was good. He might want to use the apartment again.

At the crossing of two main corridors, Cord used a screen to call Hamilton K.

"Where have you been?" the saturnine human demanded as soon as he saw Cord's face on the screen.

"Around." He did not intend to confide his secret to K. Or anyone else.

"Oh—like that, is it? Well, you'd better think up a good story for Julia McKay: she's been half insane. Keeps asking me to start a search for you. She's sure you've been murdered. I wouldn't care to be you when she finds out you've been holed up, so to speak, with another woman. She's certainly more reasonable than the average missionary, except for her abstention from all the more interesting pastimes, but like all those who take sex too seriously, she's bound to be jealous. End of lecture. Now, what are your plans?"

Cord smiled. "First, to devise a suitable excuse for Julia."

Hamilton accepted the brush-off impassively. "Keep in touch, Cord."

Next he placed a call to Julia. She gasped when she saw him.

"Hamilton K says you were worried about me," Cord said.

"Yes. Whatever happened to you? When I went looking for you in the morning, you'd simply . . . disappeared. Cord, I'd like to see you. Not this way—in a screen. I need to hold you to be sure you're all right."

"I can't come to you right now, Julia. In a little while, after I've finished, we'll have time together. I promise."

"You aren't going to do something dangerous, are you, Cord? I couldn't bear it if you—if something happened to you."

"Don't worry. I'll be safe enough. It won't take me long." He switched off the screen before she could protest more. Julia's face, white and strained, faded.

Then he started for his workroom. As soon as it was completed, he knew the way he'd use the mind reader. If he had to check everyone in the spaceport one at a time, he would. Was there anyone he could eliminate? Possibly not, but he would start with those who had been closest to Greffard—the ones who might have known what was being demonstrated.

He thought of various methods of getting close to suspects so as to touch them while carrying the telepathy machine. Perhaps it might be best if its function was known. His quarry might panic and give himself away.

It took some time to get to the laboratory wing, since he had deliberately sought out a vacant unit some distance away. Speedwalk to trans tube to a second speedwalk, and afterward on foot along another corridor. The wing was operating as usual, he saw. Technicians in coveralls and spaceport employees in ordinary dress came and went with enough frequency to supply witnesses of any attack. Some doors were closed, others open. The one to his work area was locked.

He entered without hesitation. If anyone had forced the door or even attempted to do so, alarms would have gone off. Clearly, the shop was inviolate.

Which was, as Fyrrell would have said, a fatal mistake.

As he started to close the door, something seemed to burst at the back of his head, and Cord plunged into a darkness shot with color.

An eon later, he was falling. . . .

Ancestors! He really was falling—head-first down a narrow space in darkness. His mind was still grappling with the situation when reflexes took over. Thrusting out hands and knees, Cord attempted to wedge himself into the chimneylike space. The shock of halting his momentum almost dislodged him. His hands, knees, and back felt scraped raw, and the back of his head hurt so badly he was on the point of blacking out again.

No! He wasn't going to let himself die and his parents' killer get away with it. Anger gave him strength. His ancestors would laugh at him if he gave up now. The blood seemed to roar in his head with voices like those on the Spine of Arzet, but his mind was clearing.

He was head-down in a disposal chute, he decided. Or maybe some sort of ventilating duct. The important thing was, if he fell, it would be head-first either on a hard floor or perhaps on a garbage heap, but the impact would surely break his neck and crush his skull.

There was no way of guessing how far he had fallen before regaining consciousness. He might be very near the bottom of the shaft—in which case, he could work his way down and make his exit from whatever the shaft led to. It could not be a furnace or mass-energy converter, he knew. There were disposal chutes all over the complex; they couldn't all terminate in the converter. It was possible the rubbish dropped onto a conveyor belt, which then carried it to a central point. If so, there would be service doors and walkways for maintenance.

On the other hand, if he was still many levels above the ground, he would never make it to the bottom under his own power. He was inching along steadily, but his progress was too slow, and the strain on his circulatory system was already beginning to tell. If he could make it as far as the next level—wherever that was—he might be able to push the access panel open. That assumed the door would be in the wall in front of him. If it was behind him or on one side, he might not be able to manage it. Or even know it was there. Mehirans' nightsight was better than humans', but there was no light in the chimney. Why should there be? No one was expected to be here.

First one hand, then the other. Then move the left knee forward, and the right. Once more. His breathing sounded ragged in his ears, louder than the hammering of his blood.

Now the left hand. Its palm pressed the wall, but under his fingers there was—nothing.

With feverish care, Cord felt the edge. The empty place was as wide as the chute. Now he imagined he felt a breath of air on his face. A duct?

Muttering a prayer to his ancestors, Cord braced himself with one hand while groping for the other side of the horizontal passage.

Would it be too low to admit him? Cord's hand stretched farther—there! He worked his knees closer to the duct, took a deep breath, and pushed himself into it. He fell jarringly on his back, his legs still in the shaft.

He lay for time, while his circulation slowed and his breathing returned to normal. Finally, muscles aching, he worked his way into the duct, rolled onto his hands and knees, and began to hunt for a way out.

The passage seemed to go on and on in the darkness, though Cord knew it was illusion. The distance felt greater than it was because he was covering it on hands and knees bruised and raw from the chute.

Ahead the darkness was lessening. He could see no light, but he thought he could make out a short section of the duct's floor. Ah! Another duct crossed his own at right angles, and in that duct there must be a light. A very faint one, he guessed, but bright enough to eyes accustomed to utter blackness.

At the intersection he grinned in grim relief. The cross passage was tall enough to stand in, he saw by the glow. Better yet, the illumination came from a lamp marking a ladder in a vertical tube. Where there is a ladder, there is a way out.

Cord climbed down awkwardly. In the disposal chute, the rush of adrenaline had masked the pain in his hands and knees. Now, with the hard part done, they burned so much he could not ignore them. His whole body ached. He forced his fingers to close around the rungs. He held on to the side of the ladder with his tail, too. It would be little help if he fell, but it steadied him. All his muscles felt slack.

At the bottom there was a maintenance area, as he had suspected. The only thing of interest to him was the green exit sign. He emerged in a hallway—not a main one, he observed, considering its narrowness, but the level and section were marked on the walls. This was a part of the building he had never visited. Its chief function was to keep the rest of the complex operating efficiently.

He walked slowly toward the trans tube, almost in a daze. It did not matter, he knew. Although the area seemed isolated, there was no danger because the killer did not know he was here. In fact, he remembered, the killer must be certain of his death.

The tube seemed far away. Cord plodded on in spite of rubbery muscles and bones that felt brittle. The world was receding around him and getting fuzzy at the edges. Even the sound of voices approaching did not penetrate the haze.

"Hey!"

The shout meant nothing to Cord, but it severed the tenuous thread binding him to consciousness.

Falling—again!

"Gods, what happened to him?"

". . . defector?"

"Better call security . . ."

". . . infirmary . . ."

Fragments of conversation came to him: words with no meaning attached.

"Get something under his feet, Sam'l—he's too pale."

And then there was nothing.

There was a buzzing sound. It droned on and on, and Cord thought of some swarm of insects on a warm afternoon. The great white cloud-flowers were in bloom, their sharp scent filling the air. . . .

But he was in the alien spaceport, he remembered. Cord opened his eyes. He was lying on a softly padded bed or table in a small room, with a metal shell as long as himself hovering over him. It was clearly a machine of some sort, he observed, with his mother's interest in machinery. The buzzing had come from it, probably, though it was silent now. The air bore an antiseptic tang.

"Are you feeling better?"

Cord noticed the humans for the first time. One seemed to be a physician or med-tech, and had asked the question. The other was O'as Garatua. The doctor looked concerned; she looked annoyed.

"Yes, thank you. I feel fine." It was true: whatever they'd done, it had worked.

"What happened to you?" Garatua snapped. "The men who called me got quite a scare when they saw you. Your knees and hands were dripping blood and almost in shreds. Your back and your shirt were in tatters. They thought you'd tried to sabotage something and fallen into the machinery. Fortunately, they called Security first."

Cord turned his head. He examined the palms of his hands and then looked down at his kneecaps. Both appeared freshly healed.

"I was dumped into a disposal chute."

The doctor made horrified noises.

"I don't suppose you let yourself be bundled in," Garatua said mildly—for her, at least.

"I had entered my workshop." Cord drew the memories to him, a bit at a time. "Someone must have been inside: he hit me."

"Yes, there was a bad contusion at the back of the skull. Not fatal, obviously, but it required treatment," the physician added.

"I don't feel it now," Cord agreed, touching the back of his head. "When I regained consciousness, I was in the chute, falling."

"By the balls of the Blue God," O'as said deliberately. "You simply aren't safe to be out by yourself. Leave you alone for five minutes and you almost get yourself killed." She crossed her arms and stared at him.

Cord was going to give her a harsh answer: it wasn't his fault the spaceport contained a homicidal maniac. Instead he opened his mind to her psychic emanations. It might be better to make a friend of her, if he could.

He had touched no mind in—how long? He could not remember. It was unpleasant to sense humans' emotions. Cord had grown accustomed to keeping his shields in place. Yet surely if he was speaking to his would-be murderer he would know by probing her feelings.

As he expected, Garatua's inner self was as hard and unapproachable as her exterior. But she was not unfriendly; she was angry, though not, he sensed, at him. She was also worried. There was an underlying bitterness, too, buried far down. Human emotional lives were not as controlled and as healthy as those of Mehirans. Cord realized that he knew a great deal about her from reading her emotions.

The doctor swung away the metal monitor shell and helped Cord sit up. He felt well enough to stand up. The doctor fussed about for a few moments, then pronounced him fit to leave.

He walked out slowly, the security chief beside him.

"You really aren't the one, are you?"

"What? What one?"

"Who's been trying to kill me. I'm sorry, O'as. I believe now that I was wrong to suspect you, but it was an understandable mistake. I had a grudge against you for torturing Bird. Your being guilty of that made it seem likely you were guilty of the other as well," he added. You just never knew how far a Kamean was following you. They certainly gave the impression of being a little slow.

Garatua took off at a tangent.

"You know," she replied, with the closest thing to friendliness he had seen in her, "I've been wondering about that girl. I never understood how she held out as she did. She seemed like a creampuff, but she didn't break down when anyone else would have. At least, anyone who wasn't psychoconditioned, and they usually die under questioning. She isn't . . . ah . . . insane, is she?"

"No, of course not!"

"Strange. Insanity sometimes accounts for anomalies like that. . . . You were saying you thought I was trying to murder you?"

"I have apologized for thinking so." Cord reminded himself that no one's mind, Mehiran or human, was as straightforward as it might seem at first. Certainly Garatua's reaction surprised him. She was neither offended at his admission nor flattered that he'd changed his opinion.

"That's all right." She shrugged.

He touched her emotions fleetingly, and made a guess that she was accustomed to having others think ill of her. Recalling what life was like for a Catcher on Mehira, Cord felt a certain reluctant sympathy.

"Who knew you were going to your shop?" the woman asked, as they turned a corner.

Cord's brow furrowed as he reviewed the possibilities.

"No one knew specifically that I would go there. I told neither Julia nor K, and they were the only ones I spoke with today. Of course, anyone who's been observing me might suppose I'd be there this morning—except for the festivities, I've worked in the lab every day."

"But you were late today?"

"Yes, that may have worried him," Cord agreed. "Still, I think he'd stay, don't you?—even if I didn't show up when expected. He'd have trouble leaving unobserved during the day shift. He must have gotten in before the shift began, since there would be no one in that wing earlier."

"And having killed you, or tried to, he'd wait until—" Garatua's dark eyes opened very wide.

"Until shift end to leave," Cord finished. "Let's go."

They pushed past people in the corridor without a word. As they ran toward the speedwalk, Garatua asked, "I suppose you do have a disposal chute in your work area?"

"Awkward for him if I hadn't. I wonder how he evaded my workshop's security system. Short of using a cutter beam on the lock, it should not have been possible."

"Perhaps he came up the disposal chute." O'as stole a glance at Cord as she jumped from the speedwalk.

"Is that a joke?" he asked, leaping after her. With as stolid a being as O'as, it was hard to tell. He followed her into a trans tube.

"No. There are horror stories about people—and things—lurking in spaceports. With so many passages and shafts—for ventilation, wiring and plumbing—someone could hide in a port as long as he liked."

The man who didn't exist. "How would he get here? Wouldn't you know who staffed the spaceport?"

"Officially, it's not possible. But a friendly or bribable crewman is all it takes for a stowaway."

The trans tube slowed its ascent and stopped at the office level.

"I have sometimes wondered whether it might be Hamilton

K," Cord remarked. He strode along without looking at O'as, but his mind was alert to catch her reaction.

She did not break step, physically or mentally.

"The opportunity would be present," she concurred. "However, my professional opinion is that he is not the one. Trade Agents are not bunglers. K would not have to try twice to kill you."

"You make him sound a formidable opponent."

"He would be. And he would choose a fail-safe method. If he had put you down the chute, you'd've been dead first."

"If I had fallen all the way, what would have happened?"

"The trash is sorted by a robotic system: plastic, glass, and metal to recycling, organics to be processed into fertilizer for the agri-tanks. Chances are we would never have found any trace of your body."

They reached the door of Cord's workshop before the evening exodus from the offices.

"Open the door and stand back," Garatua ordered, drawing a surprisingly large hand weapon from inside her tunic.

Cord decided not to argue. She was armed with an energy weapon, he was not. Besides, she took it for granted it was her right to go in first.

Cord pressed his palm to the lock and disengaged the additional locking mechanism, then stood aside as Garatua kicked it open. She went in crouched, eyes sweeping the room. She was good, Cord admitted. He would not make the mistake of underestimating her in the future.

The workshop was empty. It was not a large space, and there was no place to hide, except behind the door.

"Don't touch anything," O'as told him. "I'll have one of my people check for fingerprints and other traces, but we can hardly expect your attacker to have been dim-witted enough to leave any. Still, he may have been careless."

She called her department from the com-screen down the hall, ordering an amount of equipment and personnel which sounded excessive. While they waited for it to arrive, she said, "We will have to question everyone in this corridor. That room has only two exits—the door and the chute—and the suspect went out one of them. If he used the door, someone may have seen him—and remembered him as a person who normally would not be in this area. If he went down the chute after you, the situation is a little different."

"Have you ever been in a disposal shaft?" Cord asked. "Not a very secure method of escape. And I'd have heard him, wouldn't I?"

"Hanging head down and fighting to stay alive?" she countered. "As for the difficulty, there are several kinds of equipment which would make it much easier. That's one of the things my crew will be looking for—signs that someone has been climbing in the shaft. If he's left traces, we could track him."

His respect for Garatua increasing, Cord watched while she made her arrangements. Her team was trained chiefly to deal with pilferage by employees and outsiders, and with corporate espionage. On Mehira, they'd obviously been bored. With the port sealed off from the Mehirans, and no other trading company present, neither theft nor spying was a problem. The security department threw itself into the investigation with enthusiasm.

Cord noticed that O'as did not question any of the workers or technicians on the corridor herself. She assigned the task to a cheerful-looking young man. She caught Cord's expression.

"They'll talk to him," she explained. "I don't have the right personality for 'friendly' questioning. Too defensive, the psych staff says. What would you expect? People don't like Kameans: they think we're stupid, calculating, loutish. They'd react to me the wrong way no matter how charming I was." Her lips turned up in a fractional smile. "Not that I've tried that method," she added.

Cord smiled, too. He guessed he was being admitted to Garatua's circle of friends.

A moment later, she was all business again. "Now, what I want to know is, what do you believe motivated these attacks?"

It surprised him a little to realize they had not discussed the motive at all.

"It must be tied to the bombing at the demonstration." If he was going to accept her as a colleague, he owed her the truth, or as much of it as would help her find the killer. "It leaked out that the invention my parents were showing that day was a telepathy machine. Someone wanted to suppress it. The same person wants me out of the way, either because I'm on his trail or because I can reconstruct the device."

"A telepathy device, by the Names," O'as repeated. "K

didn't mention that.'' She pondered gloomily before asking, ''Are you building another one?''

''Yes. I could finish it in half a day—if I could work without interruption, and without being murdered.''

Garatua nodded. ''I think you'd better work in the security department's lab. It's no more safe than any place else, if we assume the suspect can travel through disposal chutes and ventilating ducts, but you would be surrounded by my people, at least.''

''And you trust all of them?''

''I picked them myself. I believe they are all honest, which is something I could not say for many others. If I were committing a major crime, a mind-reading machine would be the very last invention I'd want to encourage.''

''What kind of crime would be big enough to call for mass murder?'' he said bitterly.

''I can think of half a dozen,'' she replied, not unkindly. ''But I wouldn't have expected this spaceport to attract such a criminal. The fact is, this is a marginal operation as trading facilities go. In time, Mehira may be big business, but right now, especially considering how the local authorities have limited access to the port, there simply isn't much potential for crime.''

''So there's not much hope of finding the murderer by discovering what crime is being concealed?''

''I wouldn't count on it,'' O'as agreed. ''I think if there were a major criminal operation here, I'd have some clue to it.''

''So we are back where we started.''

''No—not if you're willing to trust me.''

Cord's tail switched restlessly. ''What's your plan?''

''You've been hit over the head. You have amnesia. You can't remember how to finish your device. That won't mean anything to most of the port, but the murderer apparently knows what your invention is, so he'll see it as additional time in which to finish you off. You'll stay in your unit, 'resting,' and I'll see to it you've got an invisible round-the-clock guard. We'll rig an alarm system so no one can get in without giving warning—even if he swims in via the toilet. He'll come after you and we'll get him.''

It was not a plan Cord could have used alone, but if he was willing to trust Garatua, it might work. And he would be able to sleep easy. For some nights now his rest had been troubled by nightmares—almost as though he'd been picking up the psychic emanations of other sleepers. It either meant his shaky mental control was failing under stress to the point of receiving even in his sleep or that the dreams were the product of his own fevered brain.

"All right," he said. "As long as you have no objection to my checking the alarms."

"I insist on it," O'as responded with grim humor.

# Chapter 20

Cord prowled restlessly around the room.

"This is getting no results," he said to his visitor.

O'as placidly bit into a sandwich. She had brought lunch in for the two of them, but Cord's appetite had succumbed to inactivity.

"I've been stuck here for three days and nobody has tried to kill me. We're wasting our time, and I'm bored."

"You're just horny," O'as remarked. She had refused to allow him visits from anyone, even Julia.

"Care to remedy that?" Expectant, he stopped pacing.

"As a matter of fact—"

She never got a chance to finish the sentence: the screen's beeping cut her off. O'as delayed hitting the respond button long enough to push Cord out of camera range. The security chief wanted no hint of Cord's good health to leak out.

"Chief," said the voice of one of her staff, "we've got a problem in the cafeteria."

Garatua's face darkened. "What do you mean, 'a problem'? A lover's quarrel? A spilled drink? Try to be specific, Leno."

"Specifically, we've got a corpse and seven wounded. Attempted murder and suicide."

"Balls of the Blue God," O'as muttered. "Half a lunch and no rest afterward—a sure formula for indigestion and an early grave. I'll be right down."

"I'm coming with you," Cord insisted.

The security head shrugged. "Why not? You can hardly get into trouble with half of security present."

When they burst into the cafeteria, it looked like a battlefield to Cord. People were scattered about, tables were overturned and broken, bottles and containers spilled their contents across puddles of blood. The bright-colored smears made an abstract painting of the floor. A medical team was present,

172

loading the casualties onto gurneys. Several more, with minor injuries, were being assisted to the infirmary.

"Thank the gods it happened after the lunch hour, or it would have been worse." Leno gestured toward a mound shrouded in white plastic. "He's over there."

O'as stamped over and raised a corner of the sheet.

"Industrial-use cutter," she remarked. "Anyone recognize him before he took his face off?"

"Yeah. He's Lion Pars. He has his employee card, and others have identified him."

"Well?" She hoisted a thick eyebrow.

"He was a quiet little guy who worked down in maintenance. He didn't live up to his name. Everyone thought that was funny."

Cord looked down at the oozing red slab that had recently been a face. How could life get so bad that a man would do that to himself?

"So he just checked a cutter out of stores, came in here, and started shooting?"

A wiry woman with long black hair approached O'as.

"It wasn't like that at all," the woman said, not catching the sarcasm in the security head's voice.

O'as turned sharply toward her, looking annoyed. "How was it, then?" O'as asked, her voice brittle.

"He'd been depressed and worried for a long time—a month, maybe. We used to talk sometimes. He—"

"Were you friends? Lovers?" Garantua interrupted.

"No. Li didn't have friends. He had acquaintances."

"Sorry. What were you going to say?"

"He was frightened. Today he was talking to himself and always looking around, like this." The woman's eyes darted from side to side and seemed to twitch away from objects. "As though he kept seeing things out of the corners of his eyes."

"If he was carrying on that way, why didn't someone do something? Sounds like he was breaking up," Leno observed.

Lion's co-worker looked at him pityingly.

"You don't turn someone in because he's gone comet-riding and forgotten to get back in time for his shift. Li wasn't the kind to use Happi-High or Comet Dust much, so I thought he'd taken a little too much or maybe mixed them.

Hey, you know how it is: if you aren't a regular, it's easy to make a mistake.''

"Make sure the meds get blood samples," Garatua told Leno. "We'll interview everyone he worked with, too. I'll search his unit myself. So what happened then?"

Their informant continued, "He was sitting at a table—over there, the corner one—but he wasn't eating. He was talking to himself. He passed by me earlier, but he didn't say anything to me—probably didn't see me."

"Did you hear what he was saying?"

"It was bizarre. He kept repeating that things were creeping around after him."

Things. The word hung in the air, almost visible.

"Things?" Garatua echoed without enthusiasm.

"He didn't say what he meant. Frankly, I wouldn't have wanted to know," the woman answered.

Everyone knew what she meant. . . .

"Thanks. Give your name and number to Leno. We may need to talk to you again. Come on," Garatua told Cord.

"Where are we going?"

"I want to see Lion's psych profile. And interview the people in his department."

They stopped at a privacy-shielded com-screen, used Garatua's special access code, and learned more about the subject's mind and life than his own mother had known. Most of the terminology was gibberish to Cord, but his companion translated.

"Repressed to a factor of five, as the girl said, acquaintances, not friends. No real sexual outlets. Liked to take long walks in the outdoors—a bit difficult on this world. Religion—Fourth Zen Anabaptist Church. That accounts for much of the guilt and fear. Prefers being alone. Painstaking and methodical, a delicate balance between stability and howling insanity."

"I understood personnel were screened to eliminate undesirable elements and potential problems," Cord said.

"They are. And according to his profile, there was little likelihood that Pars would tip over into instability. Granted, he was weird, but the psych-tech's opinion is that he'd go on being a little weird and not very happy but doing his job all right. Which is all the company asks."

"The psych-tech made a mistake."

"So it appears," O'as admitted.

*    *    *

They were down on the lowest level of the complex. The port grew its own food under artificial light, using waste products to feed gigantic hybrid plants. Alien—to Cord, at least—bushes and stalks towered over them as they spoke with the dead man's department head.

"Lion's job was to maintain the farm's environment. He checked the irrigation and fertilizer channels, the lighting and so forth. Most of the harvesting and planting is automated, and he had nothing to do with that. But keeping the temperature and light cycles stable and monitoring the watering and feeding is a major effort. When you're feeding as many as we do, those things are critical. We could live on Mehiran food for some time and stay pretty healthy, but a port can't afford to depend on external food supplies. And on some worlds, we couldn't digest the proteins and starches at all."

"What sort of person was he?"

The supervisor examined a half-ripe berry the size of Cord's fist before answering.

"Not easy to know. Quiet but pleasant. Or was. I can't believe he'd try to kill anyone else. Himself, yes. I can believe that. Unless . . ."

Neither Cord nor Garatua prompted him. Cord was sure the man would refuse to say more if they tried to push him.

". . . unless he began to see them as not human. Or humanoid—I beg your pardon," the human added to Cord.

"We were told that Lion talked about 'things'—creatures, perhaps. Did he speak to you about them?"

"Not much, and not at all lately. A few weeks ago he said something about things hiding in the maintenance tunnels. We laughed it off, and after that he wouldn't say any more. He got so he didn't like going into the tunnels alone. Out of orbit? Sure, but lots of people have a crimp one way or another."

Gazing around the cavernous space, dim even with the plant lights, Cord could understand Lion's crimp. The plants' huge leaves rustled with the soft breeze from a ventilator. In the silence, such sounds were almost sinister. Did Lion take long walks in this man-made "out-of-doors"? Or was he threatened by this towering primeval forest?

"You wouldn't happen to have a cutter down here, would you?" O'as was asking.

In the semi-gloom it was not easy to see the embarrassed flush on the man's face, but it could be read in his movements and his voice.

"I won't try to fool you. We do have one—you're going to find it's the one he used up there." He stumbled over the words, trying to explain. "We kept it because it's easier to have it here than to make trips to stores. When Li got twitchy about the tunnels and started taking the cutter with him . . . well—we needed him. If he dusted out, we'd be shorthanded. But I swear I never knew he'd take the cutter out of the department. I wouldn't have let him do that, no matter how many aliens were after him."

Garatua snorted in derision, but Cord's attention was riveted.

"Say that again, please."

"Huh? What?"

"About aliens being after him. Was that what he believed? Not 'things' but aliens?"

"Lion had this theory that the things were aliens trying to infiltrate the port. Rumors about 'things' are common—in every spaceport there are tales of mutated giant spiders and worms—or worse—in the lower levels."

"Port legends," O'as agreed. "No truth to any of it. Like city stories about the insane mother who put her baby down the disposal chute—" She stopped abruptly.

"The funny thing is," the supervisor went on, "Lion didn't imagine oversized spiders or worms, and on some planets it would be rational to believe aliens were trying to break in. I don't know exactly what he saw in the tunnels, but he did see a big bird outside, once. But it was night, and I guess he was seeing things."

"A big bird?" O'as repeated.

"Bigger than a man, with a sharp, curved beak. Since he saw it outside the buildings, and at night, it didn't seem so weird. We thought it was a real Mehiran creature." He looked at Cord expectantly.

Cord shook his head, swinging his heavy scalplock. "There's nothing on Mehira that fits the description."

"How long had he been out of orbit?" O'as asked.

"Like I said, it's been a few weeks since he got the idea that there were things down here following him. It's only the past week he's actually 'seen' them. Before he just thought they were there."

"Uhh," O'as grunted. "Well, thanks. You've been helpful." She turned and stalked off.

"Hell of a fine woman," the superintendent muttered to Cord. "Not too talkative, not too skinny. You say what you like about Kameans, but that girl's got grit."

"You should tell her so," Cord said. The superintendent looked as though he had a certain amount of grit himself.

"I sure would like to, but I'm not much good at meeting people. That's why I'm down here farming."

"It's not hard. In a day or two, why not go up to security to ask her how the investigation is going. Then tell her what a good job you think she's doing. That would get you acquainted."

"I guess it would. Thanks. Maybe I'll do it."

Cord went after O'as. In the dim emptiness, he began to walk faster. It was a relief to find her waiting at the trans tube.

"What next?" Cord asked her.

"We check his unit." She jumped in the trans tube. Cord was only a step behind.

The unit was compulsively tidy. A shelf held tapes—mostly of the self-improvement variety—and some family portrait holopix and a religious object or two. Garatua poked around. Cord sniffed the air. It was stale.

He found all the rooms in the spaceport somewhat musty, since the complex contained no windows. The building was sheathed in the black material that made it impervious to attack and accident; it used an efficient ventilation system instead of the Mehirans' haphazard method of opening windows. Still, however sophisticated, mechanically circulated air is not the same as a refreshing breeze. The atmosphere of Pars's room was even less fresh than usual, Cord noticed. He looked for the ventilating duct. While O'as went through Lion's belongings, Cord dragged a chair over to the wall. Standing on the chair to examine the duct, he discovered the reason for the room's closeness.

"There's something in here," Cord told the security chief. She stopped her search of the wardrobe to join him.

"I don't like to hear that word 'thing,' " she said. "There's been too much talk about 'things' already."

"It looks like a notebook," Cord said, using a thumbnail to loosen one of the screws holding the grille in place,

The screws came free easily: they had been removed and replaced often. Garatua took the book from Cord and opened it. "It's a diary," she announced.

Cord stepped off the chair and sat next to O'as on Lion's neatly made bed. He watched her skim the pages, looking for a pertinent entry. "Listen to this," she commanded.

" 'I knew I wasn't imagining it. I thought there were things down there, watching, watching, always watching me, but really there's only the one. It's nasty and slimy but it's frightened of me—that's because it knows what a cutter is. I shot at it and missed. It flattened out so fast the ray hit the wall, and I'll have to explain about that when the next maintenance crew comes around. Then it slid into a duct and I didn't follow it.' "

O'as flipped the page and read another section:

" 'I can't tell anyone about it. They'll say I'm crazy—the letters say so, and the others laughed when I said there were things in the tunnels.' " "what does he mean by 'letters'?" O'as asked herself. " 'It's a trial sent by Providence to test me. If my faith is great enough it can't hurt me. I've got to keep doing my job and pretend I'm not frightened. If I tell everyone what's wrong, they'll ship me offplanet to a hospital and take my brain apart. Everyone here will laugh at me for not doing my duty and having faith. I wonder if it will come up here looking for me.' "

Cord, reading over Garatua's shoulder, saw the man's deterioration in his handwriting. It had been precise, easy to read even for Cord, who was not yet familiar with script. Now the words sprawled across the page. If O'as had not been reading aloud, Cord doubted he could have deciphered the diary. She turned another page. "Ah," she said triumphantly. "Here's our answer."

" 'Someone knows. Another note was under my door when I came home from work. Got to try harder to be calm. If they drug me I'll be helpless—it could get me then. Tomorrow I'll bring the cutter with me.'

"Well," said Garatua, "That's that. There's more, but I can read it later. There are one or two more places here I want to check, and then we can go."

"Your investigation is completed, then?" Cord asked. Certain points still seemed obscure to him.

"Not quite. I'd like to get a look at the poison-pen letters he received and find out who sent them. Let someone start that in a community as isolated as this, and it's bound to lead to trouble. Pars may have been half cracked to begin with, but I'll bet it was the letters that pushed him over."

Cord nodded agreement, then was startled to hear O'as say, "Now we pay a visit to Julia McKay." At his expression, she explained, "Since Lion was religious it makes sense to think he went to a missionary for advice. Besides, it's important that no mystery be attached to his death: this port is cut off from civilization—Terran/human, anyhow—and things get magnified out of proportion in isolation. If the pressure builds and rumors start, this port could go off like a string of firecrackers."

O'as did not speak again, and Cord did not intrude on her thoughts, verbally or otherwise. Out of self-preservation—and habit—his shields were now up all the time. This was an unthinkable insult among Mehirans, but among the uncontrolled violence of the Terran minds, Cord would go mad. The drawback was that the shields prevented him from finding his would-be assassin.

Julia admitted them to her unit, greeting them with an inquiring and obviously puzzled smile.

"Lion Pars killed himself this afternoon," O'as said abruptly. "Did he ever come to you for spiritual counseling—or whatever you call it?"

Julia's eyes went wide. "Lion killed himself? Oh, no . . ."

"He wounded several others. He went berserk in the dining room." Garatua waited for a response.

"You aren't surprised, are you, Julia?" Cord asked, when she did not speak. It earned him an approving nod from the security head.

"No, I'm not. Here, sit down," Julia invited. O'as sat on the chair, and Cord and Julia took places on the bed. "I suppose you want to know about him. He came to my services, of course. Like my own sect, the Zen Anabaptists place emphasis on group worship. He also came to confess, or 'share' as we call it."

"Confess what?"

"Nothing of importance—the small deviations from righteousness of a person with no great sins or great virtues. But lately he did not come to confess so much as to talk. He needed someone who would listen to him.''

Garatua frowned slightly. "Anything not covered by the seal of the confessional?"

Julia hesitated. "Many religions require that a chaplain maintain professional secrecy, but exceptions are permitted in some cases. My own religion leaves it to the discretion of the minister.''

O'as waited with what was, for her, patience.

"I don't think it can do poor Lion any harm to tell you part of what he told me," Julia decided. "Maybe it will help you to understand.''

"Go ahead.''

"He was always rather nervous, but more so in the past month. He was frightened to be alone in the tunnels where he worked.''

"Oh? What did he think was down there?" O'as phrased the question casually.

"He imagined there were monsters." The word "imagined" was accented. "I think he realized that it was all a product of an unhealthy mind, but when your heart is pounding and you're trembling and sweating with fear it might be hard to remember it.''

"So there wasn't really anything to it but craziness.''

Julia smiled. "He was a nice little man, but he should never have gone to work for a trading company. Lion was afraid of aliens. He should have stayed on his own world, surrounded by other Zen Anabaptists and no aliens at all. Or else he should have had psych counseling to cure him of it.''

"And when did you last see him?"

"It must have been the day before yesterday—yes, after his shift he came to the chapel.''

"Did he do or say anything to indicate that he was reaching his breaking point?"

"No. It was obvious he wasn't in good shape mentally, but if I'd had any clue that he would become violent, I would have insisted he see the doctor.''

"Did he mention receiving a letter?"

"No—but there hasn't been a ship in port for some time, so he couldn't have gotten one recently.''

"I meant a letter or note from someone within the spaceport."

Julia shook her head; the auburn hair rippled over her shoulders, and Cord admired the way light sparkled over it.

"I don't think he said anything about one. But his mind was taken up with his fears. Is there anything else I can tell you?"

"No, I guess that wraps it up. Everyone agrees he was out of orbit and he finally blew up. You know what this means?"

The question was addressed to Cord. He tore his attention away from Julia and raised his eyebrows inquiringly at O'as.

"Lion feared aliens. You're the only alien ever to stay inside the port—and you've been here almost a month. The same month Lion went over the edge. He was the one who tried to kill you—and he was completely familiar with the ducts and tunnels."

O'as stood up to leave. "Give me a call," she said pointedly to Cord, "when you have the chance. . . ."

Once she was out of the door, Cord put his arms around Julia. She returned his embrace and squeezed him.

"You're safe now," she murmured. "I'm sure of it."

Cord stroked her glorious hair; his hands moved downward. Julia purred deep in her throat and ran her fingers lightly over his muscled arms. "It's been so long."

"For me too," Julia acknowledged.

The material of her jumpsuit shredded under his strong fingers as Cord fumbled with the fastenings. It was lucky that it was disposable.

Julia laughed. "You make me do things I didn't think I'd ever do."

Cord helped her out of the tatters. "Does that mean there are some positions left we haven't tried?"

Julia pulled at his tunic. "Let's find out."

They lay side by side on the soft bed; Cord touched her pale smooth skin with his rough tongue and traced intricate patterns with it across her ample breasts. His organ had emerged from its pouch and was uncurling. Julia moved away from him. He was about to protest until she shifted her position so that they were reversed head to toe.

Gently she took him into her mouth, her tongue rolling about, gently probing, teasing. Cord moved her left leg over his broad chest and bent his head. Her alien musky scent was an intoxicating perfume from another world. His rough tongue went to work; soon she was writhing, grinding her pelvis into his body, under his own expert probing. Even with his shields up, he could feel Julia's desire.

When they could stand it no more, Julia shifted position again and lay on her back. Cord loomed above her, his engorged organ larger than ever before. He molded himself to her heaving body and slowly began thrusting. Julia moaned and clutched at him. His tail came under him and probed for the second opening; it inched in slowly.

He held his upper torso away from hers but entwined his legs with hers, holding her fast. Then with a maddening deliberation, he alternated slow thrusting. He wanted the pleasure to last forever.

Julia began to make growling noises; then she moaned, she purred, she fought, she bit him. Finally his thrusts picked up momentum, both organ and tail smashing into Julia's soft flesh while she tried to impale herself on him with equal fervor. Cord let go as Julia was peaking; their colliding bodies spasmed in unison.

They lay there, gasping for breath. Julia sighed with satisfaction. "Your life may have been in danger, but it's your tail I'd really miss." At his expression, she hastily added, "But the rest of you is important too."

They laughed and lay back in each other's arms. Cord nibbled on Julia's human, nonpointed ear. "I'm still hungry."

"Is it dinnertime?" she asked innocently.

"Who's talking about food?" He left a wet trail of kisses from her neck, along her shoulder, over her breastbone, and down to one impertinent nipple, poking up at him. "I've been confined in a small room with nothing to do but think about making love."

She looked at him seriously. "And not thinking about revenge? Not thinking about putting together your infernal device?"

Cord looked away. "I swore to my ancestors that I'd track down my parents' killer. As for the machine, I can't remember the final connections." That was the story he and O'as agreed upon; it came out without thinking. He certainly trusted Julia by now.

"What does the doctor say? Will your memory come

back?'' Julia gazed at him with worried eyes. Cord loved her deep, dark eyes, like pools of night.

"He says I'm fine . . . physically. Here, let me prove it to you.''

He stood up and pulled Julia upright too. Though she was not as tiny as Tanna, the girl from the party, he sat her astride his powerful legs. With her legs spread apart and around him, there was no obstacle to his entering her again. Then, so impaled, he tucked her feet over his calves and crouched down. She was his complete prisoner, unable to get away. His organ, which had shrunk to normal, was now able to probe her in a different way. In true Mehiran fashion, it touched her in delicate, feathery strokes as he controlled its slow, insistent probing. It probed just at the lips of the opening and deep within her. Julia shuddered at the pleasant but odd sensation. Before it began to swell and straighten, he could use it to touch any part of her that he desired.

Using his strength to support her entire body on his muscular thighs, he made love to Julia until she was wild with passion, alternately trying to drive herself deeper onto his organ or fighting desperately to get away from it. He kept thrusting without a sense of time, until they'd both come again and again, their sweat-slicked bodies shuddering at just a mere touch.

Julia finally dressed and went to buy some dinner. She brought back an assortment of packets, and they ate sitting cross-legged on the bed. She used the com-screen to punch in entertainment viewing—the first he'd had a chance to see, now that he could relax and not worry about dying.

He slept with Julia that night. They were exhausted from loving, so they talked of many different things until they fell asleep. For the first time in a long time, Cord was content.

The night wind was good on his face and in his nostrils. There were enticing scents in the rich air. Cord dreamed he was running over the marshland and scrub toward the city, leaving the spaceport far behind. There was something peculiar about his gait—he seemed to have an extra limb or two—but he couldn't see his legs. It didn't seem important—he had to get to the city.

He loped into parkland. He recognized it and yet it was

new to him. The enticing scents were much stronger here: the
aromas of life.

His running slowed to a walk. He cautiously approached
some dense bushes. A couple lay twined beneath sharp green
leaves that parted as he walked, ungainly, toward them. They
turned their faces toward the rustling, to see the one who was
so rudely breaking into their passion. Cord could see them
clearly now: two young Mehirans, naked except for identical
love-knots, woven into their braids and adorned with tiny
golden beads.

They screamed almost simultaneously, the girl in soprano,
the boy in tenor. Instead of rearing back in mutually shared
fright, Cord pressed forward. Their raw emotions filled him,
sustained him, more strengthening than food or drink. He
reached for them with huge, clawed hands/paws that slashed
across the colors of their screams. . . .

Cord sat bolt upright, sweating, his heart pounding. He
groped for Julia and made a strangled sound. She was not at
his side. The room spun around him, and then a light snapped
on suddenly from an adjoining space.

Julia emerged, naked, from the washroom and ran toward
him. "What's the matter? What's wrong?"

"A nightmare," he managed to croak. He lay back on the
perspiration-soaked pillows, and Julia stroked his head.

"It's all right," she crooned. "I'm here."

But it wasn't all right. In the back of his mind, Cord knew
it would not be all right until the last pieces of the puzzle
were solved. Like the other nightmares he'd had, Cord felt
he'd been sharing the mind of a killer. Lion was dead, so a
killer was still at large. Julia had called Lion a poor little
man; Cord closed his eyes and pictured Lion's bloody body
on the cafeteria floor. It was the wrong shape, the wrong
size—his attacker had been a huge, boxlike human. What if
Lion hadn't blown his parents to smithereens, hadn't tried to
poison him, hadn't tried to bash in his brains? What if the
real killer was still in the spaceport?

Cord would have preferred being wrong to being dead.

# Chapter 21

After a restless night and not much sleep, Cord rose early, just before dawn. Julia stirred and woke; she lay on the bed and her dark eyes watched him pace the cubicle, his tail twitching.

Wordlessly they dressed, having decided to get some fresh air. They made their way out of the building, past a few early birds, and walked toward the edge of the landing field.

"Word is out that a ship is coming in soon," Julia said. They trudged across the paved and barren field, watching the Mehiran sunrise. The sky was clear, and the breeze carried the scent of growing things.

"I won't be on it when it leaves," Cord replied, to the unspoken question. "I'm not ready. There's still so much I need to learn. And I have to accumulate more money by further trading with Hamilton K."

Julia linked her arm in his. "I'm glad you aren't leaving yet."

When they reached the glassy black wall surrounding the spaceport, Julia reached out to touch it. She traced aimless patterns on the shiny surface.

"What are you thinking about?" Cord asked when Julia had not said anything for a few moments.

"I was wishing there were no walls—that I could travel anywhere I wanted to, when I wanted to. That it didn't take so much time and money and effort to travel, when it's possible at all."

So Julia felt confined by the port's isolation. He had thought he was the only one affected by it.

"What you want is the Empire's warp." He laughed, remembering what K had told him.

Julia stopped and stared at him.

"Yes," she replied, "that's exactly what I want. How did you know?"

"Doesn't everyone want freedom? Isn't that what the idea of the warp represents?" It would be good to be able to go where he wanted, without ties.

"I wonder if it would give everyone freedom, though. You couldn't build one, could you, Cord?"

Cord grinned. "I think it's beyond my skills—even beyond my mother's. If it were that simple, someone in your civilization would have duplicated it by now."

"You must be right." She leaned against the black wall, stretching luxuriously. "I love the sunlight. It makes me feel so energetic."

Her pale skin and red hair made a contrast with the obsidian darkness behind her.

"Cord?"

"Yes?"

"It seems strange that we are so much alike, coming from such different backgrounds, such different worlds."

"Yes, it does, doesn't it," Cord replied. He had often thought Julia and he shared many traits.

Impulsively, she brushed her lips across his.

"You'd better get back to your work," she said. "I've kept you away from it too long."

It was true, but Cord didn't mind at all.

"Meet you tonight?" he asked.

"I'd like to—but I am due for a whole day's meditation and devotions. Since you came here, I've skimped on my spiritual care, I'm afraid."

"Tomorrow, then?"

Julia smiled. "By then, I will have recovered from your 'attentions.' Besides, if the ship *is* coming, we'll no doubt have a celebration. This time, I'll make sure you celebrate with me!"

Cord left Julia sunning herself by the wall and returned to his lab. He nodded at the security guard outside and let himself in. He worked most of the morning, and completed the telepathy device. Its awkwardness was a drawback, he decided. One could not walk around holding a strange object the size of a large fruit and making excuses to touch people. So he modified the shape, making it flatter, and added straps.

When he was done, the telepathic receiver could be worn around the waist, hidden under a loose shirt.

Of course, he did not know whether his prototype worked, having no assistant on whom to test it. But since he had promised to call O'as today, he would test the device on the head of security. . . .

She was sitting at her desk, staring at a pile of grubby, much-folded papers. When he entered she looked up.

"I was wondering when I'd hear from you." The words were brusque, as usual, but Cord caught an undertone of unease.

"What's the matter?" he asked.

"I went back to Lion's unit last night and searched it again. I was careless the first time. He'd kept all the poison-pen letters. Quite a nasty assortment—whoever sent them knew exactly what strings to pull. The whole idea of there being things in the tunnels was suggested *to* him. When he began to believe it, the letters began to suggest that he was going crazy."

"Not nice," Cord agreed. "May I take a look?" He reached for the notes. His hand brushed Garatua's as he took them.

*. . . hate it when people touch me . . . he didn't mean anything . . . clever . . . might help . . . wonder if he's satisfied about Pars . . . wish I were . . .*

The brief contact permitted him to read no more.

"I've been over them. No fingerprints now except Lion's. They're all screen printouts—you can use the screen to print a document without its going into the memory. Each one was printed on a different screen: there are microscopic differences in the letters."

"Do you think you can find the sender?"

"I intend to try," Garatua said. "By the way, I'm not happy with the case against Pars. It doesn't feel right."

Cord certainly knew what she meant. Catching relied on guesswork and intuition, as well as hard work.

"What are you going to do about it?" he asked cautiously.

"Right now, I'm letting Pars take all the blame. He's dead; it can't do him any harm. But his confidant—or partner, I don't know which—is still on the loose. What about you?"

"I will try to finish the telepathic receiver. If it works, we can check everyone in this port until we find out the truth."

But he did not care to mention that such an undertaking might be tedious and difficult. He couldn't line them all up and touch each one. Though he might have to as a last resort. Nor did he plan to tell O'as that the mind reader device was already operational. He wanted to catch the killer himself.

Cord had not seen Hamilton K since the night of the party. He still distrusted the Trade Agent, but it was expedient to mask his feelings. Well, he was used to it.

An inquiry about the best forms of interstellar exchange was the excuse for his visit. It was data which would be valuable when he left Mehira.

"You will find it convenient to take your pay in several ways," K told him. "And we'll make payment in any manner you specify. But if I were you, I'd opt for Ismanian notes, flame beryls, Ten Suns stock and TerraBank traveler's checks. Those things are easy to exchange on any planet with a spaceport. If you were taking a ship to an uncivilized world, you'd need trade goods. What you needed would depend on the cultural level, climate, and so forth. But I don't suppose you're thinking of setting up as a trader?"

"No. I will go someplace where my skills are needed."

"If you wish to apply for employment with Ten Suns, I'll give you a reference. There are police agencies of various sorts, too. Or bounty hunting, if you prefer to be independent."

"Thank you. I am not sure yet what I want to do. First I'll have to look around," Cord said.

"Well, you'll have enough money for a decent vacation while you do. You know there's a ship spacing in soon?"

"I've heard talk. What if I chose to leave with it?"

"Things aren't formal here. If you let the purser know at least an hour before it departs, that's good enough. Even if the passenger accommodations are full, they always have an extra cabin or two in the crew's quarters. Not as luxurious, perhaps, but not bad."

"Good. Thank you for your help, Trade Agent." As he stood up, Cord dropped a printout he had made earlier. It fell on Hamilton K's desk.

Hamilton picked it up and passed it to Cord. Their fingers met only briefly, but it was enough.

. . . *paying too little for his stuff* . . . *he'll smarten up* . . .

*reminds me of myself . . . too bad about his parents, his mother was . . .*

Cord tucked the paper into his pocket and left the office. He reflected that he had gained a great deal of data. He was not being given enough for the inventions he had to offer, and the telepathy device had a definite drawback. It was possible only to read what went through the other's mind at the moment of touching him. As far as Cord could tell at this time, K might be guilty.

Next time, Cord would mention the murder of his parents when using the mind reader.

# Chapter 22

Cord sat in the cafeteria, ignoring his meal. He doodled on a pad, drawing wreaths of leaves and vines. They interconnected endlessly, like his thoughts. Was the killer dead or alive? Did he have one murder to deal with, or two? What did a killer who worked with bombs and poison have to do with one who killed like a beast?

He gave up sketching and stared into the aquarium opposite his table. The unappealing blue thing was feeding on tiny shellfish. Someone entering the room cast a shadow on the tank. The creature froze. Its long, brilliant-blue body contracted and darkened to muddy brown. It had become a stone.

Cord left the table and went over to peer into the water, as close as the glass permitted. He wished he could touch the object, to discover whether it felt as much like rock as it looked. The experiment was impossible: the tank was sealed. Disgustedly he returned to his place and picked up his drink.

"Hello, Cord," a voice greeted him. "May I join you?"

He looked up and smiled in recognition. Tanna dimpled in return. "I wasn't sure you'd recognize my . . . face."

She set her tray down next to his. It held a large sausage, a tall, stalklike vegetable, and a pastry filled with a fluffy white substance.

"That's a very phallic-looking meal," Cord observed.

"Any of these foods could be you," Tanna said, straight-faced, "you're so versatile. But the end result is somewhat different." She nipped the end off the sausage. "But tell me, what were you thinking about so hard?"

"It was something that occurred to me suddenly. I know little of the galaxy's species. After all, everyone here at the port is either Terran or human."

"Terrans *are* humans, but the converse isn't necessarily true. Terrans are humans who come from the planet Terra.

190

There are some worlds originally colonized by Terrans, and there are planets inhabited by people of basically human stock who evolved on worlds other than Terra. Then there are the humanoid races, like Mehirans. Is that confusing enough for you?'' she asked, her eyes quizzical.

"What about nonhumanoid species? Are there any? Are any of them similar to—well, to that thing in the aquarium, for instance?"

"Marine life forms, you mean? Several, at least. Maybe more."

"Are there any shape changers?" Cord pursued.

"Oh! Like the Harno shifter in being able to alter their form—I see." Tanna finished the sausage and then took dainty bites of the vegetable. "No, intelligence and shape shifting are mutually exclusive. Although holodramas about were-animals are always popular."

"Ah." An intriguing hypothesis ruled out. It was too bad. That left the possibility of a person—or creature—hiding in the port's labyrinthine underpinnings. It explained both the man who had attacked him and Lion's monster. Such a being might be aware of K's "emergency" exits.

"A promising line of thought?" Tanna's pink tongue flicked the last bit of filling out of the remaining morsel of pastry.

"If I can tear my mind away from certain distractions," he said. "Watching that tongue of yours makes me want to peel your clothes right off."

"I've been told that before." She laughed. "Unfortunately, I'm due back at my job. Later, maybe?"

"Anytime." He should get on with his work, too. Cord thought about calling Julia but decided against it. She would still be at her devotions, and while he regarded her religious beliefs as peculiar and rather unwholesome, he owed them respect.

At the screen in his shop he made printouts of the plans of the spaceport. They took up the top of his largest table. Cord set aside all but the sheets showing the lowest levels. The rest showed a tracery of passages and ducts through which some-one might travel, but the lowest levels were likely to be its home.

It did not take long to confirm what he already suspected. It would be easy to travel from almost any part of the complex to any other part. There were even tunnels under the field to give access to the guidance systems which assisted spaceships in landing. The spaceport was a Catcher's nightmare. Venture into that maze after someone and you would run the risk of having him double back and come up behind you. Nor could Cord think of any way to block the ducts and passages. You might lead a full-scale armed expedition—if you had enough manpower. He didn't, and he suspected Hamilton K wouldn't permit it anyway. The idea of turning dozens of armed, untrained port personnel loose in the tunnel system did not appeal to Cord either. He played with a few other ideas, one of which was pumping in anesthetic gas. The drawbacks were the quantity of gas required and the danger of sedating the entire port.

So he would have to do it the hard way. He would interview everyone in the port, starting with Greffard's friends and associates. He need only ask if each one had bombed the demonstration, while using the telepathy device. It would be time-consuming but worthwhile if it turned up the killer, and Cord thought Hamilton K would back him up. Unless, of course, K was actually the killer. . . .

Once he had checked everyone in the port, if no one tested out as guilty, he again could shift his attention to the lower levels and ducts and tunnels, and have no difficulty persuading K to help him.

Now that he had determined a course of action, he felt better. He went back to the lab, where he found a message waiting on his screen, requesting that he go to Hamilton K's office at the eleventh hour.

He arrived at precisely the eleventh hour and was admitted to K's office.

Hamilton was speaking to someone—another Mehiran. Cord hid his surprise. The other's clothing and bearing told Cord he was from the Council.

"Cord, this is Mayon, who has come here representing the Council," K said. "He wants to talk to you. Would you like to use the office next door?"

Whatever the Council wished to tell him, Cord had no doubt it was meant to be secret. He was equally sure that it wouldn't be, in any room K offered.

"Thank you. However, I must check on something in my workroom. If the Respected Mayon will come with me . . . ?"

The Council agent bowed assent and followed Cord out.

They were some paces down the corridor before either spoke.

"I am grateful you made an excuse to talk elsewhere," Mayon said. "I assume we are going to a place where we will not be intruded upon?"

The man's tone was cold. Cord noticed that Mayon avoided looking at him. It wasn't surprising. He had been keeping clear of the occasional Mehiran visitors to the port to spare them—and himself—embarrassment. His reputation as a killer, as a slayer of even Catchers like himself, must have circled Mehira by now. Probably his name was being used to frighten badly behaved children into obedience.

"Of course," Cord replied, masking his feelings.

"Excellent."

Mayon did not say anything more until they were inside Cord's workshop. The Council's representative looked around at the workbenches and the tools with faint disdain.

"Well," he began, "the Council naturally assumed you had ceased to work for it."

When he paused, Cord answered as he would not have dared a short time before: "I felt sure the Council would reach the correct conclusion."

Mayon glanced at him in amazement. The Council was not used to flippant answers.

"The Council would not have sent me to contact you," he continued, "but for extraordinary circumstances. You were asked to investigate an . . . act of violence which took place near the port's wall."

"I was," Cord agreed. In the tumble of recent events, he had forgotten the strange crime he had been instructed to solve. It seemed as distant as childhood. He never had gotten the chance to examine the corpse. Was it still in stasis at Council headquarters? Quite possibly.

"After you . . . left the Council's service, another Catcher was assigned the task. He has not produced results. As you may have been told, the original crime was not of overwhelming interest to the Council. It was merely a puzzle, of concern because of the proximity of the humans' compound."

"Yes, I understood as much."

"Since that time, there have been three more killings. One was a guard at a gate near the port. And then, two nights ago, a young couple, who had been enjoying themselves in the River Park, were found horribly mutilated."

Cord's breath caught in his throat.

"What is it? Do you know something about it?" Mayon demanded.

"Two nights ago I had an odd nightmare," Cord admitted. "It concerned two love-friends in a park. They screamed."

"That's how they came to be found," the Council representative said. "There were others in the wood, of course. If no one had heard the cries, both audible and emotional, the bodies might not have been discovered at all. And their signals reached you while you slept? You must be unusually sensitive." His tone implied doubt that such receptivity was likely in a Catcher.

"I must be," Cord agreed. He wanted more details of the eerie coincidence. The man's roundabout description gave Cord an appreciation for the humans' blunt reports.

"Had the skulls been opened, as in the first case?" he asked brutally.

"Not exactly, I am told. I have not seen them, needless to say." Mayon turned pale, his skin yellow rather than a healthy gold.

"Neither have I, unfortunately. But I was informed that the first victim's skull had been sawed apart with almost surgical neatness."

"Not this time. The couple had been savaged, as if by an animal. Such ferociousness was not evident at the death of the guard."

"Had anything been eaten?"

"Yes. Parts of the brains and some of the other tissues as well. Not a great deal—there could not have been much time between the shouts and the arrival of the first people on the scene."

"They saw nothing?"

"No. Of course, they made a certain amount of noise in approaching, and between the dark and the shrubbery it took them a while to find the source of the screams."

"If the Council recognizes a similarity between the crimes, they must have been perpetrated by the same person," Cord mused. "And the Council wishes me to do something about it?"

"Yes." For the first time, Mayon looked directly at him.

Cord knew what he saw: a man with the reputation of a savage beast, a tool to be used but not respected or liked.

"I don't know what I can do," Cord replied. "I have taken up residence here at the port, and I doubt the Council really wishes me back on Mehiran soil."

"That's true. But the Council very earnestly desires the end of whatever creature committed these acts. The Council believes it comes from inside the spaceport."

Mayon must have interpreted Cord's answering stare as disbelief. He pointed out. "Nothing like this happened before the arrival of the aliens. Now there have been three violent attacks in the First District in less than half a year. Until now, there had been only four in the city in fifteen years. You must look for someone inside the port—some insane human who slips outside at night."

"And if I do?"

"The Council will pay well."

Cord shrugged and curled his tail. "The humans are paying me as much as I need or want. Really, the Council has little to offer me."

Mayon's lips tightened. "The Council will drop all charges against you so that you may leave the port and live again in a civilized fashion. It will give you an estate in some isolated region where—where your neighbors will not be an annoyance to you. . . ."

Cord smiled inwardly at the choice of language.

"And they will supply you with a woman," Mayon concluded. "What more could you ask?"

Cord thought about it. He thought about the ancestors' injunction that he leave Mehira, and he thought about all the human women who were willing to sleep with him without being ordered to do so by the Council. They didn't have lithe, saucy tails, perhaps, or velvety, upstanding ears, but they were enthusiastic, and there was a fascination in variety. And here he was respected.

"I must decline the Council's generous offer," he said. "However, I will most likely uncover the murderer in the course of my current investigations within the spaceport. You can tell the Council it stands to benefit no matter what my own fate might be."

"The Council will surely accept your kindness. I will report to it at once." Mayon seemed able to find his own way out of the port, so Cord let him. Certainly he had not sullied a Council representative's reputation by lingering a moment longer than required.

Well, Cord had made a grand gesture to show his magnanimity and yet committed himself to nothing, since he was taking no pay. Seizing control of his life while danger swirled around him made Cord feel like the eye of a hurricane. He felt stronger than ever before, and he thought of Julia's inner calm. Perhaps her alien religion did contain some truth. In any case it was time for action—time to use the telepathy device to find a killer. . . .

# Chapter 23

"I did not expect to see you again so soon," Hamilton K remarked wryly. He stared in confusion at the litter of strange devices Cord had dumped on his desk. "Did you finish your business with Mayon?"

"Yes," Cord replied. "But I didn't come to bore you with my private affairs. I have a number of questions to ask you, before we get on with our trading."

Hamilton K sighed and, nudging the devices aside carefully, put his feet up on the desk. "I can see this is going to be a long session."

Cord ignored the remark and paced back and forth in front of him, tail whipping. "Could someone leave the spaceport without being seen?" He preferred not to divulge his suspicions to a man he did not quite trust. Furthermore, he could not reveal all that was known of the outside murders without betraying the Mehiran empathic ability and its corollary aversion to violence. Even though there was no longer a tie to bind him to Mehira, he could not put his race in danger.

"Difficult," K answered immediately. "Whether or not the port is on alert, whether it is day or night, everyone has to have a pass and be let out or admitted by the guard. And we've been on alert status since the bombing."

"That's only at the main entrance," Cord pointed out.

"I assumed you meant out of the compound, not only out of the building. Getting out onto the landing area is easy enough. There are several entrances, including the loading dock—by which you entered once, I hear."

"Yes." Cord frowned. "The field is surrounded by the wall, however. There's no way out except through the main entrance at the front or by climbing the wall?"

"There is a freight entrance at the south end, where Mehiran

197

goods can be taken in. That's sealed up tighter than the main door. You could fly out. Or . . ."

"What?"

"Let's be honest. The port is designed with a few discreet exits—for emergency use only."

"I would like to examine them to see if anyone has gone out that way."

"I can't allow it, I'm afraid. Their locations are a secret. They wouldn't be any use if they weren't."

"Does O'as Garatua know about them?"

"Certainly."

"If she checks them for tampering, that will be adequate."

"I will have her take care of it," Hamilton said. "Why do you want to know?"

"That is also a secret."

K grinned, acknowledging that Cord had outmaneuvered him. With delicate irony he inquired, "Is there any other way in which I can be of service?"

"Yes. Help me catch a murderer—provided you're not one yourself."

It required neither telepathy nor empathy to read K's surprise. "Then what was Lion Pars—a coincidence?"

"Or an attempt to mislead us. O'as agrees with me."

"I find it strange that Garatua did not see fit to advise me that Pars was not the culprit," K snapped ill-temperedly. "As Trade Agent of Mehira Port, the presence of a psychopath is of some interest to me. I want him found." Then he added, "Sometimes I've the feeling you don't entirely trust me, Cord."

"I don't," Cord responded.

"In matters of trade I am trustworthy only to a point. If I give my word, I'll keep it—but you'd better be very careful about what you agree to do. If I can buy from you at less than the article's worth, I will. That's good business. On the other hand, there are things I will not do. I won't sell poison by claiming it's wholesome. I won't practice piracy. I won't deal in slaves. I won't commit murder except in self-defense."

Cord stared at the Trade Agent. The human was urbane, half smiling, but there was sincerity in the words. Cord remembered that a partial truth is sometimes the most convincing kind of lie.

"And did you?" he queried.

"Kill? I have done so when my life was in danger. Once, to save a friend. Did I kill your parents and try to remove you? No."

"Are you willing to prove it?"

"How?" The Trade Agent was too wary to agree before finding out what he was volunteering to do.

"I have a working telepathic receiver. Will you let me read your mind?"

"I would prefer to finish our business here first."

Cord smiled. "Understandably so. However, I am not interested in anything but discovering the murderer. I promise I won't take advantage of your trading knowledge."

"Good enough. What do you want me to do?" K removed his feet from the desk and stood up.

"Hold out your hand." Cord stretched out his own to meet the human's.

*. . . damnedest thing I ever—certainly led to excitement— thought this would be a dull station . . .*

"Did you kill my father and mother?"

"No." *. . . against my own interests to kill the goose that lays . . . wish she had . . . mustn't think that with her son listening in if he is . . .*

"Did you try to kill me?"

"No." *. . . sort of like the kid . . . the commission will make me wealthy—get me a different assignment . . . but if poor old Lion didn't . . . nasty situation . . .*

"It is," Cord observed, freeing K's hand.

"You really were receiving my thoughts?"

"Of course."

"Fascinating. Ten Suns will want to buy that gadget, you realize." K was doing his best to hide his excitement.

"It has drawbacks," Cord confessed.

"You have to touch the subject? Still, with some development it would be useful."

"I'll discuss the terms after we catch the murderer."

K frowned. "What about all this other stuff you dumped on my desk?"

Cord's tail whipped. "Whatever you were going to offer me—triple it and all of it's yours. Put the money in my account in notes, stock, and checks, as you suggested."

"Flame beryls too?" K grinned. "I have the safe here; I can hand some over right now."

Cord shrugged. "I've never seen them. Why not?"

Hamilton K walked over to a blank wall in his office and opened up a hidden panel. "While you're counting these, I can test the various devices as you describe their operation."

Cord nodded. "After that, will you contact O'as Garatua about the exits?"

K reached into the safe and brought out a small box. "That and other things. That woman is going to hear some pretty foul language when I give her a piece of my mind."

"Your mind is the only piece I'd be willing to accept!" O'as snapped, entering K's office through a partially opened door. She slammed the door panel closed with a savage push of her elbow.

K sealed his safe and went back behind his desk. "Won't you come in?" he asked snidely. He ignored her and began counting out the small stones. They were a coral opalescence that glittered with reflected light. K counted out ten and handed them to Cord, who placed them in his side pouch.

Only after putting the remaining flame beryls back in the safe did Hamilton K speak. "What's the matter now?"

The Kamean shot him an equally nasty look and dropped into a chair. Cord remained standing. When they both looked at him, Cord asked, "Should I leave? Perhaps this is private."

O'as raised a hand. "Stay. This concerns you—and all of us. I've been in communications." She bit out her words. "A subspace message came in from the Ten Suns ship *Maida*." In an aside to Hamilton K, she said, "The news of a ship's impending arrival has already made the rounds, but that message was from the freighter *Lady of Eire*. This message was top-secret."

Cord realized that Garatua's anger was anxiety. He wondered what could worry O'as, phlegmatic in spite of a peppery tongue, to such a degree.

"Do you mind if I explain a few things to Cord?" O'as addressed Hamilton, evidently collecting herself.

"Go ahead—as long as you explain the problem."

"The *Maida* brought in about half the personnel here. The essential staff always goes in first, and nonessential comes next. The *Maida* brought the second group."

Cord nodded. He could tell this was going to be a lengthy conversation. So he sat down on the edge of a Terran chair.

"You recall we talked about the disposal system after you

nearly went down it? Ordinarily, the recyclers work for years with routine cleaning and adjustment by the system robots. It's supposed to be self-maintaining, and it is. If it weren't, it wouldn't be reliable enough for isolated ports and starships. But the *Maida*'s unit failed. Nothing too serious, but it required human intervention. They got a crew in to empty the holding tanks so they could get at the malfunction. In the organic tank, they found bits of bone.''

"Human bone?" asked K.

"Yeah. There aren't enough fragments to fill a cup, but the *Maida*'s captain thinks she knows whom they belonged to. On their last trip to Mehira, when they brought us, they lost a crewman on one of the planets where they took on freight. They thought he'd jumped ship. Impossible to find him—the place had no government to speak of.''

"I heard something about it," K said.

"The official explanation," O'as continued, "was that he must have slipped off the ship and gone native. His crewmates didn't believe it; they thought he'd had an accident. They searched for him, but there was no trace, and the aliens couldn't or wouldn't talk.''

"It has been known to happen," Hamilton K said.

"The mystery was that no one saw him go. It wasn't a dangerous world, and the *Maida*'s method of accounting for her crew was pretty lax. It's not surprising. Checking in and out is standard practice on unstable worlds and in big ports. On backwater worlds, the rules get loose.''

"Which leads to episodes like this," K added.

O'as grunted. "Its major importance is that we know when the man disappeared. Now we know what happened to him, assuming the bones are his, and it's reasonable to suppose they are.''

"So someone on the ship must have killed him?" Cord spoke for the first time since Garatua began the report.

"Yes. The captain has questioned the crew under hypnosis and drugs, and the first officer has done the same to her. Every crew member who was on the ship then is clear.''

"Did anyone leave the ship after that voyage?"

"Yes, two. One took a post as third officer with a smaller company, and one retired to raise chickaroos on St. George. Ten Suns Enterprises is checking on them now. When the ship arrives, the captain wants to question everyone here who came on the *Maida*. Whoever killed that crewman is probably in the spaceport.''

"Quite a project," K commented.

"It will be," O'as agreed without enthusiasm. "I'll compile a list of those who arrived on the *Maida*."

There was a moment of silence. Cord's tail kept switching. To restrain it, he wrapped it about the chair leg. Something was bothering him.

"But what does this have to do with me?" he finally asked.

"It is highly likely that the possible killer of this crewman is the same person who killed your parents," O'as explained.

"You left out the person who attacked me," Cord pointed out logically. "Isn't one psychopath responsible for all the attacks?"

"I don't know," admitted O'as. She turned to Hamilton K. "The subspace message also transmitted an electronic 'picture' of the dead crewman." She reached into her tunic and pulled out a folded sheet of paper. "That's why I ran here. Fortunately—or unfortunately—Cord was here too."

She stood up and smoothed out the sheet on K's desk. Cord stood up to examine it—and recoiled. The face that stared back at him, created by millions of pinpoints, was the same man who had tried to kill him in the spaceport weeks ago!

Hamilton was on his feet too. "Are you trying to tell me that he was attacked by a dead man? Impossible!"

O'as spread her hands. "I have no explanation." She looked at Cord.

"That *is* the man," Cord said in a flat voice. "And I have no explanation."

"Resurrection? Teleportation?" asked Hamilton K.

"Or a shape changer," muttered Cord.

"It's clear," said O'as, "that we are not dealing with an ordinary crime nor an ordinary criminal."

"Then perhaps my mother's telepathy receiver will find the answer."

"And that's probably precisely why," said O'as, "your parents were destroyed."

"But why kill the first time? Did the crewman know something about the killer or the killer's past?"

K shook his head. "I know nothing of criminal investigation,

Cord, but I do know the company. Every Ten Suns employee is screened before assignment. The psychological testing would have uncovered any crime in the suspect's background. The only person here who hasn't got a psych profile on record is you."

"And you can't be guilty," O'as pointed out. "Still, the original murder may have been intended to cover up a crime initiated after the profile was taken—smuggling, for instance."

"What would be worth anyone's risk to smuggle onto Mehira?" K inquired. "And if illegal narcotics were being distributed in the port, could you be unaware of it, O'as?"

"What if he was selling them outside the port?" O'as countered. "That would explain why there were no signs of drug traffic. I know Cord has been curious about the possibility that someone was getting out."

O'as and Hamilton K continued to argue. Cord did not hear them. From the humans' point of view, the suggestion was a good one. They didn't know about the empathic link of Mehirans—or about his dreams.

Most crimes committed by humans might also be perpetrated by Mehirans, though not as frequently or as casually. Drug selling would probably be the exception, Cord thought. If the drug was not harmful, the Council would have no objections to its being sold. If it did affect the mind, its use would be impossible to conceal from other Mehirans.

His dream supplied the answer. The death agonies of Mehirans so far away should not have troubled his sleep—not enough to trigger a terrifying and detailed nightmare. The source of the signal was either much closer or else was someone he knew.

What he had experienced in the dream—the thrill, the pleasure in the victims' fear—was what the killer had felt. Oh, the murder of Fyrrell and Neteel had been for their slayer's safety, Cord was sure of it. The deaths outside the spaceport had been committed for enjoyment. And Pars? A combination of the two: first, for a scapegoat, and second, because his unhappiness and desperation pleased the one who drove him to death.

What a fool he had been. Here, among humans, he had missed the motive because it was such a *Mehiran* crime. On Mehira everyone knew that some commit violent crimes to savor the pain of others. It had not occurred to him to look for the same motivation among humans, who seemed to lack the empathic sense.

And with O'as's latest revelation, Cord was sure his quarry was a very unusual human.

"Well?" Hamilton K demanded. "You're the security chief. What shall we do next?"

"After the list is compiled," she answered, "you and I and Cord, with his clever little device, will cooperate with the *Maida*'s captain to find the killer. In the meantime, the freighter *Lady of Eire* has already landed and most of the port people are celebrating. The *Maida* is not due to land until tomorrow."

"If everyone is drunk, or otherwise engaged," K said, "it might make our investigation easier. Cord?"

"The telepathy device works whether one is sober or not. Or," he said, grinning, "otherwise engaged." Suddenly he remembered his promise to Julia to celebrate with her tonight.

O'as looked at her watch. "If we meet again at the third hour, here at K's office, that should give us enough time to form a plan—and for everyone else to be caught unawares."

The three of them agreed, and Cord left K's office, the comforting feel of a knife slapping against his leg. If he made love to Julia or anyone else tonight, it would be with his boots on. . . .

# Chapter 24

The day had passed swiftly. After leaving K and O'as, Cord found he had only enough time to stop at his unit and change clothing before meeting Julia for dinner—among other things. When he dressed in a silky-smooth tunic and trousers (altered to accommodate his tail comfortably), he left the mind-reading device in his equipment case. The chest's alarm system would keep it safe. He did not wish to be encumbered with the detector this evening—it would make undressing complicated and generate questions.

They met in the port's "restaurant." Unlike the main dining room, it was dimly lit, subdivided into smaller areas, and rather luxuriously furnished. There were also music and holographed entertainment.

Julia was quiet. She was never one to chatter, Cord knew, but tonight she seemed subdued. From their table, they could watch the recorded floor show while they sipped their wine. Its pale-green color pleased Cord almost as much as its light dryness.

The entertainment was an acrobatics/comedy/dance routine, two men and a woman demonstrating sex acts in a variety of unlikely postures.

"That one looks hazardous to health," Cord murmured. "One false move and you'd be explaining to the doctor how your spine came to be a two-hundred-eighty-degree arc. We could try it tonight."

Julia laughed softly. "You are corrupting me, Cord. While sex is permissible in my religion to relieve frustration, an . . . arrangement like that one could not be considered necessary. But I wonder what it would be like in free fall."

"Oh, Julia, I'll never understand the ins and outs of your beliefs. Or how you came to adopt them."

"I . . . was born a Centrist."

"But . . ." Cord intended to say that did not seem an adequate reason to continue to believe in a philosophy which was so opposed to her passionate nature. Then he thought of his own beliefs and decided they were in similar situations.

"Maybe I'm not suited to practice Centrism," Julia agreed. "It used to be easy, but since I met you, Cord, my control and beliefs are eroding. And I'm certainly not accomplishing anything here as a missionary. I wasn't even of any assistance to Lion."

It was all too true to be denied. He took Julia's hand and pressed it in sympathy.

"It doesn't matter," she assured him. "This doubting may only be a test of my faith. If it continues, then I'll decide what to do." She refilled their glasses. "Have you changed your mind about not leaving on the freighter that came in today?"

"No, I'm not ready to go yet. If I change my mind, I can always leave on the *Maida*."

Julia was surprised. "That's a Ten Suns ship. I didn't know it was coming back here."

Cord shrugged. "I need to sell Ten Suns a few more plans and prototypes. I have enough credits to leave now, but if I wait, I would have a small fortune. From what Hamilton K and others tell me, it appears that money is everything."

"Not everything!" Julia exclaimed with surprising intensity. "Not safety or freedom."

"No—but I would not want to be on my own in your civilization with no money."

"That's true," Julia conceded.

Their attention returned to the holos. The three sexual athletes had given way to a juggling act, a combination of fast talk and flying objects. Cord noticed that those watching were breathless with anticipation. The four jugglers were tossing cutter guns back and forth in an intricate pattern—and the guns were set on continuous fire. If any of the sixteen weapons was fumbled, someone was going to die.

Of course, it was all prerecorded, so there should be no unpleasant surprises. And yet it was impossible to watch without becoming tense. The jugglers worked with little illumination, so the cutters' opalescent rays wove a spiderweb pattern in the dark.

"This isn't entertainment, it's an art form," Cord whispered.

Every eye in the café was watching the act; conversation had ceased. Julia made no response.

The routine came to an end. Cord and Julia had finished their meal; the wine was gone.

"Let's go," Cord suggested.

"Yes," Julia said. Her breasts rose and fell. The dress she wore was cut low, exposing part of the aureolae around her nipples. Her pupils were dilated with expectation.

"Your room or mine?"

"Why not go somewhere different tonight?" she asked. "There's something I've wanted to try. Do you know what a stim-center is?"

"I've heard of it, but I haven't been there." In fact, Cord did not know what a stim-center might be, but he was willing to find out.

"Neither have I, of course, because it looks odd if you go alone—and a missionary shouldn't go at all—but I would like to see what it's like. You wear a headset which links you to a computer. You describe to the computer a fantasy you want to experience. A very simple description will do, although you can get more elaborate if you wish. Then you take a drug, and you live out the fantasy. Stim-centers are used a lot on worlds where the port staff can't go outside because of the climate, and also on ships making long trips."

"It sounds fantastic," Cord said. He could imagine some very interesting scenarios to try.

The stim-center was not far from the café. They strolled along a concourse twinkling with colored lights and advertisements for diversions. Life, Cord decided, cupping one of Julia's buttocks in his hand, could be very good.

The cubicle was small and gray, furnished only with a plastic-covered bed platform, a pair of silver bands with long cords leading to a simple console, and a small grille set beside it in the wall.

"Would you like to take a cruise on a luxury liner?" Julia asked.

"Yes, unless you'd rather do something else. It would be good practice for when I leave."

Julia laughed. "I'll never be able to travel in a starship of this class," she said. "But maybe you will."

Her fingers flew over a keyboard as she programmed the

computer. "Margravia and bound for Jeelung. With plenty of
entertainment—especially in free fall. . . ."

She led him over to the grille. "Now put your hand over
this." He followed her movements. "We've just been air-
injected with a drug. Put on the headband and lie down next
to me."

The headbands adjusted to fit snugly, Cord found. His last
thought before stretching out beside Julia was that the trailing
wires might be a nuisance. . . .

He was standing in front of a great viewport, staring at his
own planet, Mehira. He could see the continents and oceans
before him, like a living map. As the ship moved slowly into
space, Mehira became swathed in mist and clouds.

Julia touched his shoulder, and he looked away from the
viewport. They were in a lounge, large and carpeted on all
walls with a silky, many-colored covering. The ceiling and
walls were studded with strange plateaulike formations. They
were seating areas, Cord realized, for the occasions when the
ship's up and down orientation was different, and for the
times it might be in free fall. At the moment there was
gravity.

Julia stood beside him. Her hair was dressed high on her
head in an elaborate style which must involve some sort of
frame underneath. She was wearing floor-length strings of
gems falling from a collar around her neck, and not very
much more. Hip-high hose, and nothing else, he noted as she
turned to him. Her eyes were greener than the jewels. There
were bracelets of the same stones on her wrists.

He looked down at himself. He was clad in the richest
Mehiran clothing he had ever seen—far more costly than
anything Bird's father had worn. A broad neck ornament of
precious stones lay heavy on his shoulders, while he, too,
wore bracelets and rings. The soft tunic did not conceal the
beginning of an erection.

"Let's go to the free-fall deck," Julia suggested, lowering
her eyes.

The ship was lavishly fitted: no utilitarian, naked decks or
bulkheads. It was not as Cord had envisioned, yet he recognized it as being right. He could remember embarking on
Margravia amid the glitter of casinos, vast estates, and slave
markets. He knew that the door down the passage led to the

crew's quarters and the cabins for passengers' servants. This ship carried no second-class accommodations.

He knew it all, and knew that the computer link was supplying the knowledge. At the same time, it was all quite real. It would be very easy to slip into the dream and be aware of nothing else.

The free-fall room was in a lobe of the ship which did not rotate to provide gravity. Cord savored the sensation of decreasing weight. Part of the space was divided into small areas where passengers could take advantage of the novelty in privacy. Julia led him to an unoccupied one.

Freed of the restraint of gravity, the jeweled strands floated, exposing more of Julia's body. The hose and flimsy bandeau left just enough to the imagination to tease.

Sex was different in free fall. Postures which would be impossible in a strong gravitational field (or even a weak one) presented no challenge. Weightless, they writhed around each other, laughing as they recoiled from the cushioned walls.

"I've got you now," Cord said, pinning Julia against the wall. Garments floated like strangely hued clouds: here a cirrus wisp of black chiffon, there a cumulus of velvety white kilt.

The tip of his tail snaked up to stroke her. Julia lunged against him as his organ snaked up, too. The designer of the ship had thoughtfully provided handholds, so Cord was not dislodged.

"Oh, Cord," Julia sighed when they were no longer locked together. "I hope you aren't disappointed in me. I'm so many people—not all of them nice."

"Nice enough for me," Cord replied, kissing one leg from knee to delicate toes. What a position for a despised Catcher to find himself in!

Somehow, the dream changed and flowed. He heard a bell sounding high up and far away. Julia's expression changed. "We're going into overdrive."

She reached for him, and he entered her again. His clothes melted away like wax, forming little colored beads that bounced away. Julia's long strands of jewels dissolved and fell in a tinkling shower. Even the air around them changed colors, swirling around them, as the ship went into overdrive.

A thousand tiny fists pounded on his body; his brain exploded in a kaleidoscope of lights. He felt as though he were having an orgasm that was without end, and a tiny part of his mind wondered how Julia could survive this.

But she had. When the ship came out of overdrive, he looked into her glittering eyes and avid face. Their sweat-slicked bodies parted. The dream changed again.

Cord was naked except for a collar around his neck and a small chain which led from the collar to Julia's hand. She was now dressed in flimsy black stockings with an openwork pattern in them. Her firm breasts were covered by little circles of matching black. She led him down a corridor, into another lounge.

Inside, a huge table was set for dinner—the captain's table. The dishes were creamy porcelain, the tableware was inlaid with mosaics of precious stones. A gold-chased goblet was at every setting.

Julia tugged him into a chair beside her. Suddenly all sorts of humans came forward to claim their seats.

The captain was Hamilton K. Around the table sat Tanna, the little brunette from the party, and the twins May and Mary, as well. All three women wore ornaments instead of clothing, leaving bare all the necessary parts of their bodies. They licked their lips in anticipation—but not of food.

Across from Cord sat the burly large man who'd first attacked him—the dead man from the *Maida*. The crewman smiled at him, revealing pointed fangs. Farther down the table sat a young man; it took Cord a moment to recognize the young security guard who stood outside his lab. The security guard turned and fondled the dead crewman.

At the very end of the table, in apparent segregation, were three Mehirans: Bird, and his dead parents. Bird ignored everyone at the table and tended the mutilated bodies of his parents, which had a tendency to slump over as they fell apart.

Cord flinched. The dreams were turning ugly, and he wanted to leave. But Julia's silver chain prevented it. Then dinner started. Brisk stewards in crisp uniforms were in constant attendance, bringing a never-ending stream of delicacies. They filled glasses almost before they were empty and removed plates unobtrusively.

The captain, however, was served by a young woman who was naked but for an ornamental hip belt and neck collar.

Another slave, Cord realized, and then started when he recognized the woman as O'as Garatua.

O'as spilled a few drops of wine on the table cover while filling the captain's goblet. Hamilton K backhanded her across the mouth without interrupting his conversation with a flirtatious Tanna. O'as fell back against the wall, a trickle of blood on her lip. She managed not to drop the decanter, however, and returned to her place behind the captain's chair. O'as furtively wiped away the blood with the palm of one hand and stared hatefully at the back of K's head. No one else seemed to take notice of the incident . . . they were too busy stripping off what there was left of clothing.

The stewards ripped off their uniforms and eagerly reached for O'as, holding her down as she fought them. The twins and the nameless security guard formed a threesome on the floor. Julia stood up as Hamilton K and the *Maida* crewman approached; Cord watched as each male human entered her front and back. Dispassionately, he realized he'd not quite seen the human male organ; it was substantially different from his, but only in the beginning, before it swelled and grew. But unlike a Mehiran's, it jutted forward in a curve. His own organ hung down between his legs, as he realized something was touching it, making it grow even larger. He saw the top of Tanna's head between his thighs; somehow she'd crawled under the length of the table and now her inventive pink wet, warm tongue was busy.

A whirlwind of emotions assaulted him, hitting against his barriers. Something was pressing at his mind. A hunger, an avidity for experience, a lust for pain, terror, and the keen knife edge of emotions. The sensation was not like the instant, massive burst of psychic force from a violent death. It was pervasive, steady, and sharp as acid. It ate away at his shielding. He made an extra effort to block the signal, but he was having trouble concentrating—distracted by Tanna's insistent tongue and the steady hammering of the alien trace.

It was the same alien emotion that came to him during the dreams. As his shields slowly disintegrated, his mind finally accepted what he'd suspected all along but refused to admit— the signal came from someone close to him, someone whose emotional closeness heightened psychic receptivity. . . .

He looked up into the face of the killer. Julia smiled back. "Not enjoying yourself?" she purred. "I thought we had much in common: you Mehirans are so amoral, in heat all the time." So Julia hadn't understood Mehiran culture and abilities; she didn't know he was empathic! For all her own powers, and her fear of the telepathy machine, she didn't realize he could still detect her fatal flaw—her alien trace!

It was so incongruous, Julia standing there, talking to him in a sweet, low voice while two human males made love to her; the slapping sounds of flesh meeting flesh counterpointed her words.

She reached out and tweaked his ear. "My fuzzy alien lover and his wonderful tail. So polite all the time, so entertaining. I liked you and I was sorry about your parents. But I couldn't let them reveal me, could I?"

Her voice still dripped honey, but the dream flowed and changed again. Hamilton K's body altered and shifted. His nose and mouth grew longer, into a hairy muzzle, as he shrank in height and length. His smooth human flesh sprouted hairs, his eyes grew dark and beady. He changed into a small animal and scurried away.

The *Maida* crewman shifted also. His skin flayed away in strips, the capillaries and veins spouting little fountains of blood; the fat and muscle and sinew melted and ran off in puddles until only bones remained. The skeleton stepped back and stood there, an insane grin on the skull.

Julia jerked the silver chain, and Cord staggered upright. Tanna scrambled to her feet.

"Who are you? What are you?"

Julia tsked-tsked. "So many questions. How can I possibly explain?" An image of a cold, rocky world with a dim sun penetrated his shredded barriers. Was this Terra? He didn't know.

"You're not Julia McKay," he accused.

"But I am. I'm Julia—and I'm everyone, and I'm no one. I can't take the chance that you'll remember how to put together your infernal device—not that it would answer all your questions anyhow. . . ."

Julia turned and handed the silver chain to the skeleton. She blew Cord a goodbye kiss. "Pleasant dreams. You may not survive, but at least you'll die happy. If you do live, well"—she shrugged—"I might even be glad. . . ."

Julia faded slowly from view; with her disappearance, the cold alien trace withdrew from his mind.

The skeleton jumped forward and wrapped the silver chain around his neck with one hand and reached under his tail with the other. Something hard and cold penetrated him, pressing insistently against a crucial gland. It caused his organ to throb; he arched his back, plunging it even deeper into a writhing Tanna, who by now had impaled herself on it.

Cord dug his fingers under the chain to dislodge the skeleton's grip. Tanna had wrapped herself around his body, weighing him down; the skeleton stepped to one side as Cord staggered, withdrawing his bony hand. Cord threw himself to the floor, jerking on the chain at the same time. The skeleton fell in a heap, on top of Tanna.

For a while, the skeleton remained motionless, moving only because Tanna's body moved, but not taking any action of its own. Tanna heaved and moaned, her muscles tightening around him; unwillingly, Cord felt himself orgasm at the same time. During that moment of weakness, the skeleton came to life and tried to reach around Tanna for Cord's throat. With a mighty thrust, Cord desperately threw them both to one side and rolled away.

Leaping to his feet, he wrapped the trailing chain around one arm. Grabbing a chair, he swung it with all his strength at the skeleton, which was laboriously getting to its feet. With hollow snapping sounds, parts of bones came apart, and splinters flew in all directions. The upper torso scrabbled away from what was left of the lower. Cord continued to pound at the quivering bones until they were reduced to shards. He kicked the skull away, and it went rolling.

He stood there panting, leaning on the remains of the chair. Almost wraithlike, the blond twins approached him, floating past a spent Tanna, still lying on the ground. Trailing them was the nameless security guard. The three surrounded Cord and caressed him lightly, trying to coax his organ out again. When the security guard tried to unwrap the chain from his arm, Cord—knowing he could not go through the same scenario again—lifted up the splintered chair and tried to stab the human with it.

The man stepped back; Cord advanced. May and Mary threw themselves at his back; one of them managed to untangle the chain and pull on it. Cord swung the chair around and sank a jagged piece into the nearest twin. She vanished. He quickly jabbed the remaining twin, and she also disappeared.

His strength and mental alertness increased as each adversary was vanquished. Only the guard remained; he launched himself at Cord, who whirled around just in time. As the human speared himself on the chair and faded, the circular movement of Cord's body inadvertently whipped the chain around his own neck.

As he fought to unwind it, the entire dream sequence faded from view and everything went black. A dim light then penetrated the darkness, and Cord awoke to find himself fighting the trailing headset cord. He ripped it from his head and dragged himself to his feet. The effects of the drug lingered—his movements were ataxic. How much time had passed? He managed to hit the "Time" button on the terminal and the screen showed the date—port reckoning, of course— and the hour. Four hours or a little more had elapsed since he and Julia had entered; he could not guess how much time had passed since Julia had altered the program and left him.

He breathed deeply and called to mind a Mehiran hymn intended to calm the worshiper. Then, moving deliberately because his muscles still responded only sporadically, Cord typed security's number.

"O'as Garatua," he grated, vocal cords stiff.

"Sorry, she's not in. May I have her call you back?" responded Garatua's cheerful young assistant.

"It's urgent. Where can I find her?"

"On the loading dock. I'll transfer you, if you wish."

"Yes." Speech was returning, Cord found. He wondered why Julia had not killed him outright.

The screen blanked. After a pause, the security man's face reappeared.

"Sorry again—their line is busy."

"It's all right. I'll go down there." Cord cut the connection and called K's office.

The Trade Agent's screen was in message mode. Anger tautened Cord's body.

"K, Julia McKay is the killer. I'm going to the loading dock to find O'as. We've got to find Julia before she gets out of the port."

He made his way to ground level, dodging others on the walkways and chafing at their slowness. If he arrived and found O'as gone, it would be the last stroke of the whip. But she was probably settled there for a time, perhaps to investigate pilferage or some such matter.

The atmosphere of the loading dock was relaxed, however. Several people in grubby coveralls were standing around, drinking vending-machine coffee. O'as was leaning against a crate, watching the screen. The loading-dock door was sealed, Cord saw, so the screen provided the only view of the field.

"In case of an accident," O'as said as he joined her, seeing his curiosity. "This way, if she blows, we lose a couple of monitors—not the whole shipping department."

Cord's attention shifted to the screen.

The ship standing alone on the field was not large. It looked old. Understanding came in a rush: someone saying, "There's a freighter due in a couple of days."

"O'as! You've got to stop it," Cord shouted. The last words were lost in the roar of its rockets, loud even as transmitted and muted by the monitors.

"What's wrong?" O'as called.

Cord made his way to her side where she stood in front of the screen. The ship stood on a pillar of flame.

"The killer is on board."

The freighter rose on its bright column until fire no longer washed the field beneath it.

"Balls of the Blue God," Garatua muttered. "I wish you'd found out five minutes sooner—they'll really moan if we make them come back. Not that we can force them. All we can do is ask politely. Who is it?"

"Julia McKay."

The ship seemed no more than a comet tail now.

O'as repeated her original oath and added a few more. She blanked the screen, and her square hands moved over the keyboard with surprising speed.

"Port control? Garatua, security, here. I've been informed there's a murder suspect on the *Lady of Eire*. Radio the *Lady* and advise. If they will come back, we'll take care of the problem. If they choose not to return, ask the captain to detain their passenger Julia McKay and we'll communicate with the authorities on E'aij regarding extradition. Copy? Out."

In spite of the urgency of the situation, Cord still found it amusing that Garatua's terminal manner was as brusque as her conversational style.

"Now," she said, "I hope you're right. If not, I just made a fool of myself. What makes you think she's the one?"

"She actually admitted it to me during a session at the stim-center. When I came to, I went looking for you, to organize a search and seal the port. I'd forgotten there was a ship in. When I saw it, I realized she hadn't killed me outright because she expected to be long gone by the time I woke up. She probably planned her escape when she heard the *Maida* was returning."

Someone said, "It's beautiful, the way they rise. My father was second officer on one of those."

O'as smiled. "My grandfather was a pirate on one." She added to Cord, "Well, what do you think of your first launch?"

The urgency of the moment had overshadowed the liftoff for Cord. Now, looking back, he was able to appreciate its incandescent and fierce beauty.

"Incredible," he answered. "It's like sex, the first time. You can't believe how good it is until you've experienced it."

"Yeah." Garatua's fingers typed out a number; Cord recognized it as K's.

"It's only taking messages," Cord told her. "Or was when I tried—"

The message-mode response did not bother O'as: she keyed in one more number.

"Private code," she explained. "It transfers the call to K's current location. Which is probably beside his girlfriend."

There was no picture; K evidently had the camera turned off. But the voice that answered was unquestionably Hamilton K's.

"Hamilton, something has occurred. Meet Cord and me at port control."

"I'll be there."

In the background, a female voice murmured, "Do you have to go right now . . . ?" before O'as broke the connection.

Port control was on the top floor. To enter the room was startling; for an acrophobe it would be terrifying, Cord thought. The entire outer wall was transparent; it was as if there were nothing there at all.

"It's quite safe," the chief controller assured him. "The

wall is as thick here as any place else. The difference is that it's been made transparent rather than black. Something to do with aligning the atomic structure. It's a very expensive process, so not many places can afford it. But we have to be able to see the field, in case the instrumentation fails."

"Never mind that now," O'as said. "Has there been any reply from the *Lady of Eire*?"

"It's coming in now." The controller peered at the terminal screen, grunted, and tore off the sheet of hard copy. He handed it to O'as without comment.

" 'No passenger McKay on board. Check for stowaway has turned up nothing. Is there some mistake? Advise.' Name of Names," O'as exclaimed. "Cord, if this is a mistake, I'll—"

Hamilton K strode in, interested but detached as always.

"Julia McKay is the murderer, so says Cord," O'as announced. "She may be on the freighter *Lady of Eire*. Can we order it back?"

"I have no authority over that ship or her captain. But surely the captain will return if he is aware he is carrying a suspected murderer?"

O'as said, "He denies Julia is on the *Lady*."

"If they can't find her, they haven't searched carefully enough," Cord retorted. She was aboard the ship; she could not have stayed in the port, and she could not have gone over the wall to vanish on Mehira. He was sure she knew the ship was her only chance of escape.

"Then there's nothing to be done about it," K said.

Cord saw that K did not believe—or only half believed—that Julia was guilty. It was not difficult to follow the Trade Agent's mental processes as he fitted together the pieces.

That sweet lady? A Centrist missionary? Still, she was on the *Maida*; as a nonemployee she was responsible to no one in the port for her time or whereabouts. She had helped Greffard arrange the demonstration. . . .

At last Hamilton asked, "Do you have any proof?"

"She admitted killing my parents!"

"But it was during a stim-dream," O'as pointed out.

Hamilton K raised his eyebrows. "Sorry, Cord, but much of this is circumstantial evidence. It won't be easy to convince most people that a Centrist missionary, especially one

as quiet and likable as Julia, could be a cold-blooded
murderer.''

"I will have proof when I catch her."

"Why would she kill? What sense is there in it?" K
demanded.

"I don't have all the answers. But you know I'm right: you
can recognize the truth when you see it. Think about it. Pars
talked to her, and she gave him advice. Read his diary again,
and think about what effect her spiritual counseling would
have on a man who was already half crazy with fear. You,
O'as—you once mentioned her behavior when you were questioning Bird. Somehow she encouraged Bird to hold out. Was
Julia enduring the sight of her pain with noble fortitude—or
was she drinking it in?''

"I don't know," O'as muttered. "I don't know. Maybe."

Their resistance was without conviction. The explanation
was so *right*.

"Why did she leave?" K wanted to know. "She couldn't
have guessed the *Maida* had discovered the bones and was on
its way."

"I told her about the *Maida*," Cord said sheepishly. "And
even though I pretended to her that I was unable to finish the
telepathic receiver, she was afraid I'd remember sooner or
later. She would not have wanted to take the chance of
staying on here, although I let her think Pars was guilty. A
freighter came in, she knew I wasn't leaving on it—so she
decided to. And because I trusted her—slept with her—I
overlooked so much. . . ."

"What now, Cord?"

Cord returned Garatua's gaze levelly.

"I will track her down and kill her."

"It's a big galaxy," Hamilton K said.

"Not big enough to hide her from me."

# Chapter 25

It was two days until the *Maida* spaced in. As Cord anticipated, the ship's captain insisted on personally questioning the previous passengers. She was not willing to accept data from Cord's telepathic receiver, though it would have speeded up the investigation.

"Hypno-interrogation is admissible in a court of law almost anywhere. Your mind reader isn't—not yet. You say this Centrist is the one we want. I say, let's eliminate the other suspects first."

Working at fever pitch, it took three more days to demonstrate that the crewman's killer was not in the port. Even then, the captain was not completely convinced of Julia's guilt.

"However," she conceded, "we'll notify the Ten Suns home office and any ports in subspace radio range. They can take care of advising the local authorities and getting in touch with your missionary."

"The local authorities may or may not pay any attention," O'as observed.

"It won't matter," Cord told her. "I am leaving on the *Maida*—with the captain's permission?"

She gave it with a nod. "If you can pay your passage, you're welcome to a berth."

Hamilton K laughed grimly. "He can pay. He could buy a ship of his own, if he wanted one."

"Oh?" said the captain. She was tall and heroically built, with a wide, humorous mouth. "Do you play games of chance, young man?"

"I could learn."

"Good. We'll leave orbit as soon as we've finished loading. K, if you've got any documents to send to Ten Suns, be sure I've got them by the twenty-first hour. There's no point in wasting my time here.''

The *Maida* was a "great ship," never meant to enter any planet's atmosphere, unlike the freighter on which Julia had escaped. If it wasn't as sybaritic as the cruise ship in the stim-center dream, it was quite adequate for Cord's purpose. His only interest was in following Julia.

"We aren't scheduled for E'aij," the captain said, "and I've already deviated to come to Mehira. That was necessary, once the murder was discovered. But I can't justify rerouting to E'aij. We're bound for Kikal. From there you can get a ship headed out to E'aij."

"You don't feel any obligation to track down your man's killer?"

The captain shook her head, making her iridescent green hair swing.

"I've narrowed the field down to four: two former crew members, your missionary, and Lion Pars, the one who killed himself. I don't have the means at my disposal to do more. It's up to Ten Suns Enterprises now."

Cord smiled, a mere twist of the lips.

Let Ten Suns find Julia if it could. The company would have to act fast to get to her before he did.

# Postlude

He whipped the ray wand back and forth across the other side of the room. The smell and sizzle of vaporized plastic filled the air. The surgical bed collapsed, its support severed. Cord slithered into the room, flat on his belly. The suite might be a wreck, but his quarry was still alive. There had been no psychic death scream. The alien presence remained, utterly inhuman, without any hint of fear or panic.

Cord worked his way forward, clammy with sweat. Where was she hiding?

The flurry of explosive darts startled him when it came, because they were not aimed at him. He registered the *pop-pop-pop!* as they were fired, and then the lights went out, the luminescent panels blasted.

Cord snarled and swept the ray wand almost in a half circle, low enough to catch the other even if she were pressed to the floor as he was.

The stench of molten metal was overpowering. Fire alarms began to keen, drowning out all other sound. Thick yellow foam gushed from the ceiling as the suite's own protective system went into effect. As it covered him, Cord thought of pus.

Deafened and blinded by the froth, Cord only sensed the scramble of movement. Something leaped past him into the corridor. He twisted frantically and fired, but the ray caught only the wall, leaving a deep fissure.

He struggled to his feet, but it was too late. There were people in the passage now, alerted by the fire alarm. In the jumble of different minds and species, all of them radiating anxiety and surprise, Cord could not feel the one he wanted. Its touch was masked by all the rest.

Dripping foam, he leaped into the corridor—and bowled over a frightened technician. He jumped over the man and

searched the passageway for his quarry. He saw no one that
looked like Julia—if that's what the killer still looked like
now. He couldn't be sure if she'd changed her face or body
yet. Nor did he understand why she would have to, if she was
a shape shifter. What other reason could have brought her to
Brunan, noted chiefly for its body sculptors? There had been
some talk of an archaeological discovery of traces of an
Imperial installation, but so far no find to attract tourists. Not
that Julia was a tourist. If she was . . . but what Julia was
remained a mystery. Uncertainly, he stood in the corridor, as
various workers milled about in similar confusion. A stern-
visaged woman with "Xavier Clinic" embroidered on the
breast of her smock approached him. She was followed by
two uniformed guards. Her emanations were louder than the
tumult around them: great anger.

Cord put away his wand. "I can pay for the damage,"
Cord said before she spoke. "In any form of exchange you
prefer. Plus much more for the, ah, mental anguish, perhaps."

Her frown smoothed out as she evaluated the offer. "In
that case, if you will come to my office, we'll discuss
compensation." She gestured to the guards, who now flanked
him and then turned and called to a technician scurrying by:
"Maeve, there's no cause to evacuate the entire building.
Things are under control. Get our patients back to their
rooms. This way, please," she added to Cord.

He fought down his own vexation. If he did not observe
the custom by buying off the clinic, he would lose still more
time in Brunan's courts. He had been so close to trapping
her! How had his fire missed her? Cord scarcely heard the
clinic's director extolling the virtues of the destroyed equipment.
In spirit he was already tracking his enemy. He assumed she
would be on her way to the spaceport by now. As soon as he
could, he would follow.

No matter what planets in the galaxy Julia fled to, he
would follow. He would catch up to her and kill her, no
matter how much it cost nor how long it took. Even if it took
from this life into the next. . . .

H. M. MAJOR guards his privacy jealously. However, he is said to sport a bushy, salt-and-pepper mustache and to speak with a faint accent evocative of British colonies and whiskey-and-soda. His favorite sports are archery and fencing, which he feels has been spoiled by the use of blunted foils. He speaks several languages, but only when forced to. He lives alone except for a temple-trained Siamese guardcat. And where he lives is not really known, but it is probably not in the States.

## JOIN THE ALIEN TRACE READERS' PANEL

Help us bring you more of the books you like by filling out this survey and mailing it in today.

**1.** Book title:_____

Book #:_____

**2.** Using the scale below how would you rate this book on the following features.

| Poor | | Not so Good | | | O.K. | | Good | | Excellent | |
|------|---|------|---|---|------|---|------|---|------|---|
| 0 | 1 | 2 | 3 | 4 | 5 | 6 | 7 | 8 | 9 | 10 |

Rating

Overall opinion of book............................._____
Plot/Story ......................................._____
Setting/Location ................................._____
Writing Style ...................................._____
Character Development ..........................._____
Conclusion/Ending ..............................._____
Scene on Front Cover ..........................._____

**3.** On average about how many Sci Fi books do you buy for yourself each month?_____

**4.** How would you classify yourself as a reader of Science Fiction?
I am a ( ) light ( ) medium ( ) heavy reader.

**5.** What is your education?
( ) High School (or less)    ( ) 4 yrs. college
( ) 2 yrs. college           ( ) Post Graduate

**6.** Age_____        **7.** Sex: ( ) Male ( ) Female

Please Print Name_____

Address_____

City_____State_____Zip_____

Phone # (       )_____

Thank you. Please send to New American Library, Research Dept, 1633 Broadway, New York, NY 10019.